A KILLING FROST

**Center Point
Large Print**

**This Large Print Book carries the
Seal of Approval of N.A.V.H.**

HANNAH ALEXANDER

CENTER POINT PUBLISHING
THORNDIKE, MAINE

This Center Point Large Print edition
is published in the year 2009 by arrangement with
Harlequin Books, S.A.

The text of this Large Print edition is unabridged.
In other aspects, this book may vary
from the original edition.
Printed in the United States of America.
Set in 16-point Times New Roman type.

ISBN: 978-1-60285-354-6

Library of Congress Cataloging-in-Publication Data

Alexander, Hannah.
    A killing frost : a river dance novel / Hannah Alexander. -- Large print ed.
        p. cm.
    Originally published: Don Mills, Ont.: Steeple Hill, 2009.
    ISBN 978-1-60285-354-6 (library binding : alk. paper)
    1. Missouri--Fiction. 2. Large type books. I. Title.

PS3551.L35558K55 2009
813'.54--dc22

2008044145

In loving memory of Don (Teddy) Keebaugh, a
hero in our hometown, whose spirit will live on
through the lives of all the students he inspired.

Acknowledgments

This is an exciting time as we leave Hideaway behind and begin a new series in a new town, new location, new characters. We have received nothing but encouragement from our editor, Joan Marlow Golan, and the talented people who work with her: Krista Stroever, Lee Quarfoot, Megan Lorius, Sarah McDaniel, Maureen Stead, Amy Jones and Diane Mosher. From editing the inside to covering the outside of our novels, we have received top-notch care and professionalism. What an amazing team!

Thanks to our agent, Karen Solem, for her constant challenge for us to dig more deeply.

Thanks to the friends who helped us brainstorm this book on a cold January morning: Colleen and Dave Coble, Nancy Moser, Judy Miller, Rene Gutteridge, Deborah Raney, Doris Elaine Fell, Dan and Steph Higgins (Stephanie Grace Whitson to her many adoring readers).

Thanks to Mom, Lorene Cook, for her constant love, prayers, encouragement and endless promotion for our books.

Thanks to Mother, Vera Overall, whose love for her son and pride in his accomplishments is never-ending.

Thanks to Tim Puchta, of Puchta Winery in Hermann, Missouri, who was a great help to us as we researched last year's killing frost in wine country along the Missouri River. Any mistakes in this book are not his fault. He's the expert. We're simply enthusiasts.

As always, our deepest appreciation goes to God, who has placed the blessing of stories in our lives.

Chapter One

Doriann Streeter had never been kidnapped before, but if she'd ever tried to imagine what it might be like—which she hadn't—she'd have been wrong. She would've expected to be brave, but right now she couldn't stop shaking. If she weren't trying so hard just to breathe, she'd be surprised that she'd never expected anything like this, because she had a good imagination.

Her hands shook as she clenched them in her lap.

What had she done wrong? Why was she stuck inside a stinking, rattly old pickup truck between two dirty people with black beneath their fingernails, who reeked so badly she thought she might puke?

And what if she did puke? It could happen.

She dared a glance at the dirty man's pocket. It was where he'd stuck her cell phone when it rang. He'd grabbed it, turned it off, shoved it into his pocket with an ugly chuckle, nearly driving the truck into the ditch when he forgot to watch the road.

Some things just never occurred to a girl.

The call had to have been Mom checking up on her. Or Aunt Renee. *Please, God, make them worry when I don't answer. Please!*

They knew she always answered her calls, even when she was up to something she knew they didn't want her to be doing.

She gagged again at the smell that filled the hot cab of the pickup. She had a decision to make. Get sick in the truck and get killed, or ask for some fresh air and get killed.

"Could you open a window or something?" she asked finally, after working up her nerve to speak. She hated the way her voice shook. Not strong, the way she'd always thought she'd sound during a crisis, but scared, like a little kid. She hated that these two loser bullies scared her.

Neither of them said a word.

Doriann crossed her arms, holding them tightly against her stomach.

The windows stayed up.

This was not the time to throw a tantrum the way her cousin Ajay would do.

She dared a glance to her right at the skinny woman called Deb, who had teeth missing.

Maybe it was better that these two bullies didn't listen to her. If they saw her as a threat, then she'd be tied up and thrown into the back of the truck. But since she was just a kid to them—as if an eleven-year-old who'd already graduated from her trainer bra and had a 153 IQ could possibly be considered just a kid—they figured they could handle her between the two of them.

Doriann's face still stung from the slaps the woman had given her for screaming. Tears had dried on Doriann's face. The farther the dirty man drove from Kansas City, the faster the tears had come for a while. She'd even been afraid to ask for a tissue, so she'd had to wipe her nose on the sleeve of her jacket.

Can't panic. Don't let them see how scared you are. Think of something else.

Deb's teeth, maybe. Deb was a stupid name for a kidnapper. Deborah was a name from the Bible, a judge and prophetess in the Old Testament. Deborah was Mom's hero, because she "held a position of honor in a world that honored only men."

Good thing Judge Deborah was in heaven now. She didn't need to know how her nickname was being besmirched down here in Missouri.

Besmirched? Yes, that was the word.

They passed a road sign on I-70, and Doriann felt her eyes go buggy. Could that be right? Hadn't they just left Kansas City less than an hour ago? According to the sign, they were almost to Columbia. Halfway across Missouri. She knew this road well, because she traveled it with Mom and Dad whenever they went to River Dance to visit Grandpa and Grandma Mercer—which was never often enough for Doriann.

But if that sign was right, that meant they'd been on the road for *two hours!*

How could that be? During homeschool study hour, Aunt Renee always said that time crept by when a person was in a state of high stress, so if Doriann and her cousins would just relax and be

11

quiet, they could complete their lessons in half the time, then go out and play.

This wasn't right, because time was passing way too fast, and if Doriann was any more stressed, this stinky cloth seat would be drenched with her pee.

Maybe she was in the middle of a bad dream.

The road blurred, and Doriann blinked. She couldn't cry again. The woman and the man called Clancy might enjoy it. They were the kind of people who probably liked to make kids cry. Clancy would laugh at Doriann's tears, and Deb was probably waiting for a reason to slap her again.

And so, as they drove past the sign for Columbia, Doriann counted billboards and reworded them to make them rhyme, and added the mileage in her head, while taking slow, steady breaths until her vision cleared.

They'd just passed the exit to Columbia Regional Hospital, leaving the city behind, when the corroded old scanner in the truck's open glove compartment hissed and spat, and then a tinny male voice said, "We have report of a . . . pft . . . pft . . . pft . . . male and female, possible hostage situation . . . pft . . . last seen two hours ago in the vicinity of Swope Park, possibly headed east on I-70 . . . pft . . . pft . . . pedestrian reported seeing a child being forced into the pickup—"

"That would be me," Doriann said, voice wobbling like a baby's. "You should let me—"

Deb slapped a dirty hand over Doriann's mouth. Hard. "Shut up!"

Doriann blinked to keep the tears from falling. She breathed slowly. Tried to stay calm. Not panic. Who'd have thought it would be so hard?

". . . pft . . . FBI's most wanted couple . . . at least six already dead . . . possible sighting at a convenience mart at exit . . . pft . . . could be en route toward St. Louis."

"Six." Clancy spat on the floor.

Doriann grimaced in spite of her fear. Eeww!

"People can't even do their job right. The count's at least nine. No, wait, that's eleven."

Deb took her hand from Doriann's mouth and reached across her to smack the man on the side of the head. "Didn't I tell you not to grab the brat?" Her voice sounded like the crackle of a campfire built with green cedar branches. "And I told you not to stop for gas along the interstate!"

Doriann nodded. That was right. Deb had told him. But Clancy seemed to be the kind of person who did exactly what he was told not to do.

"What was I supposed to do, let the truck run out of gas?"

"You could've taken an exit and found a place out of sight of cruising Feds, but, no, you had to park right out in plain sight, where anybody watching for us—"

"Everybody's watching for us!" His voice clattered like a chain saw in the truck cab, making

13

Doriann wish she could disappear into the seat cushion. "It doesn't matter where we are, they're after us!"

Doriann held her breath as Clancy's fingers turned white on the steering wheel. She peered sideways at him, though trying to appear as if she wasn't. His lips disappeared in a red streak, and his eyes narrowed to the point Doriann wondered if he could see the road. She knew that look. Her cousin Ajay looked the same way just before one of his screaming fits.

"I'm making you famous." He spat the words at Deb as if he was shooting bullets.

"Being on the FBI's Most Wanted list isn't my idea of fame," Deb snapped back.

He cut a look at her. Would he punch her in the stomach again? He'd already done it once, when they'd stopped for gas. Doriann braced herself.

He held his cold stare on Deb, as if his eyes controlled a razor blade. And then, one by one, slowly, his fingers returned to their dirty pink color as he relaxed his grip on the steering wheel. His lips regained their shape. He stuck out his jaw, took a deep breath, blew it out—the way Doriann did when her cousins were getting on her last nerve.

"Why didn't somebody call the police on us sooner?" he asked, sounding almost normal. "We're heroes, that's why. Those idiots deserved to die, and people realize it," he snapped, then muttered, "Bunch of rich thieves who make their living on the backs of the working class. Bloodsucking scum. That's why this country's in the state it's in."

Doriann stared at the dashboard. So this guy hated rich people.

"Think again!" Deb said. "The callers were probably scared. Or stupid. Or just found out about the search for us. But they called, all right?"

Clancy turned his attention to Doriann, and his eyes narrowed again, but not as if he was mad. It was as though he became a different person all of a sudden. Very weird. Very scary. Doriann couldn't take a breath.

He patted her leg, leering at her as if she was a banana split with extra nuts and chocolate syrup. "This here's our little protector. They can't get to us without coming through her."

Deb pounded a fist against the passenger door and spat out a stream of words that made Doriann's eyes bulge, and started her breathing again.

Doriann was proud of her vocabulary, and always tried to use words properly. These didn't sound like words she'd need to know, but the anger behind them scared her. They were crazy.

Jesus, help me, please! These people are killers, and I know I shouldn't have lied about being sick and skipped out to the zoo today. Oh, yeah, and I know I shouldn't have drank coffee after Mom and Dad told me I couldn't have it. But I was so far ahead in my studies after this weekend, and I was so tired of Danae and Ajay and Coral and the baby all being so noisy at once, and now the coffee's going right through me, just like Mom said it would . . . Oh, Jesus, please don't let these people kill me, and don't let me wet my pants.

"Got to get off this highway," Deb snapped. "Now!" She reached in front of Doriann and grabbed the steering wheel.

Doriann wished she had a seat belt; there was no exit. The truck bounced off the road and nearly hit a tree and Doriann closed her eyes and focused on not screaming as her chest bounced against Deb's arm.

Clancy was going to kill somebody for sure this time.

Doriann thought about home and Mom and Dad and the great work both her parents did at the hospital, and about how Jesus was always with her, and about how she loved her cousins even though they drove her crazy, and about her schoolwork, and the great future Aunt Renee said Doriann would have when she graduated high school early and—

Clancy jerked the wheel hard to the left. Deb's head hit the window. Doriann screamed.

Chapter Two

On Monday morning, when Dr. Jama Keith stepped from her ten-year-old Subaru Outback onto the gravel parking lot in front of the brand-new River Dance Clinic, a chorus of birdsong

16

merged with the familiar splash and gurgle of multiple waterfalls. A serenade. Like old friends welcoming her home.

A wave of unexpected hope and longing struck her.

She fought the hope. This would be a temporary stop. An extended one, yes, but temporary. She had to keep that in mind.

Maybe memories would be short for the citizens of River Dance, her tiny, isolated childhood home. Maybe, at least, those memories would be gentle, smoothed over and worn down by time.

"Hey, Dr. Keith!" someone shouted to Jama from across the street.

She turned to see sixteen-year-old Kelly Claybaugh on her way to school. Jama waved and smiled, surprised that she recognized the kid after so many years. And that Kelly had recognized her. And called her "Doctor." Very cool.

"How's your great-grandpa?" Jama called to the pretty teenager.

"Still at the nursing home. He said you visit him every time you come to town."

"I'll be by to see him in a couple of days."

"He'd love that!" Kelly said, and Jama guessed by the perky sound of her voice and the bounce in her step that the girl must be a cheerleader at River Dance High. Her great-grandfather, Ted Claybaugh, former teacher and football coach, must be proud.

Jama was an hour early. She needed time to adjust before putting on her professional face for the new director.

River Dance, population eight hundred and thirteen, was a picturesque town built into the hillside above the northern bank of the Missouri River. The location's charm and beauty drew tourists in spite of the remoteness from more commercial river towns such as Washington and Hermann and the state capital, Jefferson City.

River Dance had inspired more than one calendar company to feature the quaint, restored homes, gift shops, waterfalls, gardens and vineyards. The new clinic was within sight of two rivers, if one could catch a view through the trees. The scent of pine needles wafted over Jama, along with the moist perfume of fresh water and rich, freshly tilled soil.

The whisper of the wind in the treetops harmonized with the mad waterfall rush of the rocky Show-Me River as it danced steeply downhill and into the mighty Missouri. The springlike gentleness of the air belied the weather forecast of a freeze tonight.

Someone honked from the street, and Jama waved instinctively before she recognized Mildred Lewis on her way downtown to her café. Best pies on the riverfront for fifty miles in either direction.

Jama's new, thick-soled shoes crunched gravel as she strolled to the log building that had recently replaced Charla Dunlap's sprawling old bed-and-breakfast. To Jama's joy, the construction crew had managed to preserve five of the seven grape arbors that Charla had so lovingly tended on her property over the years. Grapevines were the lifeblood of this town.

The solid pine porch of the new River Dance Clinic echoed Jama's footsteps as she strolled past the wooden rockers to one of the multipaned windows and peered inside. The waiting room was well furnished, with tasteful prints on the walls.

She hoped Mayor Eric Thompson had arranged for enough staff to support this place. She grinned to herself. Eric Thompson. Who'd have thought that wild rascal would someday be mayor?

The racket of a loud engine broke the tranquility of wind and water. Jama turned to see a faded blue pickup slide into the parking lot and lurch to a stop barely three feet from her Outback.

She'd have known that farm truck anywhere—she ought to, she'd learned to drive in it. And the brawny sixty-year-old rancher inside had been her teacher out on the dirt tracks that crisscrossed the vast Mercer Ranch.

"Monty?" Jama rushed down the wheelchair ramp at the side of the porch and approached the truck as Monty Mercer slowly opened the door to the sound of protesting metal.

Though Monty's short beard had aged from black to salt-and-pepper over the years, the big, strapping rancher had barely a touch of silver at his temples. "How's my favorite blonde?"

"Nervous." She stepped into his arms and hugged his weathered neck.

He patted her back instead of giving her his usual, bone-cracking bear hug. "First-day jitters?"

"Just settling in."

"This is what you've been preparing for all these years. Kinda scary, huh?"

"Kinda." What an understatement.

He narrowed his eyes at her. "What's up, kid?"

"Aren't you still a city council member?"

He nodded.

"So you met Dr. Lawrence?"

"Can't say that I did. She's apparently a friend of the mayor's, and he did most of the footwork on that one. Her credentials are in order, and she is well suited to the town's seclusion. Eric said she'll be driving back and forth from Hermann until a rental opens up in River Dance. You talked to her?"

Jama hesitated. "On the phone. Twice." The woman had been curt to the point of rudeness, which boded ill for a comfortable working relationship.

Did Monty realize, knowing Jama so well, that she had already decided she would chafe under the leadership of Dr. Lawrence?

"You'll be fine with her," he said.

Yep, he'd realized it.

"Give it a chance."

Jama glanced up at him. Okay, reading her so well, did he also know about her recent drama with his son? Had Tyrell said anything to him?

And did Monty understand her trepidation over returning to a place where everyone was aware of all her past sins?

Or at least most of them.

Monty kept a heavy arm over her shoulders as he turned to walk with her toward the building. "Got any keys to this place yet?"

"Nope. Dr. Lawrence is supposed to show up before nine, but I . . . thought I'd come early. This is the first time I've seen the building all completed and ready to go."

Monty released her and sank slowly onto one of the wooden rockers on the front porch with a muffled groan.

She eyed him critically. "Been working too many hours again?"

"Something like that."

"I know you're a hunk in top form, but even you have your limits, and—"

"And I'm not getting any younger," he muttered, without the dry humor that typically laced his tone. "The latest studies show that people who remain active throughout their lives will—"

"I know, I know, but I'm just saying—"

"We'd hoped you'd stay with us at the ranch last night, maybe even agree to lodge with us for a while. Do you know Fran hasn't seen you in at

21

least a month? And you haven't returned her last two calls. She's reminded me about that at least twice in the past twenty-four hours. She's eager to see you."

Jama sat in the other rocker and allowed the motion to help calm her as she listened to the sound of wood gently moving against wood. "Sorry. My housemates decided to throw a party for me last night, so I stayed in Columbia and drove here this morning."

"And the calls?"

"Sorry about that, too. It's been a hectic few days, settling my affairs at the hospital, trying to find someone to sublet my share of the house in Columbia, staying—"

"Staying away from Tyrell." Monty gave Jama a look. "He's at the ranch now, you know."

Her rocking motion stopped. "He's back in River Dance already?"

Monty rested his head against the pine rocker, closing his eyes to the early-morning sun. "He's staying in the apartment over the garage. He's ready to shove all kinds of new ranching ideas down my throat."

"He told me a few weeks ago that you'd already purchased that new tractor he showed you."

"I didn't say I disagreed with his ideas." Monty opened his eyes and fixed his attention on Jama again. "What's going on with you two? Last we saw of him, we were sure he would pop the question."

Jama studied the wooden floor of the porch, but she didn't see wood grain; she was seeing Tyrell's face, the light of love in his dark blue eyes. She heard his voice so clearly telling her that he wanted her in his life for as long as he lived. He'd asked her to marry him.

How could it all have gone so wrong? A dream she had nurtured for so many years finally coming true, and she'd been unable to embrace it.

And when she looked up at Tyrell's father before her, she felt the throbbing ache inside.

"Is that why you came this morning?" she asked Monty. "To heal the breach?"

"At least you admit there's a breach," he said. "Tyrell won't admit that much. All his mother and I know is that he's changed. He's not his usual, cheerful—" Monty grimaced, and his face whitened.

"Monty?"

He held a hand up and gave a brief shake of the head.

"Seriously, what's up with you? Did you pull a muscle or something?"

"I'm not feeling the best, okay?" As he said the words, Jama spotted a streak of blood seeping through the blue sleeve of his chambray shirt.

She sprang from her chair and dropped to her knees beside him. "What happened?" She reached for his arm.

"Had a little accident with a ladder out behind the barn."

23

"You fell from the ladder? And you didn't tell me about it immediately?"

"It wasn't at the top of my list."

"I'm a doctor now, remember? We need to see to this." Jama unbuttoned his sleeve.

"Think that director of yours will be here any time soon?"

Jama slid his sleeve up. "I'm not sure, but I'll call and find out. Tell me exactly where you're hurting. How did you land?"

"Think I might've busted a rib or two." He grimaced again.

Jama saw a superficial cut on his wrist. The arm didn't appear to be broken, but she would delay judgment about that until she had an X-ray. "Why didn't you say something when you got here?"

"I wanted to meddle in your life while I had the chance, before you could pull out the doctor's bag."

"You can meddle as soon as we get you taken care of."

"Promise?"

"Sure, whatever. First, I've got to get you inside. Sit tight." She clipped her Bluetooth to her ear and punched in the new director's number on her cell phone. She hadn't bothered to incorporate the voice recognition for Dr. Lawrence's name, because she had, without doubt, subconsciously hoped that somehow the director would just go away before the need arose to connect with her again. The woman was as cold as a well digger's—

24

"How far did you fall?" Jama asked as she waited for Dr. Lawrence to answer the call.

Monty looked up at her, his face a frightening gray. The director picked up the call just as Monty slumped over, unconscious.

"Monty!"

Chapter Three

Jama felt for a pulse at Monty Mercer's throat and watched the rise and fall of his chest. "Dr. Lawrence," she said into her earpiece, "this is Dr. Jama Keith. I've arrived early at the clinic, and I have a patient on the front porch who just lost consciousness."

"Call an ambulance." The clipped voice of Dr. Ruth Lawrence had not grown warmer since the last time Jama had heard it. "We aren't open for business."

"I can take care of him if I can get him inside. We do have supplies, don't we?" Jama gave what vitals she could. "Where can I get a key? And when is the staff due?"

"I'm at least thirty minutes out, and no one else is scheduled to be there. Either get a key from the mayor or get the patient to the closest facility. That would be Jefferson City or Fulton."

"I know that," Jama snapped.

"I highly advise transfer." No emotion. Not irritation at Jama's shortness. Not concern. Nothing.

25

"I'll call the mayor for a key." Jama clicked off, then spoke the mayor's name into her Bluetooth. Why was no staff scheduled to arrive?

With one call, Jama discovered Eric Thompson was out of town for a meeting and wouldn't be back until later in the morning. She dug her only credit card out of her purse, doubting she could jimmy the lock as easily as she had at the high-school gymnasium on her graduation night. If this failed, she'd break a window.

"Hang on, Monty. I'll take care of you." She placed another call as she knelt before the front door and slid the card between the door and the jamb.

A deep male voice sounded in her ear. "Jama? Are you at the clinic yet? What's up?" Caller ID.

"Hi, Tyrell, where are you?" She was surprised by the relief she felt.

"Getting the Durango serviced down at Joe's."

Good. That was only a few blocks away. He could walk from there. Or run. "I need you to come to the clinic. Your dad's been injured."

"What happened?"

"He fell."

"I'm on my way."

She closed her eyes, allowing herself a few seconds of comfort . . . followed by regret.

By the time Jama had the clinic's front door open—Mayor Eric Thompson was welcome to

26

withhold the cost of the broken window from her first paycheck—a crowd of two men, a woman and two children had noticed the activity and now clamored to help. They moved Monty into the clinic and settled him on a bed in the first treatment room.

They continued to hover while Jama ran from room to room, looking through cabinets for supplies to stop the bleeding and assess the damage, slamming doors and tripping over equipment. Where was the EKG machine?

"What can we do, Dr. Keith?" Harold Kaiser, the local grocer, had known Jama since she was a toddler. Her new title sounded odd on his lips. "Just tell us and we'll do it."

"Sure thing," said Carol Saffer, the town postmaster. "I had some first-aid training a couple of years ago."

Jama grimaced. Sweethearts, both of them, but she needed somebody who really knew how to help. "Hey, guys, doesn't Zelda Benedict still live across the street?"

"Sure does," Harold said. He and Carol often competed over which of them knew more citizens of River Dance, and who knew them better. "She walks three miles on the Katy Trail every morning she doesn't work, then smells up the neighborhood every night before bed when she sits on her front porch and smokes her cigar, if she doesn't have a night shift."

Some things never changed. "Would somebody run across the street to see if she's back from her walk?" Jama asked. Though Zelda was retired from her job as an RN at the nursing home, she had recently told Jama she still did part-time nursing.

To Jama's great relief, just as she found the EKG machine behind door number three in the largest treatment room, all the would-be helpers were scrambling out the clinic entrance to search for Zelda.

Monty's eyes opened when Jama began to attach the leads from the machine to his chest. He looked around the room, grimaced and tried to sit up.

"Don't you dare move." She pressed him back. "I've got work to do, and you're hindering me. You don't want me to look bad my first day on the job, because I will make you pay."

He studied her a moment, then relaxed as well as any man could relax when he'd been stripped half-naked and attached to wires by a woman who'd once been a child he'd helped raise. "Did I bleed all over that nice, clean front porch?"

"I wouldn't know, but you can help pay for the window I broke to get you in here."

His answering grin was more of a contortion of the face. "Did this on purpose, you know. Wanted to break you in right as soon as you arrived here."

"So you're saying you didn't fall from the ladder, you jumped."

"That's got to be it. I've climbed plenty of ladders. Never fallen before."

"So what happened this time? Did a rung break? Did the ground shift under the—" The lines on the EKG machine caught her attention.

"Monty, you said you thought you might have busted a rib or two."

"Chest hurts."

She swallowed and tried to keep her breathing even. "Did it hurt before you fell off the ladder?"

He paused. "I'm not sure, but it might have."

"Think about it. This is important."

"Why?"

"It'll give me a better idea about the source of your pain." She searched through the cabinets for IV supplies and fluids while she punched in the preprogrammed number on her cell phone for the airlift service for St. Mary's Hospital in Jefferson City. She would need a blood thinner and other meds . . . "Where was that pain located?"

He pointed to the middle of his chest.

When the line connected, Jama requested a helicopter, explained the situation and location. The emergency personnel would have to land in the parking lot of the winery, the only large, paved surface in River Dance. The gravel on the clinic lot would spray in every direction if the chopper landed here. Jama needed help to make sure the winery lot was cleared. This early in the morning, it should be empty except for employee vehicles.

She disconnected and returned her attention to Monty. "I've checked you over, and can't appreciate any obvious deformities. There was a lot of blood, but it was superficial. Since I don't have an X-ray tech, I can't get a film right now, but, Monty, your EKG shows classic ST elevation. I'm going to establish a large bore IV and—"

"English, Jama." He was looking gray again.

"Sorry. It looks like you're having a heart attack. I've called for an airlift, but—"

"Somebody need a seventy-six-year-old nurse?" came a screechy shout from the waiting room. Zelda Benedict.

Jama was flooded with relief. That voice, recalled from Jama's past, brought to mind memories of strength and calm assurance. "In here," Jama called. "Second room to the left. When's the last time you established an IV in a patient?"

The tall, slender woman entering the room wore orange jogging shorts that matched her hair, dusty tennis shoes and a light green tank top that matched her eyes. She had a green jacket that matched her tank top, but it was tied by the sleeves around her waist. Zelda Benedict looked closer to fifty than seventy-six.

"I did one yesterday, that recent enough for you?" Zelda peered at the monitor, then clucked her tongue. "Large bore? Tell me where everything is."

"I can't. I just got here, myself. We aren't exactly open for business."

"You got that right. If you're the one who broke that glass, the mayor's gonna tear you a new one."

"Tear a new one . . ." Monty mumbled. "That's it, Jama. That's how my chest felt."

Zelda patted his hand. "We'll get you feeling better. An aspirin, a little heparin, a little trip to the hospital, and you'll be fixed—"

"Hold it," Jama said. "Monty, what do you mean? You felt something tearing in your chest when you fell?"

"Felt that way. Something seemed to rip, but I didn't think much of it—didn't have time after the fall."

"So you're saying you felt this tearing pain in your chest *before* you fell?"

He nodded.

Jama closed her eyes. She'd heard of bad first days, but this was becoming a nightmare. "Zelda, find the sublingual nitro."

"Where do I look?"

Jama turned, scanned the glass-doored cabinets and pointed to one. "Try there. And locate the heparin and aspirin, but don't get them out yet."

"Why not? If this is a heart—"

"Wait a minute, will you?" How could this be happening, today of all days? Was this punishment from God so many years after the original sins?

Jama checked Monty for neurological deficits and found a decided weakness in his left leg.

Zelda brought the nitro. "Here you go. Now, how about the—"

"Forget the heparin," Jama said.

The nurse arched a finely drawn eyebrow that matched her hair. "An aspirin, at least?"

"Can't risk the bleeding."

"What bleeding?" The question was threaded with the steel of Nurse Zelda's teacher voice, honed from her years of being nurse director of River Dance Nursing Care. "This arm isn't bleeding enough to warrant withholding blood thinners."

"Something about this doesn't seem to be a simple MI," Jama said.

"So what is it? We need a diagnosis before we can treat."

Jama touched Monty's arm. "The ripping in his chest could be a clue about what caused the MI."

"Did you call Fran?" Monty asked, eyes closed. Under the harsh, bright lights, his pale, grayish skin and leathered wrinkles from years beneath the sun made him look suddenly aged.

"I called Tyrell. He's on his way here."

"Don't let him bully you." Monty's words had begun to slur. "Tell him you'll take good care of me."

Jama met Zelda's inquiring look, and all the years of training fled. She was just Jama Keith again, the girl who tagged after Zelda Benedict at the nursing home like a lost puppy, finding acceptance from the elderly patients she loved, even before she began receiving pay as an aide.

Who was Jama Keith now, standing here making life-and-death decisions for the man who had been her second father? How could she—

"Dr. Keith?" Zelda's soft green eyes held only respect. "What are your instincts telling you?"

"Dissecting aortic aneurysm. A tear in the wall of the aorta—"

"What do you need for a positive diagnosis?"

"I need to see if he has mediastinal widening, and for that, I need a chest X-ray."

"You've got no tech scheduled?"

Jama shook her head. "As I said, we're not open yet."

Zelda's frown finally showed her age. "Well, folderol. I knew I should've taken that course at the university."

"If we treat him for a classic MI with blood thinners of any kind, and this is a tear in the aorta—"

"I know," Zelda said. "He could bleed to death."

"I've called for airlift to St. Mary's."

"How long do we have?"

Jama looked at the large wall clock. "They should be here in ten minutes."

"I'll contact the hospital for an accepting physician."

"I need someone to clear a landing space for—"

There was another shout from the waiting room—one Jama recognized. For as far back as she could remember, that voice had meant comfort, friendship and much, much more.

And now? Tyrell Mercer's voice stirred conflicting emotions, but she didn't have time to deal with anything but Monty.

"There's our man," Zelda said with a wink. "Just in time, as always. Go put him to work, and tell him his daddy's being well cared for by the best doctor and nurse in River Dance."

Jama rushed to intercept "our man" and fill him in.

Tyrell was in the middle of the large waiting room, his six-foot-three broad-shouldered bulk cutting a swath across the polished wooden floor and area rug toward the treatment rooms.

He stopped when he saw Jama, his expression apprehensive. "What happened?"

Jama felt drawn to his comforting strength. She wanted nothing more than to step into his embrace and let it engulf her. Today, however, she needed to be the strong one.

She stepped forward and placed a hand on his arm. "It's his heart."

Chapter Four

Doriann mustn't throw up. If she did, Deb would for sure kill her—though nothing could make this truck stink any worse, so it shouldn't matter to Deb. Doriann tried to focus on the white dotted line in the center of the road, and on the distant hilltops, not the trees that raced past on both sides in a blur of spring green.

Think, Doriann. Got to think! Where are we?

She glanced at the speedometer. Eighty-two miles per hour.

Speedometer . . . speed. That was what Aunt Renee had been teaching about during Social Studies lessons for the past month. Speed was a nickname for an illegal drug. Doriann would probably know all this stuff so much better if she attended public school and had friends besides her cousins and other homeschooled kids at church.

Mom and Dad always worried about the development of Doriann's social skills in a home-schooling environment, but they wanted her to be able to learn at her own pace. In public school, she'd be in sixth grade, not ninth. Who would have thought teaching her about illegal drugs might save her life?

If her life got saved.

There was a drug that stank like dirty socks—the way this truck stank—when it was being cooked, and one of the words for it was speed. Methamphetamines. Meth. Crank. It made sense. Had these people been cooking meth? Dopeheads? All kinds of terms for that drug. Missouri outranked every other state in the country for meth lab busts per capita.

Doriann felt that could be a good thing, or a bad

thing. If the busts were because the police in Missouri worked harder than police in any other state to find the meth labs, then that was good. But it could also mean there were more meth labs to be busted.

Aunt Renee said that someone on meth would do anything for another fix. Since this truck had nearly turned over when they left the interstate before waiting for an exit ramp, Doriann bet that either these two freaks were crazy or high on something.

Think, Doriann! How do you get out of this mess?

Aunt Renee said more than once that Doriann was the smartest kid she'd ever known. More like a little grown-up than a kid. Of course, Aunt Renee believed in positive reinforcement. But still.

Aunt Renee had made that statement yesterday, right after Doriann had told her cousins a scary story and made Ajay cry. That meant the statement wasn't being made in a positive way, but to heap on the guilt.

Mom said Aunt Renee was good at guilt trips. Mom should know that about her twin sister.

So if Aunt Renee says I'm a great storyteller, tell Clancy a story. He does everything Deb tells him not to do. He's a lot like my cousins, and I know how to handle them. What do dopeheads want most in all the world? More dope, right? And what do I want most in all the world? Out of this truck!

Clancy blasted through an intersection without even slowing at the stop sign, or checking for traffic. Had to be scorched on speed. Right?

"You missed the turn," Deb said. "94. That's the road that'll take us to St. Louis."

Doriann perked up as Clancy stomped the brake with a screech of tires. They were taking Highway 94. *Thank you, Jesus!* She suddenly felt less like crying. If she could get Clancy to take the exit to River Dance . . . Uncle Tyrell was there, and Grandpa and Grandma, and even Aunt Jama, who was supposed to start her new job today.

Uncle Tyrell was big and tough and could take on a dinosaur. He wasn't afraid of anything. And Grandpa wouldn't let anybody hurt her, over his dead body. But how was a kid supposed to get Clancy to take River Dance Road?

She cleared her throat. "We're going the wrong way."

"Shut up," Deb snapped.

Doriann braced herself to be slapped again. "I'm just warning you, is all."

Deb didn't slap her, but she looked as if she was about to.

"I have to warn you about one of the towns we'll be passing," Doriann continued. "River Dance. It's a bad place. W-we don't want to go there."

Clancy's jaw tightened, and he flexed his right arm. "That's not where we're headed."

"This road will take us right past the turnoff to—"

"Why don't we want to go to River Dance?" Clancy growled.

"Don't talk to the brat," Deb said. "Don't listen, and don't talk."

"Why not? If she knows something about this place—"

"She's a kid, and she doesn't know anything. Who takes directions from a stupid kid?"

"I might be a stupid kid, but I know somebody who's been to River Dance, and you don't." Doriann braced herself.

Still no slap.

"They have a lot of drugs in that town," she continued. "That's always been a problem there." Her family would kill her for slandering their hometown this way . . . That was the word, wasn't it? Slander. Yes. Not libel. Libel was slander in print.

"My friend says it isn't all bad," she said. "I mean, there's this great winery on top of the hill, and there are some cellars below the main building where wine barrels are stored, and some of the high-school kids sneak in and steal some of the wine. And there are old, abandoned farmhouses."

"So you know this town, huh?" Clancy asked.

Deb wrapped her hand around Doriann's arm. She squeezed. Hard.

Doriann winced. She realized she'd better be careful. "My friend did . . . until she moved to Kansas City. My friend used to play in one of those farmhouses until she found out she was in one of the places where drugs are made. Scary people hung out there." That should get their attention.

"Scarier than me?" Clancy asked with a laugh that blasted his rotten breath through the cab of the truck.

Doriann nearly gagged. "People like you." She wasn't going to pretend she thought he was a good guy. "It's creepy around that town. There are lots of trees along that part of the river. A person could get lost in those woods and never get out."

That should convince him to turn there. Didn't he and Deb need to hide from the FBI agents and police? And if they thought they could find drugs in River Dance, why go farther?

"Sounds like a place I might want to visit," Clancy said.

Doriann slanted a look at Deb, who didn't look mad at all. Good. She had their attention.

She sank back into her seat, trying not to show her relief. *Grandpa, here I come, ready or not.*

Doriann watched the trees whiz by, so fast that she was reminded of her mother's blender concoction of yogurt and green vegetables—an awful drink that made her feel sick just to remember the taste.

Clancy gave her another narrow-eyed look, making her squirm. "So. You think you know your way around this River Dance?"

She kept her eyes on the road—something she

wished Clancy would do. "My friend told me all about it."

"Then you could be our tour guide?"

"Don't even think about it," Deb snapped. "Somebody could recognize her."

"Nobody knows me there." Doriann figured if she was going to lie, she might as well go all out, as Grandpa would say.

Deb seemed to space out. She blinked, gave Doriann a confused look, closed her eyes as if the day was too bright.

Yep. Meth.

"It sounds like a good place to hide until the heat's off. Besides—" Clancy rested his hand on Doriann's leg "—with little Dori here as a guide, we won't get lost, will we, darlin'?"

Doriann cringed at his touch. "No, but it's a bad place." *How am I getting out of this truck?*

"She's gotta go," Deb said. This time she studied Doriann with a sly look of hidden intention that was scarier than slapping or curse words.

"Not till we're through with her," Clancy growled.

Doriann swallowed. Through with her? Through doing what with her? And how was she going to "go," as Deb said? Did she mean they were going to kill her?

"We're gonna crash soon if we can't get some stuff," Deb said. "What are we gonna do with her then? I'm telling you, Clancy, she can't be here."

"Wait a minute, will you?" Clancy's voice shot through the cab with a force that told Doriann there was more where that came from. Violent killer.

And they were talking about what to do with her? She was sorry she'd said anything. Why couldn't she have kept her mouth shut?

"We'll tie her up or lock her in one of those old buildings she's jabbering about," he said.

"That's stupid," Deb said. "She could get away and we could wake up in jail. Just dump her and leave. And slow the truck down! What if there's a speed trap? These backcountry roads are known for traps."

Doriann felt a flare of hope, but then the speedometer needle dropped.

She couldn't depend on a traffic cop to notice Clancy's reckless driving and rescue her. She was going to have to think of some way to save herself.

Chapter Five

Tyrell Mercer stood frozen as the love of his life looked up at him with tender concern, touching his arm with her warm hands. Jama's expressive blue-green eyes were dark and troubled.

"Is it a heart attack?" he asked.

"Not exactly." She described the morning episode, and he heard the hesitation in her voice. For the second time in three weeks, he wished he didn't know her so well. And he wished she would look into his eyes more often instead of just past his left shoulder or at the ceiling or out the front window.

"How bad is this tear you're talking about?"

"No way of knowing," she said. "I'm not even sure that's what it is. Marty mentioned a sensation of ripping in his chest, and his left leg is weaker than his right."

"He's had weakness since his stroke."

She hesitated, then her gaze met his straight-on. He didn't like the look of alarm that flashed in her eyes, and as quickly disappeared. "Monty's never had a stroke."

"It happened right after . . ." It was his turn to hesitate. "Dad had a small stroke four and a half years ago, a few weeks after Amy's funeral." Just saying the words brought back the horrible grief of his sister's death. He saw it affected Jama, as well. Of course it did. Amy had been Jama's best friend . . . her foster sister. The whole family knew Jama had never recovered.

"The rest of us had already returned to our homes and jobs," he told her. "Mom and Dad decided not to burden us with it. I only found out about it this year."

He saw Jama's eyes darken further, and he fought down his own rush of anxiety. Calm. Stay calm. But he knew from her response that, for some reason, Dad's stroke could somehow complicate everything. He just didn't know how.

"Why didn't he tell me?" she asked.

"You know Dad. Never wants anyone to worry, just like today, I'm sure. What's the significance?"

She closed her eyes briefly.

"Jama?"

She looked up then, and he could see that she was mentally adjusting her expression for him. It was in this brief change—this infinitesimal moment—that he saw the flash of loss and longing in the depth of her eyes.

"As I said, that tear he felt in his chest is classic for dissecting aortic aneurysm." Professional again, she looked away, speaking with calm authority. "That means there's bleeding that could get worse with blood thinners."

"That's why you couldn't treat him for a heart attack?"

"Exactly. But one symptom I was using to help me make the tentative diagnosis, since I had no capacity for any other kind of test, was the weakness of that leg. This is often a symptom of the condition I suspected. With no X-ray tech available, I couldn't know for sure." She sought Tyrell's gaze again.

"Explain a little more, sweetheart." The endearment slipped out, and he didn't care. "All of it. You're scaring the bejeebers out of me, so the plain truth can't be any worse." Jama had finished second in her med-school class. He trusted her judgment, because he admired her intelligence

43

and her logic. But when that judgment came without complete knowledge of the facts, it could be faulty.

"This shouldn't be happening," she said. "Monty's too active and healthy for heart trouble, and so that's the knowledge on which I based my decision not to treat. I didn't know about the stroke. If this isn't what I've suspected, and if this really is an MI, then there could be further damage to his heart because of the delay in treatment."

"So it's up to you to decide, based strictly on your medical judgment."

"That's right."

Jama shouldn't be forced to make life-and-death decisions about someone she loved. "Where's the other doctor?" Tyrell asked. "I thought there was a director—"

"The director isn't here, yet." Jama raised a hand to her eyes just long enough for Tyrell to see with relief that it was not shaking. He also saw she understood that he didn't doubt her expertise. She knew him that well. "I have an airlift on its way that will most likely arrive before Dr. Lawrence does."

He groaned softly. "Where do you need me right now? At Dad's bedside, or—"

"I need the parking lot cleared at the Dancing Waters Winery for landing."

"I'll call now." He pulled out his cell phone.

• • •

Throughout her internship and the early years of residency training, Jama had had doctors, nurses, fellow interns and residents looking over her shoulder as she worked with patients. By the second year of her family practice residency, however, she had gained the trust of her colleagues, and no longer had anyone looking over her shoulder and critiquing her work.

Now, as the flight crew switched Monty from the clinic equipment to their own, she was the authority who stood in the middle of the action, observing every movement. Had any member of the crew made the slightest misstep, she'd have tackled that person and completed the job herself.

As she watched and tried hard to contain her worry, a fresh layer of remorse pressed down on her shoulders like a boatload of river silt.

Monty's stroke? Had it been caused by the black grief of Amy's death, and not some clot in his brain?

Medical science was learning more and more about the impact of emotions on overall health.

The male flight nurse, nearly as big and intimidating as Tyrell, frowned at the display on the monitor, then scowled at Jama.

"Dr. Keith, why hasn't this man been stabilized for transport?"

The man's attitude startled her. She resented his questioning of her judgment. "He's as stable as we

45

can make him under the circumstances," she told him.

"He hasn't received any—"

"I have reason to believe he has a dissecting aortic aneurysm, which will need to be ruled out before medication can be given for—"

"How did you determine that?" the nurse demanded. "You have no—"

"That's my clinical assessment," she snapped. "I'll take responsibility for it. Don't stand here arguing with me while this patient needs immediate transport."

"Excuse me." Tyrell entered the room. "I'm this man's son. I believe the doctor has made her diagnosis. If you have any questions, you can take them up with me after you've flown my father to St. Mary's."

The staring match lasted a few seconds. The nurse backed down. He was, after all, a professional, and it was obvious he took his job seriously.

The crew completed the switch and transferred Monty to a gurney for transport while Jama tried hard to maintain her resolute demeanor.

The nurse was knowledgeable. He knew what he was doing. Jama would not, however, change her diagnosis.

She followed the crew out the front door and across the parking lot, and she might've followed them all the way up the hill to the helicopter in the winery parking lot. Before she could do so, however, an ancient station wagon entered the lot and pulled next to Jama's green Subaru.

If she wasn't mistaken, the new director had arrived to ramp up the tension a few more notches.

Dr. Ruth Lawrence was at least four inches shorter than Jama's five-eight. She looked to be about ten years older. She wore her dark brown hair in a braid down her back. Her angular face, free of makeup, didn't appear to have ever exhibited a smile except for telltale laugh lines around her golden-brown eyes. Her royal-blue scrubs looked well used, as did her lab coat. She'd had the sense to dress for comfort.

Jama altered her course and stepped toward her. "Dr. Lawrence? I'm Dr. Jama Keith."

The woman nodded without smiling or offering her hand. "I saw the helicopter arrive. Do you have a report for me?" She turned and started toward the clinic, brisk steps, economical movements, no evidence of cordiality, obviously expecting Jama to keep pace.

Once more Jama reported about Monty and her judgment call. When they reached the broken windowpane, Jama promised to pay for the damage.

"I'm sure you will." Dr. Lawrence paused at the clinic door, which had been anchored open, then she looked at Jama as if to ask why.

Jama didn't reply.

Dr. Lawrence stepped inside. "Under the circumstances, I believe the mayor will be magnanimous," she said over her shoulder, "but paying might remind you next time that you aren't Dirty Harry."

Jama was beginning to feel a little snarly. "A key might be nice *next* time."

Dr. Lawrence stepped into the comfortably spacious reception room and studied the fully equipped business office behind glass. "Would a key have kept you from making a questionable diagnosis?"

Jama pressed her lips together to keep angry words from spilling out. Definitely snarly. "Are you trying to tell me I'm *not* going to have my own key to the clinic?"

Dr. Lawrence wandered back toward the broad hallway that led to the treatment rooms and private offices, ignoring her.

"Don't you think the key would have prevented the broken glass?" Jama persisted.

"Couldn't you have decided on a less destructive way to see to the patient?" Dr. Lawrence asked over her shoulder.

"Are you questioning my diagnostic skills, or my decision to break a replaceable piece of glass for the sake of patient care?"

Dr. Lawrence paused to peer into the first treatment room, where Monty had recently been, and where Zelda was cleaning up as if she had suddenly become a member of staff.

"I did the best I could with the diagnosis," Jama said. "I'm not a radiology tech, Dr. Lawrence, and we didn't have one on-site, so I made the best call I could under the circumstances."

The director turned back to her. "Let's drop the formalities. They're stuffy and awkward. My name is Ruth, and I expect to be called Ruth, not Dr. Lawrence, and certainly not Dr. Ruth." There was no humor in her voice.

"I'm Jama."

"Yes, Jama," she said, her voice suddenly softer, as if she'd discovered where she had mislaid her manners. "I'm not saying we will be chummy—" so much for the manners "—but we need to establish some simplicity. It's going to be a hectic few days as we hire our own staff, develop our management systems, train the team to—"

"There's no *staff?*"

Dr. Lawrence . . . Ruth . . . blinked. "Who did you expect to do the hiring? The mayor?"

"It might have been helpful."

"I won't have a small-town mayor hiring medical personnel. I specified this before I agreed to work here."

"Then it might have been nice if someone had informed *me,*" Jama complained. Just because she'd had no voice in the decisions and plans that had been made for the next two years didn't mean she wanted to be treated as if she didn't exist.

"I will make my own choices and judgments

about the people with whom I will spend a huge amount of my time," Ruth said.

"Mayor Thompson hired *me.* You didn't have any choice about that."

Ruth turned to rearrange a stack of magazines on the center table in the waiting room. "Your situation is different, but since you mentioned it, just because you have a forgivable loan from this town does not mean you may behave any way you wish. Your behavior the next two years will determine whether or not you stay on after that probationary period."

Jama pressed the tip of her tongue against her front teeth. Why on earth would she want to stay on? "A probationary period of *two years?*" That was a nasty slap in the face. She would make Tyrell Mercer suffer badly for getting her into this.

She could have paid back those school loans on her own. Eventually. But Tyrell would not hear of it. Without telling her what he was up to, he'd proposed this arrangement to the city council, and the decision was made before she had time to think about it.

Sure, she'd signed the stupid contract, but she was under duress at the time. Thinking about finances made her crazy.

"Depending on how things work out," Ruth said, "the two-year probation could be greatly reduced."

Jama wondered what response she'd receive if she were to share her thoughts at that moment.

"During this time," Ruth said, "you will keep in mind that I am your supervisor . . . director . . . whatever you want to call me. You will respect my orders and do as I say when on duty. When off duty, you can say anything you want to me. You will report to work when you are scheduled, and you will do nothing to jeopardize the reputation of this clinic."

Heat warmed Jama's face. The mayor had obviously not remained silent about her youthful escapades. But at thirty-two, she was far removed from those days.

The sound of squeaky footsteps echoed from the corridor, where Zelda in her orange shorts and green shirt and dusty running shoes came toward them with a familiar glint in her eye.

Chapter Six

Jama braced herself as Zelda held her hand out to Ruth. "Couldn't help overhearing. Thought I'd introduce myself and give you a proper introduction to our little spitfire here."

Jama nearly groaned aloud. "Zelda, she doesn't need any incentive to extend my probationary—"

"Hush, kid. The good doctor just needs some pointers about handling you, is all."

Handling? "I'm not a farm animal."

Zelda ignored her. "Dr. Lawrence, our Jama has one of the tenderest hearts in the river valley, and she has a special affinity for the elderly. She was so devoted to our nursing-home residents that she missed class a time or two so she could help out when we were shorthanded, or when one of her favorite patients was dying."

"Yes, skipping school seemed to be a habit of hers," Ruth said.

"Unfortunately," Zelda said, "she was caught and suspended a couple of times, which cost her approval points with some of the River Dance citizens."

"Zelda, must you rub my nose in it?" Jama asked.

"I can introduce you to a lot of people who feel differently." Zelda continued to ignore Jama. "She's always had a special insight when it comes to anyone in pain. She needs to be given a lot of leeway. The child's been gone from here for fourteen years, and—"

"I'm not a child."

"Excuse me," Ruth said, turning to Jama, "but why fourteen years? I was under the impression you just completed your residency training, and it doesn't take fourteen years—"

"Actually, Zelda," Jama said, "it's been fifteen years since I left. I was seventeen, remember? And I took an accelerated course through college. But I took a hiatus from residency training."

"For what reason?" Ruth asked.

None of your business. "I changed specialties."

The golden-brown eyes sought Jama's and held them, probing. Jama stared back.

"That doesn't mean she's flighty, Dr. Lawrence," Zelda said. "Far from it. She doesn't deserve to be treated like the teenager she was when she left home."

Jama groaned aloud.

"She *especially* doesn't deserve to be placed on probation for two years."

"I'll make my own judgments about that," Ruth said. "I don't know everyone in town, as you obviously do."

"Then you've got two of River Dance's own to help guide you through the process if you'd just trust us a little," Zelda said.

Ruth met the nurse's gaze. "Give a stranger some time to settle," she said softly.

Jama had always appreciated Zelda's outspoken devotion—the same devotion she'd given to her wayward grandchildren when they were in trouble—but now was not the time. The new director obviously needed no more ammunition.

"Uh, Ruth," Jama said, trying to stop Zelda's runaway tongue, "you might consider Zelda for the nursing position. That is if you don't mind being bossed around by a woman who's been treating patients since before either of us was born."

Suitably distracted, Ruth returned her full attention to Zelda. "Have you applied?"

"Not me," Zelda said. "I've done my full-time

and moved on to choosing my shifts more carefully."

"Then I don't see that there's anything to discuss."

"We could use your help," Jama told her old friend, warming to the idea. "You could help us break in the new staff. It isn't as if you'd have to take the position permanently, but—"

"Have you told the director that I'm seventy-six?"

Ruth studied Zelda with renewed interest, and Jama, in turn, studied Ruth. "What does age have to do with anything?" the director asked. She didn't smile, but her expression warmed by several degrees. "I've seen men and women considerably older participate in clinic work with excellent results. Good experience is more valuable than classroom training any day."

"Well, anyway," Jama said, intrigued by Ruth's sudden thaw, "I have a report to fill out. I need to find the forms, and I have no idea where—"

The front door flew open, and Tyrell rushed inside, dark hair mussed, probably by the wind from the helicopter. "Jama, I can't find Mom, and I need to get to the hospital in Jefferson City to be there for Dad as soon as I can. He said he wants to talk to me before he goes under. I know he's worried about the ranch, and I need to reassure him that I'm not going to—"

"Why couldn't he talk before they put him on the chopper?"

"He wasn't in any shape to talk, and that flight nurse is a piece of work. I'm not sure if he's really a nurse, or a runaway from World Wrestling Entertainment. At any rate, I need to get to Jeff City as quickly as possible, but I don't want Mom driving there alone."

"I'll find Fran and drive her there."

"She's grocery shopping. You know she refuses to carry a cell phone."

"Where's she shopping?"

"She didn't say. Could be here in River Dance, could be in Fulton."

"I'll find her, then meet you at the hospital," Jama said.

Ruth cleared her throat behind them. "The city police should be capable of finding the patient's wife."

Jama turned to her director. "I need to do it myself."

"Do you feel you're the only physician who can handle his case?" Ruth asked. "We have interviews set up nearly every hour for the rest of the day."

Jama bristled. What was she, a mushroom? "Nobody told me that."

"I need you here."

"The patient has been my foster father since I was fifteen," Jama explained. "He's also a city council member, and since the personnel in this clinic are answerable to the city government—"

Ruth raised a silencing hand. She glanced at

Tyrell, then at Zelda. A weight seemed to drag down her features briefly, but her neutral mask returned.

"Then go," she said.

"Zelda can help with your interviews," Jama told her.

"I'll make my own decisions about who will help me."

Jama shrugged and nodded to Tyrell. "I'll find Fran, then meet you in Jeff."

River Dance, 14 miles. Doriann blinked at the sign, then stared down the empty road. They hadn't passed another car in miles, but a deer had jumped in front of the truck, and Clancy had almost run over a cat. He was a horrible person. He'd aimed the truck toward the cat and tried to hit it. They'd almost run off the road before Deb had screamed and smacked Clancy, gouging Doriann's chest with her elbow as she swung. Deb and Clancy were both wicked, evil people.

Please, God, oh, please, Jesus, I'll never skip school again, never lie to Aunt Renee again, never talk to strangers in the park again, and if you want, I'll even promise never to go near the zoo again, although that would be awfully hard. I mean, the animals are already in those pens and cages, and I didn't do anything to put them there, so what's the harm in going to talk to—

"Little Dori Streeter." Clancy gave a low chuckle.

"My name isn't Dori."

"Of course, it isn't. No kid of Dr. Mark-Streeter-who-thinks-he's-God's gonna use a nickname. But your father isn't here now, and you're Dori if I want to call you Dori."

Doriann stared straight ahead. *He knows Dad!*

Don't show fear. They didn't grab me just because I was there. Did they follow me?

"Do you think we're rich, or something?" she asked. "Because we're not. Hospital residents don't get paid—"

"Shut up!" Deb slapped a hand over Doriann's lips. Hard. "Your mouth is gonna get you killed, brat."

Doriann shut up. *Killed.*

"You're not stupid," Clancy told Doriann, still with that smooth, fake friendliness. "Now you know I'm wanted for murder. I bet you didn't know it was your dear daddy's fault."

Doriann didn't want her mouth slapped again. She didn't say anything.

"If your daddy wants to see you alive again, he'll do whatever I say. The Feds are closing in, and I'm not going back to prison."

"Back?" Deb exclaimed. "So you've been in—"

"Now it's time for *you* to shut up." Clancy cut a nasty look at Deb. Then he looked back down at Doriann. "I'm gonna make your daddy sorry for what he did to me. And then the government's going to make a trade with me. They'll give me a one-way ticket out of the country, and I'll send you back home."

"What about me?" Deb demanded. "You're going to leave me for the dogs to tear to pieces?"

"I didn't ask you to come with me." Clancy shot her another look that could've been a reflection of the devil.

Doriann felt her head buzz. For the next few minutes, she stared at the road ahead, all the curves and hills and flat, wide-open valleys. She caught a brief glimpse of the Missouri River on the right. She had to do something to get out of this truck. She wished she had the nerve to grab the steering wheel away from Clancy and stomp the brake on a curve. It would cause a wreck, and maybe she wouldn't go flying through the windshield, even though she wasn't wearing a seat belt.

Drugged killers didn't use seat belts. The truck didn't even have them.

Another curve, and she braced herself. *You can do this, Doriann. To save your own life, you can do this.* She raised her hand to grab the steering wheel, but Clancy snorted, scaring her so badly she peed a little.

"Yeah, your superdad's not gonna think he's so high-and-mighty when he finds out he's the reason his precious, spoiled little girl's gone missing. No E.R. doc's gonna sic the cops on me and—"

"My father isn't an E.R.—"

"Shut up, both of you!" Deb's sharp, rattly voice

shot through the cab. "How many times do I have to tell you, talkin's gonna get us in trouble? The less the brat knows, the safer we are."

Doriann frowned. That didn't make sense. "If everybody's going to know soon, anyway—"

Deb smacked Doriann's cheek, then grasped her chin with the same hand and leaned down to stare hard into her eyes. "And when will you learn to keep your sassy trap shut? We don't want to hear it."

Doriann glared into the wicked witch's yellow-green eyes until the grip tightened more painfully on her face. She looked away. When Deb let go, Doriann didn't speak, but she did reach back and flip open the catch on the sliding rear window.

When neither Clancy nor Deb stopped her, she slid the window open. She didn't believe Clancy. He wasn't going to let her go; he would kill her just as he'd killed others. Crazy, drugged, violent criminals didn't make bargains, they killed. But before she died she wanted at least one more breath of fresh air.

Silence was settling into the cab again when Doriann glanced toward the curve ahead. She nearly choked. Another animal had stepped into the road at the bottom of the hill. Bigger than a cat, littler than a deer. It was a dog. And Clancy stomped the accelerator.

Doriann braced herself. No! No!

"You moron, don't you see that curve?" Deb

braced herself against the door frame and the dash. "You're gonna wreck this truck!"

Without speaking, Clancy swerved into the other lane toward the dog—a red-and-white-speckled hound, like Humphrey, Grandpa's hunting dog, who followed Doriann everywhere when she visited Grandpa and Grandma. She'd rescued him from a ditch when he was a puppy. This dog just stood staring at the truck as it approached, his floppy ears perked with curiosity.

They were headed straight for it, and Deb started shouting again, using all those words that Doriann wanted to not have in her mental vocabulary. Clancy whooped, as if he was on a roller-coaster ride.

Doriann couldn't let this happen. She couldn't!

They were close enough to see the dog's eyes when Doriann lunged at the steering wheel and kicked at Clancy's leg, trying to reach the brake pedal. He shouted and elbowed her chest. Deb leaped across Doriann, screaming.

The truck jerked. The steering wheel spun. Doriann's face was squished into Deb's bony rib cage. Everything went crazy.

The truck bounced, nosed down a long bank, hit a tree, bounced again, slid sideways and rolled back. Trees streaked past the windows, faster and faster.

There was a sudden jerk, then a splash. Doriann saw water surge over the windshield, and panic gripped her. Was this the Missouri River? Were they all going to drown?

Clancy and Deb cussed and hit at each other, squishing Doriann between them.

She had to get out! But Deb and Clancy blocked the way to the doors. She twisted around and looked at the open back window. Not the Missouri. This was one of the nearby swamps.

She reached toward the open window. A hand grabbed her leg and jerked her back.

"You killed us!" Deb screamed. "We're gonna die!"

Something shoved Doriann's bottom upward. She didn't look to see what it was. She grabbed at the edges of the window and tugged herself toward it, kicking at the hand on her leg. The grip relaxed as Doriann squeezed her shoulders through the opening. Freezing water splashed her face, shocking her as it poured into the cab.

With all her might, she dragged her way out of the tangle of arms, plunging face-first into the pickup bed. It was filled with cold water, weeds and rotten, floating logs. The swamp probably was filled with snakes and leeches and the bodies of other people who'd crashed and drowned in the slimy pit. She kicked hard against the cab and swam through the gunk toward the weedy bank.

She heard Deb's and Clancy's angry screeches as her feet sank into the mud. She fought her way through the undergrowth beneath the trees. The splintering tinkle of breaking glass reached her as the voices grew louder, as water splashed.

Doriann crashed through the reeds and cane as fast as she could, and she didn't look back.

Chapter Seven

Doriann had no idea where she was, or where she was going, but the road had to be just ahead. Briars and branches caught at her hair and her soaked jacket, and the mud that filled her shoes squished with every step. She pushed her way through the briars, ignoring the pain. She'd worry about the blood later. She couldn't think about that now.

In fact, if she was bloody when she reached the road, someone would stop for sure. Who wouldn't pull over for a bloody, lost little girl?

Okay, maybe not a little girl, but she sure was lost, and if she kept getting caught in blackberry brambles, she'd be as bloody as a victim in one of the horror movies Mom and Dad never let her watch. Now if only a car would pass on that lonely road . . . if she could find the stupid road.

She stumbled, looked down and glimpsed a tire rut in the ground. Must be going the right way if that was from the truck. They'd hit the ground hard a couple of times. She plunged through another thicket of trees at the top of the hill. The road was here, it had to be right here. . . .

The ground sank beneath her. She fell on her

bottom in soft mud, saw the broad, silvery sparkle of the Missouri River spread out in front of her, flowing in the morning sunshine. She gasped.

It wasn't the road! She'd been running in the wrong direction! The ground sank farther, and she scrambled backward to keep from plunging into the water.

She looked up to see sunbeams streaking through the tree limbs to her left. So that was east. There were no straight lines in the woods, and that crazy river went every which way.

Aunt Renee said when you got lost in the woods without a fancy GPS device, then you had to look for the sun. If it was cloudy, you had to follow the water. It was the only way to find civilization again. Water followed the path of least resistance, and creeks drained into rivers, and there were people at the rivers, especially the Missouri.

Doriann glanced back the way she had come, and heard the rustle of brush, a voice, swearing and yelling.

She was trapped! She looked down where loose, muddy dirt had sunk beneath her feet. She couldn't jump into the river; though she was a good swimmer, it was too cold. Aunt Renee said Grandpa was worried about a killing frost harming the vineyard this year. Tonight was supposed to be the killer. It had been a warm spring, but the past two days had been cold. It was a bad combination.

The rustling noises grew louder, the angry voices

sharper. She rolled to her side to duck behind a bush. At least the warm spring had produced early buds and leaves for cover.

Unfortunately, the pale green buds and brambles stuck to her clothing, and every time she moved, the whole bush quivered.

She tugged off her bright purple jacket, dropped it onto the ground, then rolled onto it. Maybe her light green T-shirt and blue jeans—now covered with mud—wouldn't show up too much . . . and maybe her red hair would blend with . . . what? The sky? The river? Nothing!

Okay, but her hair was drenched, so it was darker, and might not be so obvious.

Clancy and Deb were getting closer. They would see her for sure. She was toast.

Think, Doriann, think!

Okay, what did people do to hide? They climbed trees. But Clancy and Deb were already too close; she'd be seen if she tried to go up a tree trunk.

She glanced along the riverbank again. Where had she seen someone hiding . . . Yes! In *Lord of the Rings*, in the first movie, the hobbits hid beneath the bank's ledge when the ring wraith was looking for them. There were roots . . .

She studied the bank in both directions, searching for a tree teetering at the very edge . . .

Nothing. And there was no one on the river this morning who would hear her call for help. Even if there was, she couldn't call loudly enough to get anybody's attention without giving herself away to the killers. Besides, what if they killed whoever tried to rescue her?

She was toast.

Jama drove the familiar main thoroughfare of her hometown, looking for a light blue Honda Civic. She could probably call Kaiser's grocery store and ask if Fran Mercer was there, but Jama wanted to deliver the news about Monty herself.

Several kindhearted women in River Dance had undertaken the responsibility of mothering Jama after her own troubled mother had left. Tilly Kaiser, who ran Kaiser's Grocery with her husband, Harold, had watched every Saturday morning when Jama did the weekly shopping, ensuring that the young girl chose nutritious food—fruits and vegetables, lean meats, whole grains, milk. Tilly allowed the occasional candy bar or small carton of ice cream, but no sugary breakfast cereals. Tilly could claim credit, during Jama's early adolescence, for neither Jama nor her dad developing cavities.

Ellen Schiska, who owned the Second in Time clothing and shoe store, always set aside the nicest—and most modest—recycled apparel in Jama's size. By selecting clothing that had come from sources out of town, Ellen protected Jama from ridicule by school peers.

Thanks to these women, few of Jama's class-mates realized the struggle Dad had supporting the two of them after Mom left. Few knew the debt Mom incurred for Dad in her state of mind. Dad never spoke to anyone about the night job he held in Fulton as the elementary-school janitor. To everyone in River Dance, Richard Keith ran the local farm implement sales and repair, and managed a thriving business.

And then there was Zelda Benedict. She had a full-time job, a louse for a husband and the responsibility of raising her two willful grandchildren after her daughter's death from a drug overdose, but Zelda had found time to notice Jama often enough at the nursing home to teach her about patient care. It was partly due to Zelda's professional recommendation that Jama was accepted into med school.

Despite the kindness of the women in Jama's youth, it was Fran Mercer who held a mother's place in Jama's heart.

One day during Jama's sophomore year in high school, Monty and Fran Mercer had pulled Jama out of her chemistry class. They walked with her to the counselor's office and sat with her while she was given the news that her father had been killed in an accident, delivering a tractor to a customer.

Fran had held Jama while she cried, and together, Monty and Fran assured Jama she would never be alone. They took her into their home when she was fifteen, and she became a part of the family.

Jama could never hope to repay Fran's motherly kindness. She'd loved Jama the most when Jama was the least lovable, the most angry over life's losses, seething at a mother who'd abandoned her, and at a fate that had taken her father from her far too soon.

And so it was Fran for whom Jama would risk anything, including her job.

Jama found her moments after leaving the clinic. Community-minded, Fran preferred to do as much of her shopping in River Dance as she could.

When Jama drove into the parking lot of Kaiser's, she immediately spotted Fran's bright red hair, which had been inherited by three of her five grandchildren. Fran was carrying two bags of groceries toward her car. When she saw Jama, her face broke into a wide smile. She rushed to her car, placed the groceries inside and was waiting with arms open wide when Jama reached her.

"Sweetie, I was just thinking about you." Fran smelled of the lavender soap she had used for years. The yarn of her pink sweater tickled Jama's chin.

"Fran, I've got—"

"I know you must be on your way to work." Fran checked her watch. "I bet you ran off without breakfast again, didn't you? I was going to deliver some sausage quiches by the clinic, knowing your

67

habits haven't changed much over the years." She patted Jama on the back. "Too bad I didn't bring them with me to the store, but—"

"Fran." Jama took her sixty-year-old foster mother's hands. "I had my first patient at the clinic. It was Monty."

Jama explained the situation, slightly surprised that Fran hadn't already heard about her husband by way of the lively River Dance grapevine.

Fran's fair skin paled visibly.

"You took care of him yourself?" Fran asked.

"I was the only one there or I'd have requested someone else—"

"Nonsense, I'm glad it was you. Sounds to me as if you made the right call, hon."

"Harold Kaiser helped carry Monty into the clinic," Jama told her. "Haven't you seen him this morning? I'd thought he might tell you."

"You know he hired that new manager. He and Tilly don't come in until the afternoon now. I'll just go see if the store will hold my groceries for me until I can collect them."

"You can ride with me, and we'll have Tilly take the groceries to your house when she's off her shift. She still has a key to your house, doesn't she?"

"Yes, but I never lock my doors, you know that. Honey, I can drive myself to the hospital. You have a new job, and a new boss who needs your—"

"My new boss doesn't need me as much as my

family does right now. I would be little help to her when I'm worried about Monty."

Fran's gentle gaze rested on Jama. "No reason to worry. He's receiving excellent care, I'm sure. It's in God's hands."

Jama carried the groceries back into the store, explained the situation to Anita, the cashier who had worked the register for twenty years, and returned to the parking lot. She opened the passenger door of her Outback for Fran and waited. Fran was not driving herself, and that was final.

Fran relented with grace—more likely for Jama's sake than for her own.

"I don't know how you do that," Jama said as she pulled out of the parking lot and drove north toward Highway 94.

"Do what, hon?"

"Place everything in God's hands and let Him handle it."

Fran paused, staring out across a portion of the family vineyard to the left of the road. "Sounds like a simplistic Sunday-school answer, doesn't it?"

Jama grimaced. That was exactly what she'd been thinking, and she was ashamed. She was a believer, but this bit about trusting her loved ones and her future to God . . . that was a hard lesson to master. She'd failed repeatedly at the faith walk that Fran made look so easy.

"Did you ever think it's the Sunday-school

answer because it's the right one?" Fran asked. "Oh, wait a minute." She fluttered her fingers over her mouth. "I forgot I'm talking to the original Missouri mule. Little Jama Keith always had to develop her own theory about everything from cooking a breakfast of fried potatoes, eggs and mountain oysters, to understanding God."

Jama cast her foster mother a stiff grin. "Some things—"

"Never change. I know. But, honey, I trust in God's power and in eternity. Otherwise, they'd have buried me with Amy."

Jama turned left onto the highway and headed west, her hands a little tight on the steering wheel, a lump swelling in her throat. She swallowed and focused on the road.

They rode in silence for several miles, and Jama struggled to think of something besides Monty's gray face, and her instinctive decision to withhold treatment for the most obvious symptoms.

"When I was a young mother," Fran said, once they were a few miles from River Dance, "I used to worry about how my children would turn out as adults, what I was doing, the decisions I might make that could scar them for life."

Jama glanced at her. "You were a great mom. Your kids always loved you."

Fran nodded. "I never doubted that. I finally realized that the worry didn't do anyone any good, and it took too much time—I was too busy raising my children, keeping house, helping Monty in the fields and vineyards to spend much time worrying. I still struggle with it occasionally. Who doesn't? I mean, it seems the motherly thing to do, you know. To worry about your children. A loving gesture."

Jama swerved to miss a dog, honked at it, glanced at it in the rearview mirror. "That looked like Monty's hunting hound."

"Probably is. He wanders away sometimes. Monty likes to hunt on Andy Griswold's property, so Humphrey knows the area. There's no leash law in River Dance. I suppose there should be, but you know Humphrey, he loves to wander."

Jama cast Fran a quick look, saw that she was gazing at the Missouri River to the left. Her lips curved downward, her eyes seemed to have dulled in the past few minutes. For all the talk about not worrying, she appeared less than serene. And then she saw Jama's expression.

"Okay, you caught me."

"You doing okay?" Jama asked.

"I'll be fine. How about you? It can't be easy, making the kinds of decisions you have to make."

"All that expensive training has its advantages. If I had worried about every patient I saw during residency, I'd have been no good to anyone."

"But this is Monty," Fran said gently.

"As I said, that's where the training kicks in. I've seen enough cases like Monty's to be able to read signs that might not be immediately apparent to others." She thought about the nurse who had questioned her skills.

Jama glanced toward the river—that steady, curving constant in her life. The Missouri River Valley, lush and fertile, contained the winding force of nature with some difficulty. The flatlands produced high yields when the weather cooperated, but the farmers had to "get while the gettin' was good," as Monty would sometimes say. Flooding could wipe out a season of work in a few hours.

Farming was always a risky endeavor, though Monty had done well over the years, supporting his family in comfort through hard work.

Much like medicine. It was never a sure thing.

Jama cast another glance at her foster mom. Monty would be okay. He had to be okay.

Chapter Eight

Doriann's lungs felt filled with the hot glue Aunt Renee used for the homeschool art projects. From behind the bush that didn't hide anything, she watched the two creeps approach. They looked bigger and scarier than they had in the truck.

They were mad, for one thing. Both kinds of mad—crazy mad and angry mad. And they shouted at each other while they called for her. How stupid. As if she was going to answer them? Run to them through the trees like a lost puppy?

Strange, all that brush had seemed so much thicker when she was trying to push through it. Now, with the sun higher, it seemed that she could see for miles in every direction. Which meant, so could the goons.

Clancy stepped around a tree branch, and looked in Doriann's direction. Toast. She was—

Deb swore loudly. "You just had to go after the dog, didn't you? Swerve off the road and nearly get us all killed. I guess you know she's gonna find the cops and lead them straight to us."

Clancy turned an ugly look on Deb. "That stupid kid's not even gonna find her own way out of this jungle."

"You'd better hope not," Deb muttered. "If that frost hits tonight, we could all freeze to death."

"What frost?"

"Don't you ever listen to the weather report? There's supposed to be a killing frost tonight that could wipe out all this year's crops. Where do you live, in a tree stump? The kid could freeze to death."

"Then that'll be one more problem we don't have to deal with. I've got enough to worry about. I'm soaking, I'm starved, and I need a hit."

Deb swore again. She did a lot of that. "You think you're the most important person in the world?"

Doriann saw their heads appear more clearly over some bushes as they drew closer. She saw

Clancy give Deb that ugly look again. Deb was too stupid to back away.

He grabbed her by her shirt with one hand and socked her in the face with the other. Doriann heard the smack of flesh, Deb's low grunts. "I'm the only person in the world." Clancy growled the words like a mad dog.

Doriann caught her breath. There was a fiend in that man, and for once, Deb apparently agreed with her. She said nothing.

"All the rest are slobs and morons who don't deserve to live," he said.

Doriann cringed.

He shoved Deb to the ground. She grunted again, and stayed where she was. Maybe she wasn't as stupid as Doriann had thought.

"Well, this slob plans to live whether I deserve it or not." Deb didn't sound so sure of herself now. Her voice shook a little. "I need a place to crash and I need it soon. We can't sleep in the truck now that you've decided it would make a good submarine."

"It's my truck, isn't it?" Clancy snapped, his voice still hard and dark.

Deb slowly got to her feet, then walked in the other direction. "No, it's a stolen truck."

"It's mine now," Clancy called after her. "I can do what I want with my things, just like I can do what I want with you, and with the kid. Out here in these woods, there ain't nothing you can do about it. I'm going to find little Dori, and then her self-righteous daddy's going to be sorry he tried to ruin my life."

Doriann couldn't breathe. She felt like a hardening clay model, ready for the kiln. Deb wasn't looking as scary right now. Sure, she looked as if she ate kids for breakfast—but that couldn't be true, because she was too skinny. And her teeth were too bad.

"Did you see that old abandoned barn a couple of miles up the road before you ran us off?" Deb called over her shoulder.

"I didn't run us off the road, you and the kid did that. I was doin' fine till you grabbed the wheel."

Deb stopped suddenly, and Doriann froze as the woman turned facing directly toward her. But she didn't look up. She sat down on a fallen log. "I'm going to crash. We need to find a place. That barn would—"

"You can't."

Deb didn't look at him. Instead, she spread her hands out and studied them. Scraggly strands of blond hair fell into her face, mingling with the blood on her cheek.

"You're not forgetting what the brat said, are you?" he asked. "There's stuff in the area, and I'd bet she knows who has it. We won't have to crash if we can—"

"I don't see her anywhere, do you?"

Without warning, Clancy stalked over to Deb

and grabbed her by her shirt again, jerking her up. "Get out there and start looking."

Doriann shrank as small as she could get, and prayed harder than she ever had in her life.

After moving in with the Mercers at the age of fifteen, Jama had developed a special ability to sense when Fran was going to become serious and initiate a mother-daughter talk. That sense had never disappeared, and as she and Fran hit a straight stretch in the road, Jama felt one of those little talks in the air. Maybe Jama was alerted by the way Fran glanced at her every few seconds. The wonderful, strong, loving woman could speak volumes through her silence.

"You're handling everything so well," Fran said. "And in spite of what I said, I'm truly glad you insisted on coming with me."

"So am I. It would have been hard to stay in River Dance today, waiting for a phone call, wondering about the results of the chest X-ray."

Fran gave the barest shake of her head. "You know I'd have called you first thing."

"So now there's one less phone call you'll have to make."

They rode in silence a few more moments, and Jama relaxed enough to admire the dazzling light of the morning sun illuminating the pale green of new spring foliage, the white blossoms of dogwoods and the magenta of redbud trees. How many times over the past fifteen years had she longed to leave the classroom or the hospital and drive to the river, perhaps park at a Katy Trail lot and just walk for miles, maybe rent a bike and ride until she was far from everything and everyone? Of course, it was impossible to run or bike far enough.

Fran rested her hand on Jama's arm. "Other than this morning's events, how do you feel about being back in town?"

Here it came. "I haven't had time to decide."

"You had time to think about it before coming."

Jama flexed her hands on the steering wheel. "Why think about it? I had no choice. I couldn't pay back the loan, not with all my other out-standing school debts." Sometimes she felt as if she'd never get out from under. She had to admit to herself that Tyrell had done the right thing for her.

"You didn't want to come?"

Jama hesitated.

"You have a home and a life in River Dance, if you'll accept it, Jama. You've succeeded, just the way you and Amy dreamed you both would. That's in spite of the odds against you, which weren't your making."

"I can't blame anyone else for my behavior in high school, the drinking, running away from home, experimenting with drugs, vandalizing the school."

"You did not vandalize the school," Fran chided, conveniently ignoring the other self-recriminations that were right on target. "You simply climbed a tree with branches that were too slender to hold your weight. I don't think breaking tree branches on school grounds constitutes vandalism."

"The principal did, and it's on my school records." Besides, Jama had been drunk at the time.

"Nobody pays any attention to those records."

"Except for scholarship boards."

For a moment, Fran was quiet. Jama searched her mind for another topic to redirect this mother-daughter talk.

Tyrell, the stereotypical, high-achieving elder son, had earned a full scholarship to Columbia. He had been confident and strong from the cradle, it seemed, and yet he possessed a serene humility that drew people to him like birds to the Vignoles grapes on the Mercer Ranch hillside. He'd been the only Mercer sibling who'd already left for college when Jama came to live with the family, and though he'd always been affectionate with his kid sister's best friend, Jama had never felt sisterly toward him.

Daniel, the second son, had sown his wild oats for about six months his junior year of high school, gotten it out of his system, and qualified for a scholarship, as well.

Heather and Renee, the twins, had surprised everyone. Inseparable through high school, they had pursued decidedly different careers. Heather

78

and her husband, Mark Streeter, were both in the cardiothoracic surgery residency program in Kansas City. Renee, homeschooling mother of four, had completed two years of college, then pursued her lifelong dream of being a wife and mother with a large family. She even mothered Heather and Mark's daughter, Doriann, while they worked their long hours at the hospital. Renee was a natural nurturer.

"Your kids have always been so encouraged to succeed," Jama said. "You and Monty helped them follow their dreams. What a difference that makes in a kid's life."

"We're so glad that Tyrell chose to follow in his father's footsteps," Fran said.

"He always loved the ranch. The rest of us chafed at the chores, but he really loved the work."

"Yes, he did, but one reason Tyrell decided to return to River Dance and take over the ranch was because he knew you'd be here," Fran said.

Jama glanced at Fran, then braced herself. Here it came again. "He told you that?"

"Didn't have to. I'm his mother. Besides, he isn't a hard man to read. I think you've probably developed that skill, as well."

"There's no way he would have quit his job at the university extension center just because I'd be here. We talked about it, and he wanted to come back, anyway. He loves the ranch."

"He's always loved the ranch, but can you tell me

why else his arrival back home would coincide with the arrival of a certain young, beautiful doctor?"

Jama couldn't answer that. She hadn't asked him to come back.

"So things might become a little awkward now," Fran said with a slight lift in her voice. It was a gentle question.

"Nope."

From the corner of her eye, Jama could see Fran watching her.

"Not just a little?" Fran asked.

"Not at all. We're both adults, and we know how to handle ourselves with maturity and grace. Or at least, Tyrell does."

"You're not going to give up information easily, are you?" Fran asked. "What's going on between you two?"

"At this moment, we're both focused on Monty."

"Jama."

"Nothing awkward, we're both just concerned about something more important."

"You know what I mean. What happened between you two that Tyrell won't talk about to anyone?"

"Tyrell proposed, I didn't accept. End of story."

There was a brief silence, then Fran said, "I find that hard to believe, sweetie. That it's the end of the story, I mean."

"It's true. It's difficult to talk about, and I know it hurt Tyrell as much as it hurt me."

"Are you telling me the crush you've had on him all these years didn't evolve?" Fran asked.

Jama suppressed a sigh. Growing up, Jama never could conceal her feelings, and certainly not from Amy and Fran. "It's me, Fran. It isn't Tyrell's fault that I'm not ready for the commitment of marriage."

"For goodness' sake, you're thirty-two, my dear. When will you be ready?"

"Some people never are. I may be one of those people."

The silence swelled inside the car as Fran waited for further explanation. None came.

"Oh, honey," Fran said with a sigh. "If you're afraid of marriage because of your poor mother, then you can rest assured that you aren't going to do what she did."

Jama cast her a brief glance. "How can you know that?"

"Why, look at you. You're the age she was when she left, and you've had the strength to make a success of your life. You're steady and dependable. I know you still have regrets, but don't we all? You've got to look forward to the life waiting for you, not backward."

"Dad never told me much about Mom's departure. He only said that she was sick and not able to be the mother I needed."

"I remember the day Amy brought you home with her after school."

81

Jama nodded. The memories of that time were branded on her mind, too. Everything in her life had changed in one afternoon when she was seven

For years, she'd had nightmares about arriving home that day to find all the doors locked. She'd shouted and screamed and pounded to get in. Then she'd caught sight of her mother's face in the window, just watching her. Cold and remote. Later Jama had heard her mother tell her father that she didn't want to be a mother anymore.

Amy had found Jama that day outside the house. Jama remembered walking beside Amy down the long lane to the Mercer home. She remembered seeing later in Amy's bedroom mirror that smudges of dirt and tears had been streaked across her face.

How was a second-grader supposed to understand the dark world of the adult mind? Jama understood mental illness now, but she still wondered about her role in creating her mother's sadness, and she still felt the pain of abandonment.

Fran touched Jama's shoulder. "My dear, something tells me this chapter in your life isn't quite over yet. Give it some time. And thought. And give it a lot of prayer. Whatever is standing in your way with Tyrell affects your entire future."

Jama swallowed hard.

"And when you look forward," Fran said, "I suspect you'll see Tyrell as an important part of it."

Jama grimaced.

"Okay, sorry, honey. This is a conversation you should be having with him, not his mother. I cannot imagine a better match than the two of you."

Jama could easily imagine just such a thing.

Chapter Nine

Tyrell paused in the threshold of his father's cubicle in the E.R. at St. Mary's Hospital in Missouri's state capital. It was a busy place. Medical dramas were taking place around him in every direction. Despite the federal regulations about patient privacy, there was no way every word spoken in this department could be kept private.

Monty Mercer opened his eyes and looked up, motioning for Tyrell to come closer.

Tyrell stepped to his father's bedside, willing away the anxiety in his stomach. He didn't attempt a smile. His father would see through it.

Dad remained awake, but it appeared to take an effort. "Glad you made it. D'you bring your mom?"

"Jama's bringing her."

Dad nodded and closed his eyes. "Then maybe you two can work things out while she's here."

"Dad, we need to focus on getting you better right now."

"Something's up with her."

"She's not talking to me about anything," Tyrell said.

"Then you need to help her start talking. If you're wanting to become her husband, you'd better find out how to get her to open up."

"I guess it's a good thing I majored in agriculture instead of psychology."

Dad nodded his agreement.

"I've given her every opportunity—"

"She turned you down, right?"

Tyrell nodded.

"Did she say why?"

"She said she wasn't ready for marriage."

For a moment, Dad was so quiet that Tyrell thought he had fallen asleep again.

"You remember that young pup Doriann found in the ditch, half-dead, three or four years ago?" Dad asked at last.

"Humphrey?"

"He turned out to be the best hunting hound I ever had, even if he does run off on his own rabbit trails every so often."

Tyrell waited. Sometimes his father had a round-about way of getting to his point, but he usually had one.

"You remember the shape that pup was in when Doriann first brought him home? Couple of broken ribs, blood all matted in his fur, and he was afraid of everything, even the barnyard kittens."

"I doubt Jama would appreciate being compared to a stray dog."

"I'm too sick to joke right now."

"Sorry. Look, I know Jama had a hard childhood. I was there, remember? I want to be there for her now."

Dad winced, reached for a tube in his arm, adjusted it.

Tyrell placed a hand on his father's shoulder. "Now is not the time for this discussion."

Dad ignored him. "That dog never did completely get over whatever happened to him as a pup. Any time somebody shouts or raises a hand suddenly, poor Humphrey cowers as if he thinks he'll be hurt again. That's how Jama's been acting."

Tyrell thought about that. His Dad was usually very perceptive. So why hadn't Tyrell seen this wariness in Jama for himself? As close as he and Jama had grown over the past few months, and with so much shared history—

"Sometimes, I guess a fella can have trouble seeing through the haze of all those romantic feelings to a festering problem," Dad said.

"Maybe, but—"

"Especially when that fella might be struggling with the same problem."

"You're talking about Amy's death? How can that be connected to Jama's childhood traumas?"

"It's a resurrection of everything bad, son. Help her through it. That's what a man does for his woman. Give her time."

"That's what I'm doing."

"But don't just go all silent on her. Draw her out."

"Okay, Dad, I'll twist her arm and beat it out of her. Now, you relax and I'll go talk to the doctor."

Dad glared up at him.

"Sorry. I'm not going to bully her about anything today. She's got her mind on one thing, and that's your health. That's my focus, too. So you need to come through this and prove her diagnosis correct. Now will you let me talk to the doctor about—"

"One more thing," Dad said. "There's supposed to be a freeze tonight."

"I know. I'll see to it as soon as *you* come through this surgery."

"Nothing you can do to help the surgeon except pray, and you can do that at home on the ranch."

"Think I don't know my job? What you didn't teach me, the university did."

Monty closed his eyes and moaned.

Tyrell leaned over him, alarmed, until he saw the very faint lines of a smile around his father's eyes.

"Dad, the ranch will not be ruined by the time you get back home. I promise I won't make any changes without your permission."

"Those shoots are fragile right now. You can't cover the vines or they'll break off."

"Dad—"

"And I don't know that burning hundreds of dollars worth of hay will even make a difference."

"We can place the bales along the road at the bottom of the hill. The heat will rise."

"Not evenly."

"Dad, if you meant what you said about wanting me to manage the ranch, now's the time to prove it."

To Tyrell's relief, his father finally gave a faint nod and released a quiet sigh. "Just remember, though," Monty said, "if this heart problem doesn't get better, it'll be your decisions from now on that make or break the future of our ranch."

"Don't write yourself off yet, Dad. It's going to be okay." He trusted Jama's instincts.

Clancy's angry voice filled the air with ugly words about the people in the world who didn't deserve to live. Doriann knew she was imagining the smell of his bad breath from twenty feet away.

She also knew that her prayers were being answered, because anybody else would've seen her in her hiding place.

Thank You, Jesus. She had lain trapped, waiting for Clancy and Deb to move for what seemed like forever, and her right leg was cramping so badly she was about to cry.

When she could stand it no longer, she shifted. Brush rustled. Dirt crumbled beneath her left knee. She peered across to see if Clancy and Deb had heard. Apparently, Clancy's voice had masked the sound.

Doriann tried to straighten her leg a little more, and more dirt fell.

Deb turned to walk in the other direction. Clancy followed.

Doriann remembered to breathe.

The ground sank a little more beneath her left knee, and she felt her right knee sink, too. She heard the scattering of pebbles far below, and felt herself sliding.

She grabbed at the base of the bush that barely camouflaged her. It rustled.

"What was that?" Clancy growled.

Both of them stopped and turned, but Deb pointed up into the trees. "Squirrels."

Doriann's eyes squeezed shut as the dirt kept crumbling beneath her. She could let go of the bush and fall into the river and freeze to death, or she could be killed by the beasts nearby.

"Look at the great blue heron," Deb said. "It just took off."

The Missouri River was Doriann's friend. She let go of the bush and braced herself.

The ground stopped crumbling. Clancy told Deb how stupid she was for bird-watching. Then he blamed her for letting "Dori" get away.

Thank You, God. Now He was answering prayers Doriann wasn't even praying.

"No runny-nosed brat's gonna outsmart me," Clancy said.

Doriann pressed her lips together. *Want to bet? A slug could outsmart you.*

"We need to find a hiding place," Deb said.

There was a pleading note in her voice. "You may be macho man, but I'm fading."

"You told me you knew how to cook a batch." His voice was getting harsher with every word. Aunt Renee said that would happen when someone was tweaking. Needing a fix. Craving a jolt, unable to think straight, and totally stupid.

"Only if I have something to cook!" Deb snapped. "The stuff for that's in St. Louis, and we're a long stretch from there, with no ride. I'm headed for that barn. You can stay here and argue with yourself."

"I'm going to get that kid."

"She's gone!" Deb shouted. "Look around you. See anything moving? You can come if you want, or you can get lost in the woods and be rescued by the FBI." She turned and plunged back into the brush in the direction they'd come.

For a moment, Clancy stood watching her leave. He said a few ugly words under his breath, stuffed his hands in the back pockets of his ratty jeans and glared at the ground.

Doriann watched him. His shoulders gradually slumped. He took his hands from his pockets and crossed them over his chest, still watching Deb walk away. He looked up into the trees, as if he thought something might jump down on him.

Doriann heard a thump nearby, and she nearly cried out. But Clancy didn't hear it. He was rushing after Deb along an overgrown path through the woods.

There was another thud, and again the sound of scattering pebbles. It wasn't the twig-snapping buffalo tramp of Clancy's or Deb's footsteps. What she heard was behind . . .

She leaned on her left elbow and turned to look back to where the river flowed. It wasn't until she felt the dirt disappear from beneath her right leg that she realized what was happening, and then it was too late.

This time the ledge crumbled.

Her mouth opened to scream, and she gulped it back, choked as the dirt beneath both legs gave way, then fell from beneath her belly, then she tumbled down with a slide of rocks, dirt and mud.

Chapter Ten

The white capitol building in Jefferson City was visible for many miles, standing out against the vivid blue of the Missouri sky, before Jama and Fran reached it. They wouldn't arrive at St. Mary's Hospital for another ten minutes.

"I can't believe Tyrell hasn't called," Jama said.

"There obviously hasn't been any news about Monty, or he'd have let us know," Fran assured her. "And you know cell phones aren't allowed in certain parts of hospitals."

Jama could feel her tension building with each mile.

"I remember the last time I rode in a car to a hospital for an emergency." Fran's voice came soft and gentle, as if her mind had been sifting through photos of the past.

"You're talking about when Monty had his stroke."

Fran nodded. "I thought I'd lose him, too. Only God knows how badly I lost my cool that day. Even though Monty's recovery went well, I still had this nagging sense that something was wrong. The trip to the hospital, the emergency room, the medical staff, all reminded me of our trip together to the hospital only weeks earlier for you and Amy."

Jama stared straight ahead at the road.

"The sheriff came to the house about midnight Christmas Eve," Fran said.

Jama didn't want to hear this. Yet she owed Fran a listening and compassionate ear. They'd seldom spoken about that horrific night because when it came up Jama either had someplace else to be, or she changed the subject.

"It had to have been a nightmare for you," Jama said.

"Worse than any nightmare, because I didn't have the relief of waking up to find that everything was okay." Fran patted Jama's arm, then allowed her hand to linger, as if she needed that connection. "We got through Amy's death, didn't we?"

Jama glanced at her. Had they, really?

"We're still functioning, sweetheart," Fran said

in answer to Jama's unspoken thought. "For a couple of years after she died, I wasn't sure I could keep going."

It grew difficult for Jama to breathe normally. This was why her visits to River Dance the past four years had taken so much effort. It was a major reason that she dreaded the next two years. To be reminded over and over . . .

"We've got purpose to our lives again," Fran said. "It'll never be the same, but we've discovered life does continue."

Jama caught her lower lip between her teeth. Life had continued, but not the same way.

Not a day passed that Jama didn't have something she needed to talk about with Amy. Since losing her best friend, her sister, she didn't think the same way anymore or feel the same about anything.

She slowed for a narrow bridge. "Amy was so much like you, Fran. She had a solid strength that made everyone around her feel secure. She could carry the world. She did, too, often. Or she tried."

Fran squeezed Jama's arm, then let go. "Face it, honey, Amy was as strong-willed as you are. I worried about that tendency of hers a lot. I worried that her independence would cost her the opportunity to have a man's love, to settle and have a family. After she died . . ." Her voice cracked. She stared out the window for a moment.

Jama stared straight ahead and focused on breathing deeply. Jama never cried.

"Afterward," Fran continued, "I realized that I'd been wishing for her to live out my dreams for her. I wasn't wise enough to allow her to live her own. With all the other kids, I'd allowed them to find their own way, but Amy . . . she was different. I guess I identified with her more. I wanted her to have a happy life, and I was afraid she would burn out before she could find someone to share that life with."

"Med school and residency are tough on a marriage," Jama said. "We saw several of our friends divorce. Amy wanted to wait until she had more time to devote to someone else in her life."

Jama still felt regret that she'd never been able to say a formal, final goodbye to Amy. She'd been in the hospital, too badly injured with a damaged spleen, collapsed lung and cracked ribs, to attend Amy's funeral.

"I wonder what she would be doing now," Fran said.

"She would be saving lives."

There was grief in Fran's hazel eyes. There was also a strong faith that Jama could never hope to emulate. How did a mother like Fran cope with the death of her daughter?

How many times had Jama wished that Fran had been her mother? Not just mother of her heart, but mother in reality.

And why, after all these years, was Jama recalling her own mother's failings so often?

Jama braked at a light and turned left. She'd driven this route so many times. . . .

"Jama," Fran said softly.

"Yes."

"You know worrying doesn't help."

Jama was so glad Fran couldn't really read her mind at that moment. "I know."

"Neither does brooding about the past."

"Are you talking about yourself now? Sometimes we can't control our thoughts."

"I know. Sometimes we do it anyway, don't we?"

"Yes."

"Sometimes, maybe, it's simply a way of honoring those we love," Fran said. "A way of giving them space in our hearts. And you're one of my kids. You have one of those places of honor in my heart."

Jama negotiated a sharp curve as the pressure flooded her chest and worked its way up. Over the years of residency, she'd learned the important art of emotional detachment. She'd lost that skill for about a year after Amy's death, but eventually it returned.

Until now.

For a long moment, Fran said nothing. Jama glanced over to find her staring out the window, and the pain in that brief glimpse was dark and hard—the harsh and ugly scars of a break in the earthly bonds of mother-daughter love that weren't meant to be erased by time, or by faith. They were simply meant to be endured. At least, that was how Jama saw it.

"You were the sister Amy so desperately needed in her life," Fran said at last. "As a middle child, with two older brothers who were into their own activities, and younger twin sisters who were inseparable, she sometimes felt left out, I'm afraid. If not for you, Amy would have had a much lonelier childhood." Fran looked over at Jama. "And now you're the one who's alone."

"Now who's worrying?" Jama teased. It was time for a lighter mood.

Fran tapped her lips with her fingers. "Shame on me."

"So to give you something different to ponder, what do you think about Zelda Benedict joining the staff at the clinic? She helped me with Monty this morning, and her skills are top-notch."

Fran hesitated, and Jama caught a fleeting look of disappointment in her expression. For Fran, talking about her daughter was like bringing Amy back to life for at least a few moments. Painful as that was, it was as Fran said—those memories honored Amy's life.

"There's been no staff hired, yet," Jama said. "Zelda still keeps her feet in the water doing PRN work. What do you think?"

It took a few seconds for Fran to switch gears.

"You realize she's not as young as she used to be. She can't be on her feet all day."

"Perhaps in a supervisory role. Teaching, maybe?"

"She smokes, Jama. That's not good for the circulation."

"One cigar a day?"

"I know, I know, she says she doesn't inhale, but that's a crock, and you know it. If she's breathing the smoke that comes out of the cigar and her mouth, she's inhaling, hon. Do you know how many years I harassed Monty to give up his pipe?"

Relieved, Jama engaged in the conversation that would keep them both occupied for the next few minutes. Fran had strong feelings about smoke, and she might have some good suggestions about staffing the clinic that should already be staffed. Jama took the reprieve gratefully.

Chapter Eleven

Doriann sneezed, coughed, sneezed again, covering her mouth to keep from making noise. She'd slid to a stop at the bottom of the bank. Dirt covered her, filling her nose and mouth.

She spat and blew her nose into the mud. All kinds of bacteria were now inside her, maybe making their way to her brain.

She tried to get up, fell against a bush, scraped her arms, smacked her elbow on a rock and bit her tongue to keep from crying out.

She scrambled to the nearest tree and held her breath. She expected to hear the rustle of brush, the sound of footsteps, angry voices, and then to see Clancy and Deb peering over the edge of the bank at her.

Nothing.

For forever, she couldn't bring herself to move from behind the tree. What if she was being tricked? Maybe the goons were just out of sight, rubbing their hands together, waiting for the right moment to jump out and then kill her. And they would probably torture her first.

How could Clancy and Deb not have heard the bank collapsing? She hadn't screamed, but she'd coughed and choked and sneezed. How could that not have been heard?

For another few seconds she listened. She heard the trickle of a stream emptying into the river and the movements of a squirrel in the branches above her. As she continued to listen, she thought she heard Clancy's angry shout in the distance, up the hillside.

Wow. Okay. So the sound of her fall hadn't reached them. How implausible was that? Implausible? Yes, that was the word.

She turned to look out across the river, the bank only a few feet from where she stood. The water was light brown with mud this time of year from flooding in other states. Logs and limbs floated in it. All Doriann had to do was find someone on the river to call to, or to follow the river downstream to a town. If only Clancy hadn't taken her cell phone, she could've used the GPS system and gotten out of here easily.

She knew that the forest along this part of the river didn't have a lot of people living in it—Grandpa had said so, and he hunted in these forests.

Carefully, she wiped more mud from her face and out of her nose and mouth, then she crept through the trees toward the river's edge. She stopped at a little stream that connected with the river and plunged her hands into the icy water. She splashed her face and rinsed her mouth, numbed by the coldness. She even snorted some up her nose. It stung and made her eyes water, but she felt cleaner.

Of course, Aunt Renee said there were all kinds of bacteria in the groundwater, too, so it was probably just as contaminated as the dirt, but at least it would wash the grit from between her teeth. Ick. Besides, she'd already been plunged into swamp water, so this couldn't be any worse.

By the time Doriann stepped to the edge of the Missouri River, she realized something was missing. The Katy Trail. On this section of the river, the railroad that had been converted to a biking/hiking trail—stretching nearly all the way across the state of Missouri—was on the north side of the river, and it often appeared between the highway and the river. Mom and Dad brought her down to the trail a lot, when they could get away from work, and Doriann knew it well.

Unless the truck had plunged across the Katy Trail, it would be just on the other side of the highway that Doriann had managed to lose. But the sun was out, and she could search and find it.

She turned and pushed her way through the brush alongside the river. It was hard going, and before long she came to cliffs that rose from the water. She'd have to climb. She looked at the grass, a thick growth filled with dandelions and sweet Williams. What else was in that grass? It was cold . . . too cold for snakes?

She could leave the riverbank and look for the trail. There might be people on it. Maybe.

But thinking about it, she became concerned for those people. Clancy and Deb could be looking for people, too. Someone innocent who was just out for a morning jog or ride. Someone who wouldn't know what was happening when Clancy jumped out from the bushes, and with his temper, no telling what he'd do if someone fought him. How could anyone know he was tweeking?

Deb had kept trying to remind Clancy that the two of them would be asleep before long—they were going to crash. She'd mentioned a barn. If they'd been so involved in their argument they hadn't heard Doriann fall down a collapsing river-bank, what else might they miss?

Would they, maybe, not notice an eleven-year-old kid with wet clothes and red hair following them through the woods?

Oh, shut up, Doriann Streeter! What are you thinking? What's a kid like you going to do tracking two killers who the FBI can't even catch? Dumb, dumb, dumb.

But she couldn't stop thinking it. Since her prayers had been answered so far—she wasn't dead yet, was she?—then God seemed to be in the prayer-answering mood today.

If Deb and Clancy did fall asleep, according to Aunt Renee, they would crash hard and sleep for possibly days. *Do I have the guts to follow them and get my cell phone back?* Doriann could lead the police to the criminals and save the day—and maybe other lives.

Aunt Renee says I could be president someday. Wouldn't this look good on the campaign trail?

Doriann caught her breath. Was she really, truly thinking of following Clancy and Deb? That was suicide!

And yet, if they did find the barn, which was near the road, then Doriann might be able to flag down help at the road. As cool as the weather had become, there probably wouldn't be a lot of people on the trail today, and she didn't see any boats on the water, most likely because of all the floating logs from the floods up north.

Could she do it? Should she?

• • •

When Jama and Fran entered the surgery waiting room, Tyrell was there, speaking with a tall, familiar-looking man in a lab coat. He had graying hair, a deep, reassuring voice, and when Jama stepped up beside him and placed a hand on his arm, she felt weak with relief. She would trust Dr. Tony George with Monty's life without a moment of hesitation.

He held a hand out to her. "Jama, I've just been telling Mr. Mercer that his father has already received the best of treatment from the transferring facility. Excellent catch diagnosing the aortic tear, Dr. Keith. I take back everything I've ever said about the young pups coming out of residency programs today."

Jama introduced her favorite resident trainer to Fran, then said, "Tony, you're practicing in Jefferson City now?"

He nodded. "It appears I arrived just in time to proceed with your patient." His deep, mellow voice had been honed through years to convey comfort and confidence to worried patients and families.

He turned to Fran. "I've just been telling your son about a recently developed procedure for a torn aorta that has excellent results with much less invasion and a shorter recovery time."

Jama looked up and met Tyrell's gaze, saw the relief in his dusky blue eyes, and nodded, sharing the emotion.

"Your husband was given a CT scan as soon as he arrived," Dr. George told Fran. "Sure enough, Dr. Keith called his condition right on the money. I'm headed into surgery now. Jama, if you were scrubbed up, I'd let you observe."

Jama hesitated. "That's tempting, but I think watching surgery on my foster father might be a little too stressful."

As Dr. George took his leave, Jama allowed herself to release the tension that had been building since Monty's collapse this morning.

He would be okay. She found herself breathing deeply for the first time in an hour. Wow.

She'd made the right call. Tony George, one of the best surgeons she knew, was handling the case. All was well.

She stood nodding, grin still in place, while Fran and Tyrell conferred about calls to other family members. Their voices registered, but their words floated in the air, uncomprehended.

Jama needed to withdraw from this scene and collect herself. She felt an almost overwhelming need to take a short walk and absorb the knowledge that she had made the right call. What she really needed was a wide-open valley, or a sound-proof room, where she could shout at the top of her lungs. *Yeehawwww!*

She, Jama Keith, had made a judgment call that saved the life of a wonderful man. It was a moment to savor over and over again.

Fran gave Jama's arm a squeeze. "I think the time has come for me to buy a cell phone. This adventure today has convinced me. Tyrell, may I borrow yours for a few minutes? I'll talk to Daniel and the twins."

"Not a problem, Mom," Tyrell said. "I called Daniel when I was in the waiting room. He's standing by to call the twins, then drive here as soon as we fill him in on what's happening with Dad."

"I don't think he needs to do that. You know what your father would say. If Daniel has time to come to the hospital, he has time to help out at the ranch." She held her hand out to Tyrell for the phone, giving her son a look and a tiny tilt of her head in Jama's direction.

It was a gesture Jama realized she was not meant to intercept.

Tyrell relinquished the phone, then touched Jama's shoulder. The power of that touch vitalized her. She willed herself not to respond, either by melting against him, or by stepping away to resist the temptation. Tyrell affected her like that. He always would.

"I bet you haven't had breakfast," he said.

"Coffee." She was floating. *Enjoy it while it lasts.*

"Which is not breakfast." He nudged her toward a sign directing the way to the cafeteria.

"Coffee fortified with heavy whipping cream

packs a punch." She fell into step beside him, and allowed herself a smile. She'd done well. As the relief continued to sink in, she would soon become giddy and silly. She knew this from past experience.

"Some fruit and cereal would add—"

"Too many carbs, Tyrell. I'm doing low carbs. Trust me, I'm a doctor, I know what I'm doing." *Liar, liar, pants on fire. How much did you pay attention in nutrition classes?*

"Not if you think you need to lose weight."

She grinned up at him. "Flatterer." Uh-oh, she felt the giddiness beginning to overtake her senses. Silliness wouldn't be far behind.

"Numbers don't lie."

"What numbers?" she asked.

"The numbers of men who can't keep their eyes off you. Including me."

Tyrell was a man who knew how to make a woman feel special, no matter her size, age or appearance. He was most interested in a woman's heart. It showed in his photography. His family teased him without mercy, because his photographs were often off center, out of focus or badly composed. He took many shots from inside moving cars, where door frames, bug-spattered windshields and telephone wires were more prominent than the breathtaking sunset, the flight of an eagle overhead or a sprig of spring flowers that he'd tried to capture.

Tyrell focused so closely on the beauty he saw, nothing else distracted him.

He used that razor-sharp perception to choose his dates in high school. He could have had his pick of any of the prettiest, most popular girls, but he chose those with particularly kind spirits or sharp intellects, who were often passed over by much less discerning guys in his class.

Of course, watching him date other girls during those years wasn't easy or painless for the youngster he regarded as another kid sister, who carried feelings for him that were anything but sisterly.

"Mom grill you on the way here?" Tyrell asked.

"Like a drill sergeant."

"Dad, too?"

"Why do you think he was at the clinic this morning?"

"Oh, I don't know . . . heart problem? Fall from a ladder?"

"If not for that, I'm sure he would have invented another excuse." Jama smiled with tenderness as she thought about Monty's arrival at the clinic that morning.

Tyrell chuckled, and Jama couldn't help gazing up at him, at the warmth in his eyes as his gaze met hers, held it.

Tyrell stopped and turned to face her, raised his hand and touched her shoulder to stop her, gently, as if handling a newborn chick. And then his head lowered. For the life of her, Jama couldn't withdraw from his magnetic power over her. She wanted a kiss from him. Needed it.

Before their lips touched, she was jostled by someone passing in the corridor. Jama stepped back, and Tyrell straightened.

"What did you tell my folks?" he asked, his voice a bit unsteady.

She looked up at him dumbly. All thought of her earlier conversation had fled her mind.

His eyes filled with humor. "About us," he prompted.

Jama turned and walked beside him again. "I told Monty he could interfere in my life as soon as he was out of the woods with this heart problem."

"Did that shut him up?"

"I don't know, did it? You said he wanted to talk to you."

Tyrell shook his head. "Take your best guess."

"Okay, tell me the truth. The only reason you proposed is because Fran and Monty twisted your arm."

Tyrell slanted a look at her. Yes, of course she knew better.

"And Mom?" he asked.

"She's digging for something."

"She probably wants to know if you've lost your mind for rejecting my proposal."

"From what I understand, you didn't tell her about that conversation, she simply guessed."

"A guy has his dignity to maintain, even with his mother."

"Well, thanks a lot. Because you didn't tell them anything, I got to be the bearer of sad news."

"So you think it's sad news, too?" he asked.

"Of course it's sad, Tyrell."

"I don't think Mom and Dad are convinced you're serious." His steps slowed. "Maybe I'm not convinced, either."

"We're all dealing with a lot right now," she said gently. "I don't think we should bring up this discussion again."

"Not now, you mean?"

"Not now."

"Okay, then later." There was a promise she heard all too clearly in his voice.

"Tyrell—"

He pressed his fingers against her lips. "Shhh. As you said, not now. Later. Give me something to hope for."

Chapter Twelve

Tyrell's shoulder nearly touched Jama's as he punched the elevator button. "You seem to like Dr. George."

She looked up at him. His jaw was clenched, betraying his tension, and she felt a pang of empathy for him. Tyrell was not only a strong physical specimen—a fabulous hunk, as her roommates had always reminded her—but he was emotionally steadfast. He seldom revealed his thoughts to anyone he didn't know well and trust, but once he gave his friendship—and his love—he spoke his mind about everything. He held nothing back.

"Tony is sixty-three and never been sued," she said, "in a world where it seems every doctor gets sued at least once in a career. What does that tell you?"

"That he decided to become a doctor late in life?" Tyrell's deep voice resonated in the wide corridor, and two passing nurses gave him a second look. Admiring looks. He never noticed that kind of attention, and when Jama pointed it out, he'd always scoff at her and blush. She never stopped pointing it out. He looked good in a blush.

"He's a thirty-year veteran," she said.

"So he's lucky?"

"He's sharp, comprehensive, doesn't leave loose ends."

"Meaning?"

"He doesn't leave his operating utensils in his patients. Keeps a scrupulous field, and keeps a close watch on follow-up care to prevent postoperative infections."

Tyrell groaned. "Sorry I asked. Not a good mental picture to have right now. So his success doesn't just come from a good bedside manner?"

"He's good, Tyrell," she told him gently. "I can't

think of anyone I'd rather have operating on Monty. Would you relax?"

"That's what I'm doing, trying to relax."

"Giving me a hard time helps you relax."

"It's always worked before."

"Aha. So *that's* what you've been doing." She grinned up at him. "And I thought you were flirting."

The elevator door opened, but he didn't enter. His look lingered on her face, his dark blue eyes darkening further. "What's this, Jama?" He gestured between the two of them.

"It's me trying to keep you from worrying about Monty while he's in surgery, because he's got an excellent surgeon, and—"

"What's this between us?" he asked.

She stepped into the elevator. "Would you get in before I take a ride downstairs without you?"

He entered, the door closed. "Don't pretend to misunderstand the question."

"This is a wonderful friendship. Familial love."

"That's all? Because I could've sworn—"

"Tyrell, you're starting it again."

"Sorry. Let me rephrase that. I love you, Jama. I believe you love me, and there's nothing sisterly about the way I catch you looking at me when you think I don't see you."

"You're doing the distraction thing again, switching the subject to keep yourself or someone else from worrying so much."

"You're right. Being with you does distract me

from remembering that, at this moment, a man I've never met before today is plunging a knife into my dad's damaged heart." There was an edge to his voice.

Jama wrapped her hands around his left bicep, and squeezed. "You know the scalpel Dr. George will use is tiny. As he said, the procedure has become much less invasive than ever before, and the recovery time is shorter. In fact, Monty could be out of surgery before we finish breakfast."

Tyrell nodded, still looking grim.

"Of course," she said, "knowing the size of your typical breakfast at the ranch, he might be out before that."

Tyrell's expression relaxed, and he slanted a glance at her, raising his black eyebrows. "Especially since I'll have such a fascinating companion with whom to dine?"

"Of course."

The elevator car stopped, the door opened, and Tyrell stepped out. "Okay, we can call a truce. It's not healthy to argue during a meal." He gestured to the entrance to the cafeteria. "Let's get some real breakfast."

Tyrell had agreed to a truce, but he couldn't help continuing to probe Jama about their relationship. She deftly changed the subject every time he tried to divert the conversation to her feelings and her thoughts.

All this time he'd thought he was listening to her with his heart, but maybe he was simply talking with his heart.

Strange that, when he was with Jama, he tended to talk more than usual. With her, his words seemed to spill out. She was so easy to share his thoughts with. Nonjudgmental. Encouraging . . . loving, but tough and honest.

Tyrell had not quite finished his breakfast when Jama set down her fork, leaned back in her chair and appeared to watch the other diners. Her unfocused gaze told him she wasn't taking in details.

What was weighing so heavily on her mind? How had Dad been able to see so easily that she was preoccupied with something, when Tyrell only saw the woman he loved, and who he knew loved him?

He suppressed a smile as he lifted a final bite of sausage to his mouth. "Admit it, you were hungry."

"Of course I was hungry. I hadn't eaten breakfast," she said dryly. "Even the heavy whipping cream loses its punch after a morning like this one. Do you know it's been years since I've eaten in a public hospital dining room?"

"Where did you eat, the bathroom?"

"During residency, I seldom had a chance to have an uninterrupted, sit-down meal, and those I had were in the areas reserved for the physicians."

He wiped his mouth, took a sip of coffee. "Too good to eat with the rest of us poor slobs?" he

111

teased. "You docs always have to insulate your-selves from the rest of the world?"

Jama glanced at the biscuits and gravy he'd left on his plate.

"Go ahead," he said. "You know you want them."

She narrowed her eyes at him. "I'm just about to fit into my preresidency jeans again, and I'm not about to spoil it now."

He held his hands out. "All that good food gone to waste. It looks delicious, too."

"Actually," she said, her hand edging toward her fork, "speaking of the doctors' dining room, it goes both ways. Believe me, the general public does *not* want to be subjected to medical conversation. I could probably write a book entitled 'Dinner Date With a Doc—A Dieter's Guide to Success.' We discuss all kinds of gross subjects, and we aren't even aware of offending the vulnerable people around us."

He nodded, nudging his plate of untouched, flaky biscuits topped with fragrant cream gravy in her direction. "I know. I dated a doc, remember?"

"There you have it."

"Plan to marry her someday."

"Tyrell."

"But admit it, you also liked that feeling of exclusivity, dining with the other doctors, enjoying the nicer chairs, better food, soft music."

She grimaced. "You think I'm a snob?"

"That wasn't what I—"

"The physicians' dining room didn't have better food. We ate the same cafeteria fare as everyone else."

"But softer chairs?"

She frowned at him, then smiled at his teasing grin. "Amy tried to eat in the public cafeteria when we were first residents." Jama picked up her fork. "She told me she didn't expect special privileges."

"Jama, I wasn't serious." But whenever his sister's name came up, the mood grew somber in a hurry. He figured that was Jama's intent.

She scooped up a minuscule amount of gravy on the tines of her fork. He knew that wouldn't be enough for her.

"The second time Amy ate in the cafeteria, she hadn't had a chance to sit down for eight hours," Jama continued. "Before she could take a bite, she was approached by a patient's family, who were offended that she was taking time to eat when they had waited for fifteen minutes in the patient's room to speak with her." Jama gave him a wry grimace. "Amy joined the rest of us snobs in the physicians' dining room after that."

The first bite of biscuit, soaked with thick gravy, brought an expression of pleasure to Jama's face. Tyrell enjoyed watching her eat, but after the third mouthful, she put her fork down and sighed. Memories of Amy always did that to her.

"Didn't your mother ever tell you not to waste your food?" Tyrell gestured to the plate.

"It's your food, duh."

"You know I got it for you. I don't like biscuits and gravy."

"You're a strange man, Tyrell Mercer. Everybody likes biscuits and gravy. And since you asked, no, my mother never taught me much of anything that I can remember."

He winced inwardly, regretting that he'd mentioned her mother. He needed to be more sensitive to his woman.

Oh, brother. His woman. As if he was a caveman with a club.

"Now that I've eaten, tell me more about this surgery," he said. "What's the success rate?"

"Since Monty didn't waste any time getting to the clinic, and since we caught his condition so quickly, the prognosis is optimistic, though there are always risks."

He nodded. "Since *you* caught it, and since *you* fought off the nurse who thought he knew better than you did, my father may live."

"That nurse was only doing his job."

"No, he wasn't. Why did he question your judgment?"

She shrugged. "He could have been having a bad day, could be too sure of himself. Some male nurses resent female doctors—it happens."

"You handled the situation well."

She gave him a brief, warm smile. "You're the one who kicked things into high gear."

"Because I trusted your call, Jama. I can think of no one I'd rather have taking care of my loved ones."

Something dark entered her expression. She looked down at the barely touched biscuits and gravy, which Tyrell knew had been her favorite breakfast meal since she was seven and spent nights with Amy at the ranch.

"I can't help wondering what you're thinking right now," he said.

She didn't respond. The darkness spread.

"You know you can tell me anything, don't you?" he asked. "You know you can trust me?"

She looked up at him, her aquamarine eyes as troubled as a turbulent surf. She didn't speak, but held his gaze, staring deeply, searchingly.

He knew it was hard for her to trust in love, while he could speak about it so easily. And why not? He'd grown up in a solid, loving family with parents who were stable, hardworking and kind.

Jama's losses had been devastating, much like the bitter, killing frost that was forecast for tonight, a natural disaster that could decimate crops and vineyards throughout the Missouri River Valley.

Tragedies and grief had created Jama's killing frosts—being pushed away, then abandoned by her mother. Losing her father, losing Amy.

"Can I?" she asked. There was a vulnerability in her voice that melted him.

"You can, Jama. You know you can."

For a moment, some of her heaviness lifted. There was hope. He could give her time.

Chapter Thirteen

Doriann had wanted camouflage, and she'd gotten it. Her wet purple jacket was camouflaged with mud. She'd found it buried beneath her. As Aunt Renee would say, *isn't it wonderful the way God always works things out?*

Doriann thought that maybe it would've been a little more comfortable if the dirt had only been ground into the outside of the jacket, but who was she to complain about the way God worked? A little grit rubbing her bare arms raw was punishment for lying to her parents and skipping out of school.

She guessed that being kidnapped and terrified so badly she wet her pants, and being slapped around by sewer-breath and having her leg groped by sewer-brain wasn't enough. She only hoped God would realize she'd learned her lesson.

She shrugged away the ugly thoughts. She wasn't usually this grumpy with God, but she'd never been kidnapped before, and she wasn't sure how to behave.

A small limb snapped loudly beneath her foot,

and she froze. The hood of her jacket covered her red hair, but the sun glared down at her through the spring-green treetops. She didn't know what Clancy or Deb would see if they turned around. She'd stayed well behind them, trying to always keep them in sight. She'd dropped to the ground like a Green Beret three times when she'd noticed Clancy or Deb twisting back. She'd told herself fifty tri-zillion times that this was crazy. An eleven-year-old kid shouldn't be following drugged killers through the woods.

But she just kept reminding herself of Aunt Renee's repeated assurance that all things were possible through Christ.

Nearly every step of the way, Doriann had been tempted to run, to turn back, follow the river to the nearest town and get to safety.

But if she took the easy way out, how many other people might die?

Doriann hated to think about what Clancy might do to another kid if he had the chance.

Aunt Renee was always reminding her class that God could use her for something great, and that Doriann and her cousins should take every opportunity to be the best they could be.

This was the best Doriann could be.

Tyrell gathered all the dishes and utensils and carried the tray to the proper receptacles. Jama watched, bemused; he definitely had domestic skills.

No doubt about it, Tyrell Mercer would make some woman very happy someday. Something about a man doing household chores was a definite turn-on. And a man who cooked and did the laundry? It just didn't get any better. Any woman would be thrilled. . . .

Again, just thinking about Tyrell with another woman shot a bolt of jealousy through Jama. Whoever he married, she'd better be good to him, or she would answer for it.

He was a man who worked hard at a job he loved. For a time, that was as an agriculturalist at the state university. Now he ran the ranch and vineyard. Jama knew he loved the work, as well, but the primary reason he'd returned home was because he loved his family, and Monty had needed help.

Five hundred acres of prime, fertile bottomland and hillside vineyards was more than one man could handle, even with all the best, most modern farm equipment and hired help during the planting and harvest. With Daniel—the younger Mercer brother—now working with Homeland Security in Kansas City, and the twins, Renee and Heather, both living with their families in Kansas City, that left Tyrell. As Jama had assured Fran, Tyrell was perfectly happy to make the change.

"Do you remember the age-old question?" Tyrell settled his smoky-dark gaze on Jama again.

"What happens when an irresistible force meets an immovable object?"

"Injury?"

"Most likely. Unless the irresistible force isn't as irresistible as it seems."

"Or if the immovable object isn't as immovable."

"So which are you, and which am I?" Tyrell asked.

Jama grimaced. Here she'd thought he'd given up on that subject. "Shouldn't we just focus on Monty for now?"

"You don't think Dad will want the same answer as soon as he wakes up? Don't you want to be ready for the poor man, considering his weakened condition?"

"Have I reminded you lately that you have a manipulative streak?"

"So are you saying I would be the irresistible force? That would make you the immovable object."

"One of the theories is that the immovable object will be smashed to pieces at impact." She paused, closed her eyes. "Even if it wants to be moved, it can't."

"Or both could be destroyed," he said. "Or both could carry the scars of that impact forever. Or the two could meld together and become stronger than either was before."

She opened her eyes. He couldn't know how much she wanted the last possibility to be true.

And how frustrating it was to know that it was her own fear that prevented it.

A nurse approached the table as Jama and Tyrell prepared to leave, announcing that Monty was out of surgery.

She handed Tyrell his cell phone. "Your mother says you need to call your sister, Heather. She's asking to speak with you."

Tyrell took the phone, pressed Speed Dial and walked to a quiet corner of the cafeteria.

As he listened to Heather, Jama saw his expression turn to stone.

Tyrell's fingers went cold all of a sudden, and he felt a tightening in his chest as his sister, the solid, calm, sensible twin, sobbed at the other end of the connection.

"Missing? How long? What happened?"

"We don't . . . we don't know. Oh, Tyrell, I'm so scared. She never went to Renee's this morning. She told me she felt sick, and she was caught up on all her subjects, and the cousins were driving her crazy—you know how they can be. All over the place all at once, and they never stop talking. I can't imagine how Renee manages to teach them so much when they never sit still, but she's so good with them, and Doriann has just blossomed under her schooling—"

"Honey, slow down." As a cardiothoracic surgical chief resident, Heather had nerves of supersonic titanium. Which was why her sudden jabbering frightened Tyrell badly.

"What is it you're trying to tell me?" he asked.

"I let Doriann stay home this morning. Alone."

"That's not unusual. You've done that before." Not that he approved, and he'd made his opinions known quite strongly in the past.

"I know I shouldn't have," she said, "but I understand how it feels to need quiet time to yourself."

"What happened, Heather?"

"I called her at home, and she didn't answer. I tried her cell, and it sounded as if she answered, then hung up. I kept calling, and got her voice mail. She hasn't answered any of my calls."

Now he was getting really scared. Doriann Streeter was a strong-willed eleven-year-old, but she would not frighten her parents like this.

"Perhaps she's in a place with no cell reception," he suggested.

"You know how she is. She doesn't sit in one place for more than five minutes, and even if cell reception is sketchy, I've tried enough times, I surely should have gotten through."

"So you went home and she wasn't there, either?"

"That's right. She and I had a few words the other night about how much I'm away from home, but I thought we'd gotten that straightened out. She understands the demands of my residency program."

121

Tyrell had his doubts about that. Sure, he was proud of his sister, but it didn't seem to him that leaving a daughter at home alone most of the time, or handing her over to your sister to raise, was something any kid was going to completely understand. But what would he know? He wasn't a parent.

"She is probably still mad, and just doesn't realize you're worried," he said.

"I know she likes to go to the park alone sometimes," Heather said. "She goes to see the animals in the zoo, and she's mature enough to go by herself."

Tyrell held his reply. An eleven-year-old had no business walking unaccompanied along the streets of Kansas City, even in the bright morning sunlight. But remarking about that right now would not be helpful.

"Any ideas?" he asked.

"One, and it terrifies me. We heard a report that two people were seen earlier this morning abducting a redheaded child only two blocks from our apartment. The police are following all leads."

Tyrell closed his eyes as a sick dizziness threatened to flatten him. He felt a hand on his arm. Jama's hand. She squeezed, and he saw her eyes filling with dread.

"So if that is what happened," he said over the phone, keeping his voice calm for the sake of his sister and Jama, "are there any leads?"

"Reports are that this couple has headed east on I-70."

"Toward St. Louis, then."

There was a catch in his sister's breathing, and a gasp from Jama, who squeezed more tightly—no longer giving strength, but needing it.

"Heather Danae, you've got to keep it together." Remaining calm no longer seemed possible, yet he needed to do so anyway.

"She's everything to me," Heather said. "If I'd paid more attention to her this morning—"

"Right now regrets and second-guessing yourself won't help."

"This could be something more than a random incident," Heather said.

"Why would you think that?"

"The couple are suspected to be killers. They may be the two who went on a rampage and killed several people across state lines, two of them doctors. This couple is on the FBI's Ten Most Wanted list."

The words were a kick in the gut, and the strength went out of Tyrell. He found a chair and sat in it. Jama sank down beside him, close.

"Mark was moonlighting on an E.R. shift a week or so ago, and a man came in demanding painkillers," Heather said. "Mark didn't comply."

Tyrell understood. He'd heard enough of his brother-in-law's stories to imagine the variety of people treated in the Emergency Department.

Weekends were the worst, when "patients" tried to con the E.R. docs into giving out narcotics, opiates and other addictive drugs. Mark had been around long enough to know when he was being scammed.

"One of the other docs had his car window smashed in the doctors' parking lot that night," Heather said. "Mark parks there, too."

"You think Mark was the target, but the guy got the wrong car?"

"I do. Mark tells me not to jump to conclusions. The man stole Mark's prescription pad, then tried to have a script filled at a pharmacy. The pharmacist checked it out—saw something wasn't right. Mark called the police, and the thief, Clancy Reneker, was arrested. He went into a rage, broke away from the officers, and then he and a woman went on a rampage across Kansas, Missouri and Illinois."

Tyrell couldn't bear the thought of his beautiful, precocious niece in the hands of drugged killers, especially someone bent on revenge.

"I don't think I can take this," Heather whispered. "If those people kill my daughter, I'll die with her."

"Now stop that," Tyrell said gently. "Don't jump to conclusions. Just go with what you know. You've prepared yourselves for the worst. Let's back off a little and think where else she might be. Might she have just gone to the zoo and forgotten to charge her cell phone?"

"She charged it last night."

"Okay, then, what if she's still so upset over your argument the other night that this time she went against character and intentionally turned it off."

"She wouldn't—"

"She's eleven. She'll be a teenager before you know it, and you know how she thinks she can conquer the world."

Heather was silent for a moment. "Renee fosters that concept, you know." There was a return to poise in Heather's voice.

"Of course."

"Mark and Renee and Chet are all at the zoo looking for her now. The police are conducting a massive search of the area."

"Then I hope we'll hear very soon that Doriann has been found and is in deep trouble with her parents. I'll have a few things to say to her, myself."

There was a soft sigh. "Glass half-full, right?"

"Cup overflowing."

"I love you, Tyrell. I wish you were here. I'm just so . . . very scared."

"I know." *Me, too. Terrified.*

"Tell me how Dad's doing."

"We haven't seen him yet, but I guess you've been told he's out of surgery. Thanks to Jama, they caught the problem and it should be fixed now."

"Jama's the hero of the day. When's she going to become my sister-in-law?"

"That hasn't been decided."

"Tell her I want to be matron of honor."

Tyrell understood her need for the small talk. "Renee already spoke for it."

"I feel a good catfight coming on."

Ordinarily, Tyrell would chuckle politely at the continued, loving rivalry of his twin sisters. He couldn't work up a smile, and he was glad Heather couldn't see his face.

"Don't tell Dad about this, Tyrell."

"Not until you've found Doriann and it's all over."

"Are we going to find her?"

"Any minute."

"From your mouth to God's ear."

"You realize, don't you, that we can't tell Mom, either," Tyrell said. "If we do, it'll be like telling Dad."

Heather's silence stretched into infinity. Being a son who had long ago stopped confiding every thought and action to his parents, he couldn't identify, but he could sympathize. Possibly more than all the other Mercer siblings, Heather depended on her family for emotional support. She and Mark were devoted to each other, but their schedules were demanding and often staggered. Heather needed to talk to her mother about what was happening.

Tyrell knew this.

"Then we don't tell Mom, either," she said in a wobbly voice.

"For Dad's sake," Tyrell said. "We can fake it for a few minutes."

"Or a few hours."

"Whatever it takes. I'm here for you, sis."

Chapter Fourteen

The small amount of information Jama had heard pounded through her ears. Her heart pumped with such force that she could feel the rhythm of it as she breathed in and out. She tried hard to remain calm.

Tyrell's shoulders slumped as soon as he disconnected the call, as if he had been holding himself erect for the sake of his sister even though she couldn't see him.

"I got the gist of the conversation," Jama told him. "Fill me in."

His face grew paler as he explained. A deep chill settled in the pit of Jama's stomach as she listened.

Tyrell leaned his elbows against the table, his face more ashen than Jama had seen it in four and a half years.

Witty, lively Doriann, too intelligent for her own good, filled with faith and joy, was the delight of the whole Mercer clan. She could beat her grandpa at chess, she had a tender heart for the wounded, animal or human. One of her best friends in the world was Monty's hunting hound, Humphrey.

Fran was proud that her brilliant, redheaded granddaughter looked just like her at the same age. And had the same assertive and gregarious personality.

Tyrell continued to recount Heather's side of the conversation, numbing Jama with helplessness as she took it all in.

"I'm still clinging to the hope that Doriann is at the zoo and just hasn't been found yet," Tyrell said.

"You could be right," Jama said, in spite of her conviction to the contrary.

Tyrell reached for her hand, clasped it in both of his.

"She's resourceful."

He swallowed hard, squeezed his eyes shut, took a deep breath. "But she's still a child."

"The FBI suspects the couple is on the way to St. Louis?"

"It's only a suspicion. They could be anywhere now."

The anxiety in his expression and his voice matched Jama's own, and she knew she had to make another attempt to be strong—something at which she had failed so far today.

"You know," Jama said, "so many times these past years as we've grieved over Amy, Fran has reminded me not to look back at what could have been, because that's wasted energy."

He nodded. "Mom's always said that."

"And the unproductive remorse only interferes with the optimism that needs to be the driving force of our lives."

"That sounds great in theory, but it doesn't work when my niece may be in the hands of desperate people. I want to call out the National Guard." Tyrell punched the palm of his hand and got up to pace.

"Was there any suggestion about what we can do to help search?"

"None," he said. "Prayer is our only option."

"We can do that, and we can spread the word to churches in River Dance."

"If we do that, someone is sure to let it slip to Mom, and even Dad, and I worry about how that will affect his recovery."

"So do I, but don't you think prayer is more important right now than silence?"

Tyrell nodded, reached for Jama, enfolded her in his arms and held her close. She tried hard to stop her trembling. He didn't need to know how frightened she was. And how much comfort she felt in the circle of his strong arms.

Doriann skittered behind a tree at the edge of the woods and stood listening for a moment before peering around the trunk. The old barn looked as if it had been punched in the roof by a giant fist, and both ends of the peaked roof leaned toward the broken middle. The siding had once been red, but years of weather had washed it to gray-pink.

Doriann had her jacket zipped up to her neck, and her hood covered her hair—she'd made sure to tuck every red, wet strand underneath the muddy cloth. She wasn't taking any chances.

Clancy hadn't stopped cussing and raving since he and Deb left the river, but it was hard for Doriann to hear anything now because the barn stood half a field away from where she hid. She needed to hear. What were they planning to do? Were they really going to sleep in there?

Doriann studied a stand of bushes halfway between the tree and the barn. It was the only cover she would have if she tried to get closer. She studied the building, and saw cracks in the weather-worn wood. Could Clancy or Deb see through those? Would they even think about looking?

The left end of the barn didn't look so bad.

Clancy's voice suddenly rose again. For sure, he and Deb wouldn't be peeping through the cracks to see if anyone was there if he wasn't even bothering to keep his voice down. And so Doriann ran across the open field, past the brush, all the way to the left corner of the barn. As quietly as possible she dropped to her knees while Clancy ranted a drugged tirade. Tirade? Yes, that was the word.

"That brat was my ticket to freedom," Clancy said.

"You're free now, aren't you?" Deb asked.

"I'm being hunted like an animal."

"So what are you going to do, go find another

doctor's kid to kidnap?" Deb asked. Her voice was quieter than before, not so harsh. Maybe Clancy had her as scared as Doriann.

"No, I want *that* doctor's kid. That doctor's just a man. He's not a god. He looks through people as if they don't even exist. I've seen too many others just like him."

"People who've looked at you like that?" Deb asked.

Silence for a minute, then, "How far to River Dance? We'll get the stuff there."

"How? We don't know anybody there, and you don't just walk into a drugstore and buy—"

"You didn't answer me," Clancy said. "How far to River Dance?"

"How should I know?"

"You saw the road signs, didn't you?"

"We're maybe about four or five miles away, my guess, but nobody's going to sell us anything."

"They'll sell us wine. At least we'll take the edge off with a couple of bottles. Hide out someplace where nobody will be looking. Stay underground, out of sight for a while. We could hit a drugstore later, or a doctor's office."

"With what? Your gun's in that swamp, you moron!"

There was a loud smack and a grunt, and Doriann could imagine more of Deb's teeth flying across the barn floor.

"Don't call me a moron!" Clancy shouted. And

then he called Deb a lot of names that Doriann had never heard before.

Deb didn't argue.

"You want to know what happened to my last partner?" Clancy asked.

No answer.

Doriann wondered if he'd knocked Deb out. What if he'd killed her?

Jama had every confidence in Dr. George's ability to care for Monty. Nevertheless, she walked into the recovery room with her stethoscope around her neck, more as something to focus on than to utilize.

When she saw Monty lying, eyes closed, most likely still half-under the anesthesia, she was glad for his grogginess. If he were alert, he would pick up on her anxiety.

"So," Monty said without opening his eyes, "remember your promise?"

She couldn't prevent a smile. He could still recognize each of his kids by the sound of their footsteps.

His eyes opened then. "You promised that as soon as we got me taken care of, I could interfere—"

"I remember. You're amazingly lucid under the influence of anesthesia."

"I've been told I metabolize that stuff quickly."

"Who told you that?"

"Can't remember."

"The last nurse who took care of you in surgery?"

"Could be," Monty murmured.

"Such as the time you had the stroke and didn't tell anybody?"

"Stop stalling. What's going on between you and my new ranch foreman?"

Jama grinned and kissed him on the forehead. "Nothing right now. You got sick, and we dropped everything else."

"So Tyrell isn't harassing you?"

Jama hesitated. "Well . . ."

"I told him not to, and he's usually pretty good about minding his father."

"I know. But he's worried about you right now, and he's not thinking straight. Our concern is for you today." For a moment, Jama saw Tyrell's dark blue gaze in his father's eyes, and she saw the challenge in them. Monty's concern warmed her, saddened her and stirred her gratitude as she thought about what might have been.

"You telling me to butt out?" Monty asked.

"Would I tell you that?"

"No, you'd just sidestep my questions until I really did have a heart attack. Do you believe in long engagements?"

"I never gave the subject much thought."

"Maybe you should."

All Jama could think of right now was Doriann. Monty's beloved granddaughter.

"Your mom and I had six years of engaged bliss."

Jama loved it when Monty referred to Fran as her mom. As if she really were.

Then his words registered. "Six? Now here's something rare—a story I haven't heard."

"Long engagements are wonderful—even though the engaged couple doesn't usually see it that way. I sure didn't when I proposed to Fran. She accepted with the condition that we wait until we had both completed high school."

In spite of everything, Jama laughed. "You were in seventh grade?"

"Ninth. Our parents insisted we complete two years of higher education before we spoke our vows."

"So you waited."

"It was the best time of our lives. We had the chance to know each other well, and because our parents were so strict, Fran and I were best friends for a long, long time."

"And you're so happy together."

"Best friends always make the best marriages."

"I think you're trying to tell me something."

"You and Tyrell are best friends?"

"Of course."

"So the real problem is that my son has not given you the option of an engagement length of your choosing."

"We didn't talk about it, Monty."

"Maybe you should. It could make all the difference. If you don't feel the pressure of a wedding and marriage for four years, you can relax, enjoy one another's company, and take some time to see if this is really what you want. I think it is, and you just don't know it yet."

"Monty," she warned.

He winced, then tapped himself on the forehead. "There I go, telling you what you're feeling. I promised Fran I wouldn't do that. You won't tell her, will you? She's already upset enough today."

"I won't tell, as long as you stop now."

He grinned, then sobered. "Jama Keith, I don't like to see someone in my family carrying more burdens than even I can haul. Want to talk about it? I may have a tricky heart right now, but seeing you suffering is even harder on me."

"Montrose Mercer," came Fran's quiet voice from the doorway to the hospital room, "don't you even joke about that."

"Who's joking?" Monty asked as his wife joined Jama at his bedside.

"I don't see how you can be so intrusive to the woman who saved your life today. You're barging in on Tyrell's territory." Fran leaned in for a kiss, and then, to Jama's delight, slid her shoes off and carefully climbed onto the narrow hospital bed beside her husband.

Jama was accustomed to their affection. They used to embarrass their kids to death when they smooched in front of any school friends who might be at the house. Jama also had many memories of being shooed out to play with all the other kids so Fran and Monty could be alone.

Some of Jama's best times were spent with the Mercers, even before Dad's death. She remembered riding home with the family from a movie or dinner or a picnic. Monty would start singing a song. Fran would harmonize, and the rest of the kids, though they rolled their eyes, grudgingly, joined.

When the kids all grew up and went their separate ways, Jama was disappointed the singing ended.

How she missed those days. She would love to return to that period in her life, when she believed Monty and Fran could carry the world on their shoulders.

She knew now that they'd never done that. They were human, made mistakes, endured pain, interfered too much in the lives of their children, had bad breath in the morning and struggled with financial decisions just like everyone else.

She stepped from the room and left the loving couple alone. Jama prayed that their lives weren't soon to be shattered by tragic news of their granddaughter.

Chapter Fifteen

The day darkened. Doriann froze. She'd been studying an anthill while waiting to see what Clancy and Deb would do next, and now she had the most horrible feeling that Clancy had sneaked out of the barn while she wasn't paying attention, and was standing between her and the sun. Hovering over her. Waiting for her to look up.

She looked up. She took a quiet, deep breath and let it out just as quietly. A bank of clouds had drifted between her and the light she needed to navigate by. The clouds meant she couldn't tell which direction to go when she left here. She really needed to get that cell phone. She'd already practiced using the GPS system. She could find her way out of here and lead the police to the killers.

According to Grandpa, cloud cover also meant that there probably wouldn't be a killing frost tonight.

"This hay stinks." It was Clancy, talking as if he'd never knocked Deb silly.

Doriann listened for Deb to reply, but she didn't.

"It's moldy," Clancy said. "How can you just lie in it like that?"

"You're no rose garden," Deb said at last.

The relief Doriann felt surprised her. Deb was wicked. She and Clancy were a threat to River Dance. But Doriann didn't want to have to remember for the rest of her life that she'd been ear-witness to a murder.

"So," Deb said, her voice kind of slurred. "Why don't you tell me how you killed all these people they're talking about on the radio. Did you really do it?"

Doriann sat up straight, confused. Had that hit messed up Deb's brain? Wasn't she there when the killings took place?

Clancy snickered. It was a dirty sound, and it gave Doriann goose bumps. "They're after you, too, you know."

"Can't be. I just met you."

"Yeah, but they can't tell the difference between one skinny broad and another. I had another skinny broad before I met you. We're all just a bunch of worthless druggies to the docs and the Feds."

"So what happened to the other skinny broad?" Deb's words weren't slurred now.

"Selma got all freaky on me and got religion. Told me she was going to turn herself in."

"To the cops?"

"Who else? God?" He snickered again. "I told her the old guy in the sky wanted her dead, anyway, not just rotting in a cell somewhere. So I did God's work for Him."

Doriann's eyes went buggy.

"You killed your girlfriend." Deb's voice shook.

"You got a problem with that?"

138

Deb startled Doriann by laughing. "Guess she got a surprise visit to the great beyond, huh? How'd you do it?"

"Slipped her an extra dose in the needle."

"The best way," Deb said. "How'd you do the others?"

Doriann stared at the side of the barn, feeling sicker and sicker while Clancy bragged about his acts of murder and Deb egged him on, asking for more stories.

Doriann had to do something, or more people were going to die. She'd just have to wait.

Tyrell rode shotgun, staring out the side window as Jama crossed the bridge over the Missouri River on the way back to River Dance. He was pretty sure his thoughts mirrored hers. They'd been banished from Monty's room and reminded that they had work to do. Tyrell had left the farm truck for Mom in case she needed it. Too bad the Durango was at Joe's Auto Service; it would have been easier for her to drive.

"It's best we didn't stay, anyway," Tyrell said. "Dad's worried about the frost, so he'll feel better knowing that'll be taken care of. And Mom's worried about your job."

"Monty's going to be fine," Jama said. "The surgery was a success, barring any unforeseen complications."

Tyrell looked at her. "Is that doctor talk for 'He'll

be fine, but don't blame me if something goes wrong'?"

"I mean that it's never a sure thing, just as in life. We can't know for sure what the outcome will be in any situation."

"I wanted to hang around and make sure Mom doesn't wear herself out at Dad's bedside. She's like that, you know."

"I do." Almost five years earlier, Fran had stayed by Jama's bedside in the hospital after the wreck.

"I spoke with Dr. George before we left," Jama said. "Someone from maintenance is probably, at this minute, removing the television from Monty's room for 'repairs.' Not that he ever seems to have time to watch much, but right now he might get bored."

"Mom could hear about Doriann's kidnapping out in the lobby or the cafeteria."

"Dr. George is having meals brought to her as well as Monty, and he has instructed the staff to encourage Fran to participate in Monty's care. Dr. George will stress to her the importance of watching Monty closely for signs of decline. A sleep chair is being brought to the room for her. Everyone agrees Monty could use a few more hours, or even overnight, to heal and rest before he is told about Doriann. This is particularly important considering the stroke he had after Amy's death."

"You arranged for all this while I was talking to Dad?"

"It didn't take much," Jama said. "Dr. George understands what's going on."

"You're pretty handy to have around sometimes." Tyrell shot her a glance.

"There will also be a cease-fire on the marriage proposal discussion," she said.

"I agree. This is no time to talk about love and commitment."

"Absolutely not."

"I may regress, though, when I think about Doriann. She was the one who's been telling me for three years that I should marry her aunt Jama."

"You're such a liar."

"I'm not lying. That's what she—"

"You said you agreed to the cease-fire, and now you're firing with both barrels."

"I'm sorry."

"Then maybe you should stop trying to distract yourself and start talking about what's really bothering you."

As Jama turned onto Highway 94, Tyrell stared across the flat river bottomland, seeing the face of his niece. "Anger," he admitted.

"Of course you're angry," Jama said. "I'm afraid to even mention what I'd like to do to the creep who abducted her."

"That's the problem. Sure, I want to get my hands on whoever took her, but as much as I love my sister, I sometimes want to grab Doriann, myself, and bring her to the ranch so Mom can shower all the love and affection on her that she showered on us when we were growing up."

"It seems to me that Renee's already doing that."

He nodded. Renee, the epitome of earth mother.

Jama drove in thoughtful silence for several moments while Tyrell returned his attention to the view out the side window, the flat fields dotted by houses and silos. Some houses in the middle of the floodplain had been built on stilts.

The view of the rich green fields served only as a reminder that his father was depending on him to protect the family's livelihood. Besides the cattle, the vineyards were the main cash crop for the Mercer Ranch.

"You were good with Heather," Jama said. "I don't think she could have picked up your feelings on the phone."

"Good. Now is not the time for me to comment on Doriann's upbringing."

"You're a good brother."

For some reason, that simple statement made Tyrell feel better. Jama had a knack for doing that. She knew what he was thinking just by looking at him. It was Jama, more than his siblings, who laughed at his jokes even when others didn't catch the meaning.

It had taken his bright little niece to point out Jama's devotion to him.

And for the first time, he'd actually paid attention to Jama's expression when they were together. He realized Doriann was right.

Granted, Tyrell had never had a problem with self-confidence. Even after Jama refused his proposal, he didn't doubt her love. When he took the time to consider why he had never married, he realized that he hadn't actually loved another woman before Jama.

For some people, there was one love for a lifetime, only one match that could be right, and for him, it was Jama. It was impossible to pinpoint why he knew this to be true. She was kind, loyal, independent, and he loved those qualities in her. But he'd met plenty of women over the years who had those same qualities. She was gentle, but she wasn't the only gentle, beautiful-inside-out woman in the world.

She was the only Jama, though.

Jama reached up and touched her ear and said, "Ruth."

"What?"

Jama looked at him and indicated the Bluetooth earpiece. "I'm calling my director. I set up the voice recognition while we were at the hospital. Amy and I used to wear ours all the time at the hospital, even when they weren't on. It kept people from thinking we were crazy when we talked to ourselves."

"You did that a lot, huh?"

"Sure. We were residents, always memorizing and studying procedures, anatomy, medications and dosages. It was tough, but—" She broke off, then said, "Yes, Ruth? It's Jama. I'm on my way back to River Dance. Will you need—"

She paused, grimaced. "Okay, I'll see you in about twenty minutes. Maybe thirty. I need to drop Tyrell off in town to pick up his mother's car."

Again, the grimace.

Jama disconnected, than glanced at Tyrell. "You know, you got me into this."

"Me? What did I do?"

"This loan from the town of River Dance was your idea."

"It was a good one," he said. "You needed the loan, and you wouldn't take it from Mom and Dad. You're so independent. Admit it, Jama, you shot yourself in the foot when you disappeared for six months with no explanation about where you had gone. I'm surprised you weren't penalized for defaulting on your other school loans."

"I got an extension. The loan company knew I wasn't defaulting. The counselor knew I was recovering from the accident."

"Yes, but when you disappeared from the face of the earth—"

"We all grieve differently. The loan companies didn't need a play-by-play of my life. It wasn't anyone's business."

144

"Not *anyone's* business? You might have considered your worried family."

"I told Monty and Fran I'd be okay. They trusted me to take care of myself."

"You think they didn't worry anyway?"

Jama gave him a "back off" look.

Tyrell resisted the strong urge to ask where she'd gone. Later, maybe, she would tell him.

"So what's the deal with your director?" he asked. "She did seem a little put out with you this morning for leaving."

Jama rolled her eyes. "She's already judged me and found me wanting because our gossiping mayor filled her in on some of my . . . activities in high school."

"You'll prove to her soon enough that you're not that kid anymore."

"That's one of the reasons I've dreaded coming back home. I'm tired of having to prove myself. She's a grump."

"Give it some time. Some of the grumpiest people turn out to be okay once you get to know them."

"That's what I've heard, but I've never actually seen proof."

"So tell me about what just happened."

Jama shook her head. "She's not angry, she's just cold. The clinic is currently swamped because of a fire at the winery. Several employees were brought to the clinic for treatment instead of being sent to Fulton or Jefferson City, and I'm not there to help. I might expect some anger, but there was nothing, just the demand I return to the clinic immediately."

"Then you need to go straight there. Maybe you could use my help until it gets sorted out. I still have my paramedic license up-to-date. I can triage."

"You have crops to save."

"What's more important, crops or people?"

"Maybe I should get there and see what's needed first. It wouldn't hurt Ruth to cancel interviews for the rest of the day and see to the injuries. Let's hope she has her priorities straight."

"Put yourself in her place. She's a stranger in a town full of people she doesn't know."

"I'll give it some thought."

He studied the fine, tense features of Jama's exquisite face. "Sweetheart."

She looked at him. He lost himself for a brief moment in the depths of those beautiful blue-green eyes.

"Give Ruth some time."

"I will." She returned her attention to the road, but a faint flush turned her cheeks an alluring shade of pink.

"More than a day," he said.

"Of course."

"And give *yourself* some time, too. You've never done well with that. You're always so impatient with yourself. I happen to know everyone in River Dance will welcome you with open arms."

She glanced at him again, her eyes reflecting mild humor . . . and another emotion. Affection. More than affection. "I get it, Tyrell. Okay? Don't worry about me. We have a lot more important things to think about today."

How well he knew what they had to think about. He reached across the console and touched her arm, felt the smooth silk of her skin. He felt goose bumps form beneath his touch, and he enjoyed that connection.

Maybe he was being selfish—he needed the comfort of her touch as much as he needed her presence right now. He couldn't help believing his presence—his touch—might also lend her comfort. Encouragement. A reassurance of his love.

"You'll call me if I can be of help at the clinic?" he asked as she turned onto River Dance Road.

"I'll call. Promise."

Chapter Sixteen

Jama dropped Tyrell off at the grocery store to pick up Fran's car, her senses still tingling from the touch of his hand. He had no idea what he did to her.

Did he?

The moment she walked into the clinic, she regretted dismissing his help so quickly. The smell

147

of smoke hung in the air. Eight people huddled in the waiting room, where it seemed everyone was talking at once.

Down the hallway, Zelda Benedict rushed from one treatment room to another, still in her jogging clothes.

Ruth Lawrence stepped out of a room and caught sight of Jama. "You're here in time to suture a wrist. We've got a smoke inhalation in three." She pointed across the hallway to the room Zelda had just entered. "There are more to be seen, and more are probably on their way."

"Any that are life threatening?"

Ruth shook her head.

"If we need more help, I know a good paramedic."

Ruth's eyebrows rose. "In this town?" She said it as if she couldn't imagine such a thing.

"Tyrell Mercer supported himself through school as a paramedic, and he still takes a shift from time to time to keep his skills sharp."

"Good. We'll call him if we need him." Ruth nodded toward the four men and two women hunched together near the unmanned reception desk. All six pairs of eyes watched Jama.

She recognized several former classmates, including Jim Hammersmith, who'd been a couple of years ahead of her in school. She nodded to him, and he stood up. "Did you hear about the fire, Jama? A little gas heater we had in the storeroom exploded. Caught a couple of crates on fire, spread to a bunch of wrapping paper, and whoosh! It was an inferno in that place."

"Everybody's coming here, though, right?" she asked. "No one was sent on to a hospital by ambulance?"

"Naw, everybody's coming to the clinic. I'm a little worried about Scotty. He fell into a stack of bottles trying to get out, and cut his wrist pretty badly."

Scott Hammersmith. Jim's little brother. Jama frowned. He'd been in her class at school, and he'd had a crush on her forever—at least it had felt that way.

"Don't worry, I'll take good care of him," Jama said.

Jim's eyebrows reached for his hairline. The others seemed to grow more interested.

"You're the one who's gonna sew on him?" Jim asked.

"My handiwork's pretty good, and we'll have him numbed up so he won't feel a thing." She'd expected to encounter these misgivings from a few of the people who'd known her in school. It had to be a little uncomfortable to think that the girl who'd been sent to the principal's office more than once for sassing a teacher might now have a sharp needle in her hand.

Merilee Jacobs, who'd grown a bit more chunky, with lank brown hair, cleared her throat. "You know, Jama Sue, you weren't the best at sewing in school."

And then, of course, there was that. "I wasn' sewing on people then, Merilee, and I'm not using one of the old sewing machines. I've learned a few things since high school." Jama shot a glance at the others on her way to the treatment room, and felt as if she'd stepped back into a time warp.

It happened whenever she came to town. She tried not to imagine two years of this kind of scrutiny. She couldn't escape the stares, and her self-consciousness dredged up memories of the people who had known her.

She glanced at Ruth as she passed the director's office. "The folks here might prefer you to do the suturing."

"We don't always get what we want in life, do we?"

Jama stopped and blinked.

"You were in a surgical residency before you switched to family practice." Ruth looked up from a stack of paperwork on her desk.

"The mayor tell you that?"

"Zelda did. Someone might have given me more information about you. I'd like to know what other skills you might have that can be utilized."

"I can do the sutures."

"Do you know how to operate the new monitors, the phone system, the Pixus dispenser and all the other brand-new, state-of-the-art equipment around here?"

"Of course. You're not going to have to break me in from scratch."

Ruth leaned back with a sigh of exasperation. "Not good enough. I told Eric we needed time, but no one seems interested in giving it to us. What difference would a couple of extra days make?"

"My fault," Jama said. "I opened the barn door when I treated Monty this morning. You may not come from a small town, but word spreads fast in River Dance. Why are you so concerned that I be familiar with the equipment? Don't you know how to operate these things?"

Ruth rolled her eyes. "Where I come from, everything is secondhand ancient. Let's get with it. Don't forget we may have more patients coming from the winery. I have applicants to be interviewed, and some have waited more than an hour."

Jama glanced down the hallway to an older woman and a young man, both seated at the far corner from the winery workers. "Tyrell has already offered to help us if we need him."

"How can I reach him?"

Jama jotted Tyrell's cell number on a sticky note. "There's something else you need to be aware of."

Ruth looked up, her expression plain on her face. *What is it this time?*

Jama drew the office door shut behind her and placed Tyrell's number on Ruth's desk. "You know that man I flew out this morning? It is feared that his eleven-year-old granddaughter, Doriann Streeter, has been kidnapped."

Ruth closed her eyes and took a heavy breath as an expression of distress flashed over her face. "So that would be Tyrell's niece."

"Yes. I think he would welcome the distraction of working with patients."

Ruth nodded. "Zelda's been running herself ragged today. She needs a break. Get the suturing done, then send her home. If more patients come in, we'll call Tyrell. Meanwhile, since we seem to be up and running in spite of our lack of staff, I'll see if I can't interview someone with X-ray training. Maybe I can check out those skills with practical testing."

Doriann stared at the barn siding three inches from her nose. One day a couple of years ago, Aunt Renee had brought a real-live private detective to the house to speak to a group of homeschool kids about his job.

What Doriann had always thought would be fun and exciting turned out to sound like the boringest job in the world. The detective told the kids that he had to sit for hours in his car, or in some other hidden location, waiting for someone to make a move. Then there would be a rush of adrenaline when he hurried to make sure the person didn't get away.

Then he told them that he usually didn't chase

convicted criminals. The police did. He checked out people who might be pulling an insurance scam, or having an affair.

Unfortunately, just when his speech got interesting, Aunt Renee quickly cut him off, thanked him for his time and assured the kids that there were all kinds of opportunities for them in their future. Criminal justice was only one career option.

Doriann didn't want to be a private detective. But now it seemed she was doing it, like it or not. Clancy and Deb needed to fall asleep before she could get her cell phone, and even then, she wasn't sure if she'd have the guts to go into that barn.

But if she didn't go in, that would mean she'd wasted all this time. She'd begged Mom and Dad for that GPS navigational program on her new phone last year, and now she could use it as she never imagined. She had to get out of here, wherever she was, and lead the police to the killers.

It'd be easy to find the Katy Trail or the river or the road if she could *only get to that phone!*

This whole waiting game was worse than boring. It was deadly. What if *she* fell asleep? She'd hardly slept at all last night. What if she snored? Clancy and Deb could be all over her.

That was the way the undercover detective said it happened. If he slipped for just one minute, he could lose his case, lose his client, be out of a job.

She couldn't help wondering what that detective

153

would do if he were here now. Of course, being a big, tough man with a gun, he wouldn't be hiding here, he'd be charging into the barn with that gun drawn.

Doriann wished she was armed. But Grandma always told her prayer worked better than any man-made weapon. Aunt Renee always prayed for a "hedge of angels to surround us in our time of need," whatever that meant. Doriann had heard of hedge trees and trimming hedge bushes, but she couldn't imagine angel hedges. She'd sure love to be surrounded by angels right now, though.

Maybe she was.

And yet, she was getting tired of waiting. And she didn't have the patience of the private eye. She itched in places she couldn't scratch, even more than usual. Her eyelids were getting heavier and heavier. She could use a nap, which was crazy.

Still, she closed her eyes for just a moment.

She was feeling herself relax when a sharp cackle startled her. She jerked her head upright, realizing she'd fallen asleep enough to drool down the side of her face.

"Guess what I just realized," Clancy exclaimed. "I've still got the kid's phone."

"So?"

"Her cell phone."

Deb groaned. "What good's that gonna do us?"

"You got a cell phone with power left in it? Mine went down with the truck. We could call anybody we wanted to with this, anywhere in the world, and it'd be free."

"Who's there to call?" Deb asked.

"Your contacts in St. Louis, for one. Let 'em know we'll be there as soon as we can rustle up another car, and we'll be needing some stuff to cook."

"Wow, what a great idea." Deb spoke as if she thought that was anything but a good idea. "If I had their numbers, we'd be all set. Think you can find my contact numbers on a kid's cell phone?"

Clancy didn't reply, but he chuckled a moment later. "Oh, man, would you look at this? She took pictures. Gotta be family. There's this old couple, and a big honkin' guy with black hair, and then here's this dog. Hey, doesn't this look like that dog we saw on the road? The one I would've bagged if the brat hadn't kicked my leg."

"The one that almost got us killed," Deb said.

Doriann remembered the day she went around River Dance taking pictures with her new cell phone. She loved what Grandpa called her "gadgets."

"Stop that, will you?" Deb complained. "You're going to run the battery down. Then who're you gonna call?"

"Doesn't sound like we've got anybody to call," he grumbled, then as Doriann peered through a crack in the side of the barn, he tossed the phone aside, into the hay he'd called "stinking."

"Say." He straightened. "That did look like the hound we saw on the road. That thing had one red ear and one white, just like the one in these pictures." He reached once more for the cell phone.

"Would you leave that thing alone! We may need it and won't have the power."

"Yeah? And I told you when we first started this trip that I'm the one in charge. Keep your ideas to yourself."

Deb turned over onto her side away from Clancy. "Whatever."

Doriann could have pounded her head on the ground in frustration.

Chapter Seventeen

Zelda assisted while Jama sutured Scott Hammersmith's wrist. It was a bad cut, needing a two-layer closure, but it came together nicely, and there was no muscle involvement. Jama was relieved. Scott's whole life consisted of fishing and hunting.

"Scotty, honey, you don't know how lucky you are today." Zelda watched Jama's work with obvious admiration. "What you've got here is a family-practice doc who's got the skills of a surgeon. She knows just where to place the sutures so—"

"Uh, don't do that." Scott's face was still nearly as pale as the towels draped over his arm. "Would you please not give me a play-by-play, Zelda? If I pass out in here, the guys'll never let me forget it."

"You're doing fine," Jama assured him. "And even if you did pass out, we'd never tell a soul."

Scott switched his attention from the far corner of the room to Jama's face, clearly not wanting to observe the action. "You're as pretty as ever, Jama Sue."

"Now, Scott, no flirting with the doc," Zelda said. "You're a married man now. Besides, you don't want to distract her from her work."

"I'm not flirting, I'm just saying . . . well . . . anyway." Some color returned to his face.

"You know what, Dr. Keith," Zelda said, "I might've been a little hasty turning down Dr. Ruth's offer this morning."

Jama completed her final suture and took a second to study her handiwork. The scarring would be minimal. Then Zelda's words registered.

"Don't call her Dr. Ruth to her face. And are you saying what I think you are?"

"I might talk to her about a part-time job."

Jama and Scott exchanged a look. "Part-time?" Jama asked.

"Well, it's not like this place will be overcrowded in the first couple of weeks, is it?"

"You never know. Judging by the amount of traffic we've had so far, we could have our schedule packed."

"Still, it wouldn't hurt me to try it on for size,"

Zelda said. "It's awfully good to be able to work with you again, see how far you've come. Besides, I've got these new, high-tech shoes that make me feel like I'm walking on clouds, so it's not like I'l have too much trouble standing on my feet all day I could try it for a while."

Jama felt some of the load slip from her shoulders. She met Zelda's gaze and nodded.

Jama sent Scott out with scripts for an antibiotic and pain meds, with instructions to return. She watched with relief as he and his friends said goodbye and trooped out the front door, trailing the faint scent of smoke behind them.

She turned to find her director standing with arms crossed, leaning against the threshold of the reception office.

"He needed an appointment," Ruth said.

"He can call when we have the office set up to schedule appointments."

"You could have made one for him and entered it into the computer later, once you've figured out how to do it. And he needed printed instructions about wound care, and a doctor's pass for work."

Jama ran her tongue along her teeth before speaking. "A doctor's pass? There was a fire. You think his employer doesn't know what happened? This is River Dance. Everybody in the Missouri River Valley probably knows about it by now. Everyone also should know we're not set up for clinic hours yet."

"Keep it in mind for future reference," Ruth said as she walked toward her office.

Jama was still frowning as she entered the suture room to find Zelda wiping down the tray table.

"You heard?" Jama asked.

Zelda nodded. "It'll be okay."

"She intimidates me," Jama said.

"Maybe you should take a look at her from my end of the life cycle. She's not so intimidating then. She's a young woman, probably in her late thirties, if that, and she's overwhelmed. Probably never directed a clinic before, never had this much responsibility."

"You think she's still in her thirties?" Jama asked. "She seems older than that."

"Lots of things make a person look older. Stress. Bad experiences, whatever."

"Hello?" came a slightly annoyed voice from the hallway. "Am I being psychoanalyzed by people who don't even know me?"

Jama and Zelda looked at each other sheepishly when Ruth entered the room, arms crossed, chin out.

"Well, it was supposed to be a private conversation," Zelda said. "We didn't expect our eaves to be dropped."

In spite of herself, Jama couldn't help reevaluating her director's appearance. There was a stiffness in the way she held her mouth, a tightness around her eyes—which were, now that Jama was paying attention, pretty—in fact, Ruth looked as if she could be friendly. If she ever smiled. The lines in her face were not deep.

"I'm thirty-eight—not that it's anybody's business. And neither is my private life your business. I'll thank you to keep your thoughts about me to yourselves."

"Well, folderol," Zelda muttered. "That yanks it. Even if I did want the job, I'm not getting it now."

There was a surprised pause. "I thought you weren't interested," Ruth said.

"It's not like I'm ready to give up and sit at home, so what else am I going to do? Lately I've been working three or four times a week, long shifts, long drives to Columbia or Jeff City. It'd be easier and quicker to walk across the street than drive halfway to the moon and back."

"Then you're hired," Ruth said. "That'll get one position filled and cut down on the interviews considerably." She turned and walked out, leaving Jama and Zelda to stare after her.

"She doesn't waste much time, does she?" Jama asked.

"Suppose she's that desperate?"

"I warned you," Ruth called back from the hallway. "Jama? Are you coming? We need to get someone hired to answer the phones."

Doriann opened her eyes to the sight of gray-pink wood. She froze. She'd fallen asleep again! What if . . .

She turned her head slightly, straining to see if someone might be standing next to her, listening for the sound of Clancy or Deb breathing above her, for the sound of footsteps, sniffing for rotten breath.

All she smelled was damp dirt beneath her, and a faint green scent of grass. All she heard was a loud snort, then a quiet snore from inside the barn.

Relief.

Carefully, Doriann pushed herself to her knees and tried to see through a crack low on the barn wall. There was something in the way. She stood and rose up on her toes to a crack higher on the wall, but she heard a sudden noise, a brush of movement inside.

She froze, scared to breathe for several long seconds. Then came the snoring again. She probably wouldn't be able to see inside where it was shadowy, but if there were other cracks in the walls, and if Clancy and Deb had left a door open . . . just maybe she'd be able to catch sight of something.

She leaned closer to the wall, until her nose touched the rough wood. She saw shadows that took shape as she focused. She saw the skinny body of Deb, all angles and sharp points, where she lay on a broken hay bale. They had left the door open—or it had fallen off. Clancy was stretched out beside Deb, lying on his back, arms under his head.

Deb was the one snoring, her mouth wide-open, jaw slack.

Doriann studied the two of them. They didn't look so scary in their sleep. She wondered what kind of people they might have been if not for the speed. Aunt Renee said the drugs did awful things to people.

Of course, most people didn't turn into killers just because they took drugs. But sometimes, according to Aunt Renee and Mom and Dad, drugs could take people over and turn them inside out, make them do things they'd never do if they were straight.

So if Clancy had never taken drugs, maybe he would be a schoolteacher or a bus driver. Or maybe a doctor or a famous chef with his own cooking show. Maybe Deb would be an airline pilot or a captain of a ship or a senator.

What did their parents think about them? Aunt Renee said that if any of her kids got into drugs, she'd be heartbroken. She'd wonder what she did wrong. But Doriann couldn't understand why anybody else would be to blame for Clancy's choice to do drugs. He made the decision. Same as Deb.

But they probably had some very sad parents somewhere in the world.

The way Doriann saw it, she could never do drugs because she had parents and aunts and uncles and grandparents and cousins who would all be heartbroken. She wouldn't be Doriann any longer.

She'd be somebody with rotten teeth and bad breath and, as Aunt Renee always said, a dirty soul. Sure, Jesus could clean her up again, and make a good person out of her, but she'd still be a different person, and she didn't want to be a different person.

Doriann closed her eyes and took a deep breath. Somebody needed to call 911 and stop the killing—and only she knew where the killers were.

She crept around the side of the barn, came to the barn door—or what used to be the door. Now it was just a few pieces of wood cobbled together with barbed wire and nails.

She didn't want to make any noise so she crept on around to the other side.

She looked at a hole in the side of the barn. It looked as if some of the slats of wood had been kicked out by a horse or a mule or bull. She studied the tractor door, where the wood gaped in several places, and the side door, which hung on one hinge. She could slip through that opening without making noise.

This wasn't as easy as it had seemed when she was safely in the woods out of sight of the killers. She leaned forward and tried to peer through another crack.

Aunt Renee said that when a drug addict crashed, they could sleep for days, but still, Deb was the only one asleep for sure.

Doriann couldn't see anything. Maybe she didn't

have the right angle. She stood on her toes and pressed her nose against the rough wood.

All she saw was something white. It darkened, then whitened again.

She caught a scream before it could leave her mouth. She was staring at an eye.

Chapter Eighteen

Jama returned the receiver to the phone and braced herself. She called Ruth's office instead of walking back to break the news. Might as well practice the new system.

"Hi, Ruth. Sorry to interrupt your interview, but I just received word from River Dance Winery that we can expect at least three more patients, two with smoke inhalation, one with a possible broken arm. Zelda's gone. Want me to call Tyrell now?"

"Yes, call him. Let me know if I'm going to have to cancel interviews this afternoon. Keep taking calls if you can, try to get that appointment book filled. We need a ballpark figure of how many patients to expect next week, so we'll know how to staff this place."

"Got it. I'm getting another call."

Ruth disconnected without replying.

The call was from the mayor of River Dance.

"Jama Sue, what's going on down there?" Eric Thompson had the deepest, smoothest bass voice, which he used to good effect when running for office or presiding over a town meeting. "Yesterday, Ruth said she wouldn't have the clinic ready for a full load of patients until next week. I just heard down at Mildred's café that you've already treated some patients."

"It seems we've been forced into operation a little sooner than expected. I just hope nothing serious comes in, because we certainly aren't set up for it."

She thought of Monty. Of the fire. Serious had already broadsided them.

"How many slots have you filled in the appointment book for Monday?" Eric asked.

"Most of them, and we're working on Tuesday. What did you do, advertise in every paper along the Missouri?"

"You have a problem with that? We've got to get this clinic up and running and bringing in revenue ASAP. We've got almost every cent in the till invested in this place, and we're up to our necks in debt."

"I thought there was enough to build the clinic without going into debt."

"That was until we took you on. And I might have underestimated the cost of X-ray machines and lab equipment. I've been to the schools to promise end-of-term physicals at a discount, I've offered weekly blood pressure checks for anyone over sixty, I've—"

"Are you worried we'll fail?"

165

"With you here, hometown girl, coming back to treat the sick, I think we'll make a go of it."

"No pressure to perform, though, right?" she said dryly.

"The day you signed that contract, I could see your mind working. You'd rather be anywhere but here."

Jama didn't argue.

"I heard you hit the ground running today, and did a great job," he said. "That'll draw some business this way."

Jama smiled to herself. This clinic had been Eric's idea. He had a right to be proud. Because of his hard work and vision, River Dance had a small industrial park at the east edge of town, and other growth was taking place on Main Street. The town may not always be so dependent on the vineyards.

"Have you considered staying past the two-year period?" Eric asked.

"Nope."

"Not at all? You know Tyrell's planning to stay."

"And you're telling me this because . . . ?"

"Word gets around. You know that. He's crazy about you, Jama. I can see it in his eyes when he talks about you."

Jama sighed. She'd seen it, too. Time for a subject change.

"Eric, has Ruth ever done administrative work before?"

"Nothing like this."

"What has she done?"

"She hasn't told you?"

"There hasn't been a lot of time to chat. What's up with her?"

There was a pause. "What has she said?"

"All she mentioned was that the last place she worked had poor equipment."

"That's an understatement."

"Care to let me in on the secret?"

"She was a missionary," Eric said.

"You're kidding." And no one had said anything about it?

"Sounds to me as if she doesn't want to talk about it yet." Eric's voice was soft. "Don't ask her, okay?"

"Okay, but where was she a missionary, and why is she here now, and—"

"Tanzania. Her reason for being here is her business unless she decides to tell you. I met Ruth and Jack a few years ago when I was with my guard unit on a peacekeeping mission near their medical clinic in Tanzania. I was taken there for treatment after an injury. She's on leave from her mission for the immediate future. That's all I can tell you. Let it drop for now, okay? That poor woman's been through enough."

When Eric disconnected, Jama sat staring at the phone for a moment, then shook her head. How many more surprises could she expect before the end of the day?

She called the Mercer Ranch, and was once again amazed by the warm comfort she felt at the sound of Tyrell's voice.

"Hi," she said. "Did you mean it when you said you'd be willing to help us here at the clinic for a while?"

"Of course. Daniel just arrived. He can direct the men to prepare for tonight's freeze. Our cousin, Mae, is driving the tractor, and she's an expert. I can consult with him by phone if he needs any help."

"How soon can you be here?"

"Will five minutes work?"

Jama smiled. "I'll see you then."

Doriann heard Clancy's laughter as she stumbled over her own feet, crashing through the woods, noisy and obvious. He'd tricked her, made her think they were both asleep when he was wide-awake. Had he known she was out there all this time?

The sound of his footsteps grew louder, the sound of her breathing harder. It wouldn't help to scream, because there was nobody to hear except Deb.

Doriann stumbled through a creek, in water up to her knees, scrambled around a small cliff, then plunged beneath some cedar trees.

Grandpa always said the only good cedar tree was a dead cedar tree. That wasn't true. This was the only place to hide . . . if Clancy hadn't already seen her. Twigs and branches popped behind her. Too close!

She ducked behind a thick growth of a stickery green tree, caught the hood of her jacket on a branch that dragged at her for a second, then snapped away.

Clancy stopped a few yards away; she could hear him breathing, talking to himself under his breath. There was a footstep, then another, coming closer. Slowing near where she hid . . . whispers . . . laughter under his breath, as if this was all such fun for him. It made her mad.

She saw the toes of his grungy running shoes when he reached the stand of trees. She opened her mouth, breathing as shallowly and quietly as she could, but her heart pumped so hard, she felt sure he could hear the thrum of it in her chest.

And still he whispered. Like a crazy person. Which he was. Mad with cravings for the drugs that kept him high.

Doriann was never doing drugs. Never.

He fell silent for a moment, and Doriann held her breath. Then she heard his laughter, dark, wicked, evil . . . barely a few feet behind her.

She yelped and plunged from the cedar blind, into the woods where blackberry brambles scraped her face and hands and grabbed her jacket, as if trying to slow her down so he could catch her. But he wasn't going to catch her. No way!

She raced and stumbled past trees, through thickets, to a hillside with a tiny waterfall running down it. She scrambled over it and down the hill. There she found a stretch of road.

She didn't dare take time to stop, but she looked both directions as she crossed. This was the Katy Trail! But there weren't any people on the trail. No surprise.

The road and the river couldn't be far away.

Clancy plunged from the thicket she'd led him through, and he was angry now, not whispering but cussing out loud. There was no one to help her. She was alone.

She paused long enough to grab up some sandy gravel from the trail. Both hands full, she turned and flung the gravel into his face. With a cry of surprise, he stumbled backward, hands covering his eyes as he spewed his bad words.

Doriann threaded her way into the trees and ran as fast as she could, stumbling over roots, ripping her clothes on thorns, slipping in mud.

She couldn't tell if he was following her, and couldn't stop long enough to listen for him. She just ran deeper into the trees and prayed he wouldn't be able to get the sand out of his eyes and come after her.

Tyrell was in his mother's car, on his way back to town, when his cell phone jingled its tune from his shirt pocket. He was wishing he'd allowed

Jama to talk him into a Bluetooth earpiece when his mother's voice reached him over the airwaves.

"Tyrell." It was soft. Dead soft.

He nearly missed a turn. "Mom? What's wrong? Is it Dad? Has something—"

"Monty is sleeping peacefully. I took a walk around the hospital for some exercise, and I just happened to pass a waiting room with a television."

No. Oh, no.

"There was an announcement about a child abduction in Kansas City early this morning," she continued. "The child is still missing and the kidnappers are still at large."

Tyrell could not speak.

"These abductors are on the FBI's Most Wanted list. Killers."

He swallowed. "Mom, what—"

"The child was described as a preteen with red hair and a purple jacket, abducted in the neighborhood where Heather, Mark and Doriann live."

"Kansas City has a lot of redheaded—"

"I don't know why, but something disturbed me about the announcement. Maybe it was because of the way you and Jama wouldn't look me in the eye when you left, or maybe it was because that maintenance man who removed the television from the room couldn't tell Monty what was wrong with it when he asked."

"Mom, it's been a hard day for you and Dad—"

"I just called Heather."

He felt sick.

"She started crying, told me they had to keep that line open, then hung up. Tyrell, I want you to tell me what's happening, and I want you to tell me now."

Doriann's toe caught on a fallen limb and she fell headlong, her face landing in a soft bed of pine needles. Stickery pine needles. She rolled over, looked behind her, scrambled back to her feet, and then stopped. Listening.

A breeze whispered through the pines. A bird sang somewhere above her. It sounded like a mockingbird. She didn't hear anything else.

But the wind and the birdsong could be masking other sounds.

She looked up into thick clouds. She couldn't tell where the sun was in the sky. How long had she slept outside that barn, and how far had she run? Would it be twilight soon? It could get dark before long, and yet she knew her sense of time and direction were both wacko.

She didn't know which way to run. So she didn't. She looked around for the tallest pine tree with limbs low enough for her to reach. She saw one across a narrow, rocky creek bed. She crept to the tree and ducked beneath its branches, then reached up and began to climb.

Tyrell turned onto River Street toward the clinic as he explained to his mother what might have happened to Doriann, and then, because he wanted so badly to be able to convince himself, he said, "Mom, nothing is certain. I know how it looks. I want to believe that this is all some big mistake, and that Doriann will come walking home any time after a day in the park."

"But we both know that probably won't happen."

He shifted his cell phone to his other hand to signal a turn.

"It's four o'clock in the afternoon, Tyrell. She may be strong-willed and impulsive, and she may be desperate for some downtime, but she wouldn't worry her family like this. Not all day. She would know her parents would call and check on her frequently during the day."

Tyrell knew this far too well. He'd been driving himself half crazy with this knowledge. Denying the obvious did no one any good, but what else could he tell his family? That if Doriann had fallen into the hands of killers, she was most likely already dead? And yet . . . he prayed this wasn't the case.

"Doriann is a very mature child," Mom said. "She's bright and capable."

"She is."

"If she is in a bad situation—"

"Worrying won't help us right now."

Another silence, this one longer. "I want to know where my granddaughter is, and I want to know now." She could no longer hide the tremble in her voice.

"Mom, you've got to hold it together for Dad's sake."

"I . . . I know." There were tears near the surface; he could hear them.

"This is an impossible situation for you," he said. "Jama did all she could to keep you from having to go through it."

"But I needed to know. Don't you understand? I need to be praying."

"The news about Doriann right now could slow Dad's healing, even set him back."

Silence.

"That's why we tried to keep this under wraps until we had more information," Tyrell said.

"I understand, but Doriann's my flesh and blood. She's your father's oldest grandchild, and he would be livid if he knew he was being coddled this way."

"Let him be livid later," Tyrell said. "Right now, he needs to heal. Do you think you can keep mum until he's out of the woods a little further?" Tyrell pulled into the clinic parking lot, relieved to see only two cars. The patients hadn't arrived yet. Jama would have time to give him a quick orientation.

More silence from Mom. Longer this time. "I can do this, honey," she said. "Dad's going to be fine."

"Are you going to tell him?"

"Not before it's necessary. He's the worrier of the family, you know."

"The stroke he had when Amy—"

"I know. Let me handle him. And please, Tyrell, keep me in the loop."

"Do you have to go back to the room for a while?" he asked.

She sighed. "No. I can have a nurse tell Monty I'm tired and decided to get a room. Tyrell, you do understand I'm serious about this. I want every update. I'm going to glue myself to the waiting-room chair and watch for every television announcement."

"I'll keep you updated." Tyrell sat in the car and kept the line open, listening as she accepted the reality of this horror in her own way. Nobody was going to fix this for her.

Chapter Nineteen

For the first time all day, the phone was quiet. The next influx of patients had not yet arrived. Jama sat in her director's office as Ruth perused the top résumé of a small stack.

"Do you know Chelsea Franklin?" Ruth asked.

"Yes."

Ruth flipped the page, then frowned. "Who writes a résumé on both sides?"

"Somebody who has to conserve paper. Chelsea

is Etta Franklin's girl, and the family doesn't have a lot, especially now that Mr. Franklin decided he couldn't care for a wife with early onset Alzheimer's."

Ruth read the sheet for a few seconds, then looked up at Jama. "What else do you know about this applicant?"

"Graduated about ten years ago from River Dance High, graduated from college, worked a few years as a medical technician to save money for med school, then returned home recently."

"That doesn't tell me any more than her résumé does. What can you tell me about her character?"

"She was a sweet child. I used to babysit her sometimes. I don't think that'll help you much."

"Zelda implied today that the two of you could help me significantly. Let's test that theory."

"Maybe you should ask Zelda, then, since it was her idea. I haven't been around, myself, for a long time."

"You're here, Zelda is not, and I want to make some decisions right away." Ruth swiveled in her chair and leaned toward Jama. "You grew up here. I know you've got old friends who keep you apprised of local news . . . friends such as the Mercers, Zelda. I need you to help me decide whether or not this candidate would be a good addition to the mix we already have here."

"Which is?"

"Which is three very opinionated, strong-willed

women, who will have to figure out a way to learn to get along."

"If you think that, why did you hire Zelda, and why didn't you fire me?"

"Zelda's experience is invaluable, and Eric wouldn't let me fire you even if I tried. It would be a huge financial loss to the community to replace you."

"Thanks," Jama muttered.

"Tell me about the applicant," Ruth said.

"Chelsea's quiet. She doesn't push her opinions on others."

"So she could either be nervous working with us, or could serve as a buffer between us," Ruth said.

"She's probably anxious about coming back to town, concerned she may not find a job nearby. She needs to be able to spend time with her mother."

"Our need for the right employee is what we have to focus on. Can she do the job?"

"I'm sure she can."

"It appears to me that Chelsea's commitment to her mother shows some character."

"It's heartbreaking," Jama said.

Ruth laid the résumé aside, as if she'd made her decision. "She's probably no happier about returning to River Dance than you are."

"I can't speak for her. It would just take a few days for her to prove herself," Jama said.

"Since she's due to arrive in about ten minutes,

we may be able to put her to the test during her interview, depending on the incoming casualties."

The waiting-room door opened, and Jama got up to peer along the hallway. Tyrell stepped inside. He gave her a half-hearted wave.

"Our help is here," she told Ruth.

"It may be a few minutes before the rest of the winery workers get here. It sounded to me as if they were more interested in dousing the fire than seeking medical attention."

The telephone buzzed, and Jama rushed to answer it, waving for Tyrell to have a seat as she entered the reception office.

Tyrell stood in the middle of the empty waiting room, watching Jama and thinking about the unprotected hillside at the ranch covered with Norton and Vignoles vines. The Norton were a sturdy strain of native grape, but it, too, was at risk if the weather didn't change.

He couldn't help wondering if his brother was setting the bales properly at the base of the hillside. Too close, and the fires could scorch the vines, too far away, and a fortune in precious hay would be wasted.

His thoughts scrambled with tension as he watched Jama juggle calls: Dad and Doriann, life and death, the fragility of existence; Jama and Amy and the lost bond of friendship that Jama grieved after more than four and a half years.

He shook his head, wishing he was wiser about affairs of the heart.

He couldn't keep his attention from Jama. She was efficient on the phone, patient, which had never been a characteristic of hers when she was growing up. As she listened, counseled, reassured and jotted down appointments, he hoped that only he caught the strain in her voice.

As the calls continued and no patients entered, Tyrell stepped to the back window of the waiting room and gazed up the hillside, below which he knew fields of large, round hay bales were being transported into place for multiple bonfires.

Would these efforts save the vines?

The ranch was Dad's lifework. Mom's occasional rival.

Not that Mom would ever say anything about it, but Tyrell had always known that she'd often been lonely, even in the midst of all her children, when Dad was at a co-op meeting that ran late, or in the fields making his rows a little straighter.

Dad had always taken pride in his work. So had Mom. And Dad had spent good, quality time with his kids, and with his wife. They loved him for it. But Tyrell had suspected for years that quality time once or twice a week with her husband might not be enough for Mom. Quantity might also play a part. He knew that it played a part for him. He wanted more than even his happily married parents had enjoyed.

He couldn't help wondering if that could be part of Jama's concern about the two of them, as well. Having seen Monty's obsession with making the Mercer Ranch the best, most productive, most progressive ranch in the Missouri River Valley, would Jama be worried that Tyrell would follow in his father's footsteps?

Jama would never dream of saying a word against her foster father.

And then Tyrell thought about Heather and Mark. Was Heather simply imitating her father's example when she worked so many long hours that her daughter was practically being raised by someone else?

"Tyrell? Hello?"

He blinked and turned to find Jama standing behind him, eyeing him with concern.

"You okay?" she asked.

His first impulse was to assure her that everything was fine. But he hated lying. "No. You?"

She shook her head. "Everything okay at the ranch?"

"Daniel's carrying his cell phone. He can call me with any questions." Their cousin, Mae, and her husband had a dairy farm near Hermann. Tyrell was counting on her expertise to guide Daniel as she drove the tractor with the bale lift.

"Do you think the bale fires will work?" Jama asked.

"I think it's our best chance. We won't light the

fires unless the temperature drops below twenty-six degrees. The technique won't be foolproof, but we might save a percentage of the shoots."

"Big if?" Jama asked.

He nodded. "How many patients are coming from the winery?"

Jama sank into one of the waiting-room chairs. "Five, according to the call I received about a minute ago. Three smoke inhalations, one possible broken bone, and one of the men has a possible hip dislocation."

"Ambulance?" He sat down beside her.

"Private vehicle."

"I could have collected two or three of them on my way here if I'd known transport was needed."

"I was told it's chaos at the winery. Two fire trucks are there, and one of the first responders is securing the patients. They should be here before long. If not for the hip dislocation, I'd say we could take care of the rest ourselves. You probably have a lot more work to do at the ranch."

"Not quite as much as you'd think. Daniel and Mae can handle it."

"I heard Tom Frey's trying to hire a helicopter to protect his vineyard," Jama said.

It would cost thousands of dollars a night to have a helicopter hover over the crops and move the air to keep the frost from destroying them, but the method might be a feasible alternative to the bonfires. However, Tyrell believed that the delicate shoots were less likely to be damaged with heated air than with the strong, uneven blasts of wind caused by rotor blades.

But Tyrell's mind wasn't completely on the crops, or the incoming injured, or even on his father.

"You're thinking about Doriann," Jama said.

He nodded. "Every time I close my eyes, I can see her hair, the color of sweet potatoes."

Jama laid her hand on his. "I remember her head poking out of the hay last summer, with the widest, most mischievous grin on her face."

Tyrell stared down at their joined hands, comforted by her touch.

"If you think about it too much, the fear can eat you alive," Jama said.

Tyrell nodded. He was trying to think of everything else . . . anything but his visions of what might be happening to Doriann. He reached into his pocket and pulled out his cell phone. There was still juice in the battery.

"When she's found, you'll be one of the first to know," Jama assured him.

"Mom knows," Tyrell said.

There was a swift intake of breath. "How?"

"She saw a TV news alert."

Jama leaned close enough for him to catch the warm air of her minty breath against the side of his face. "How's she handling it?"

"She's unhappy with us for keeping it from her in the first place, and she's frantic for Doriann."

Jama stood and walked to the front window, arms crossed over her chest. "Oh, Tyrell, I thought we were doing the right thing."

"I still think we did."

"But to find out about it on television?"

"You did all you could to keep that from happening. Stop second-guessing yourself, Jama." He wanted to get up and join her at the window, to hold her close, and reassure her that all would be well. But would it?

He thought about his brother. "Daniel says Doriann's still alive."

Jama turned. "Is that just a statement of hope, or something more?"

"He told me he knows she's alive." Tyrell kept his doubts from his voice. Long ago, his sisters had labeled their younger brother the family prophet. Daniel had always had a profound faith, a deep rapport with God, it seemed. Those few times in his life when he'd stated a certain knowledge about something, he had always been right.

And yet Tyrell was afraid to believe him this time. Afraid to trust.

"She's alive," Jama said, her faith in Daniel's word apparent in her voice. "And since she's alive, there's hope. And since she's such a wily little squirt, I think she'll stay alive."

"Nice thought." Tyrell was chagrined at the cynicism in his voice.

Obviously, so was Jama. "Ted Claybaugh would have pulled you off the field for that attitude."

"Coach isn't here, and this isn't football."

"But remember what he said. 'Kids, learn the game well, and learn to do it with a strong heart and good ethics, because when you can do that in football, you'll know how to live right in the game of life.'"

Tyrell couldn't help smiling at Jama's attempt to imitate the retired coach's gruff voice. He realized, once again, how much he would lose if Jama were to ever step out of his life.

"You kept Heather from panicking this morning," Jama said. "You know, that 'cup overflowing' speech you always give anyone who'll listen. Now look at you."

Tyrell glanced out the window, where a River Dance Winery passenger van was pulling into the parking lot. "Jama, you know that I love you, right?"

She followed the line of his vision. She didn't answer him. That bothered him. A lot.

Before he could press the issue, Jama headed for the door. "You have a lot of work to do back at the ranch. If you'll just help us relocate that man's hip, Ruth and I can handle the rest."

She stepped out before he could reply. He felt the sting of rejection all the way to his toes.

Chapter Twenty

Jama watched Tyrell establish an IV on Tom Pritt's arm as she explained to the burly vineyard worker what was going to happen.

"It'll be harder for Tyrell and me than it will be on you, Tom. You'll be floating on a drug wave, and this won't take long at all." She was glad Ruth had ordered the morphine and midazolam ahead of time and made sure both were in the Pixus machine.

At Jama's nod, Tyrell pushed the drugs into the line. He hooked up the blood pressure cuff and monitor, and placed a pulse ox on Tom's finger.

"You know the procedure, right?" Jama asked Tyrell, as Tom's eyes glazed over.

"I've done it a few times."

"Then let's get this man taken care of."

Jama gripped Tom's right knee, while Tyrell anchored the patient to the bed by lying across his lower abdomen and holding on to the other side of the bed.

Jama listened to the voices of Ruth and Chelsea Franklin in the hallway as she pulled on Tom's leg with steady pressure. When he didn't wince, she increased the pressure at a forty-five-degree angle. The man was big and muscled, but as he continued to relax, she felt him move easily. There was a pop.

She smiled at Tyrell. "It's in."

He straightened and watched the monitor as they waited for the drugs to wear off. "You know, I need to keep my skills sharp. I don't suppose Ruth would consider me as a backup whenever you're shorthanded."

"You have a ranch to run," Jama said.

"Dad may be slowing down, but I'm pretty sure he'll be ready to get back to work as soon as he's well again. You know how he is."

Jama pressed her stethoscope against Tom's chest, stalling for time. His heartbeat was strong and steady, breathing was good.

"Jama?"

She looked at Tyrell.

"What do you think? I'll be nearby, I'll probably have some time on my hands."

"You'll have to ask Ruth about it."

"I'm asking you."

Jama looked into his deep blue eyes, and thought about the constant stress she would feel with him so close. She didn't think it would be any easier for him. At least . . . part of her hoped it wouldn't.

"Don't you think it would be a little awkward, considering everything?" she asked softly.

"I can handle it," he said. "Can you?"

She hesitated.

Tom yawned and opened his eyes. "You guys gonna do this thing, or am I just going to lie here all day?"

186

Jama chuckled and returned her attention to their patient, relieved by yet another reprieve.

The clinic was quiet again, as the patients departed with friends and family members. Tyrell had returned to the ranch, and Jama manned the telephones once more.

As she picked up the receiver, she saw Chelsea Franklin follow Ruth from X-ray into Ruth's office. Tall and slender, with soft black hair, large blue eyes with dark lashes and brows, the young woman had grown from an awkward adolescent into a beauty. She smiled warmly at Jama and waved.

Any other time, Jama would have greeted Chelsea with a hug and sat down to catch up on ten years' worth of life. Chelsea had always had so much potential in her future. What would happen to her now?

"River Dance Clinic," Jama spoke into the receiver.

"Dr. Lawrence, please?" It was a man's voice, and the reception was poor.

"I'm sorry, she's in a meeting right now. May I take a message?"

"If you would just tell her that Jack is calling from Tanzania. I'll wait."

Jack. Ruth's husband, according to Eric.

"I'll get her."

But when Jama stepped to Ruth's doorway and

announced the call, Ruth looked up briefly and shook her head.

"Should I take a number so you can return the call later?" Jama asked.

Ruth leaned back in her chair and tucked her ink pen through strands of her tightly woven hair. "Since Chelsea may become a part of this team, I can save time by telling you both right now that I will accept no personal calls during office hours. Africa has no connection with this clinic, Jama. I am refusing the call."

Jama blinked, looked at Chelsea, who studied Ruth with curiosity.

"You're giving me the job?" Chelsea asked hesitantly.

"If you have the skills I need." Ruth turned back to Chelsea, apparently dismissing Jama. "If I read your résumé correctly, you've had experience both as a lab tech and as an X-ray tech. We need that combination—"

"Excuse me," Jama said, "do you really want me to tell this man who is calling from the other side of the planet that you choose not to take personal calls on company time?"

"I didn't stutter." Ruth didn't look at her.

Jama shrugged and turned away. She didn't have time to argue. "We have a patient coming in."

"I said no more patients," Ruth called after her.

Jama turned back to the doorway. "A local farmer had an accident. We can at least check him out and stabilize him before sending him on to a hospital. He's driving himself."

For a moment, their gazes collided.

Ruth didn't look away. "Who is the director here?"

"You are, but he's coming by here anyway, and it wouldn't hurt for me to take a look at his foot."

Ruth sighed. "Take a look, but that's it. Nothing more."

"I'll tell Jack to call back after business hours."

"Tell him not to call at all," Ruth said, her voice growing sharper, warning Jama not to push further.

Jama returned to the phone, only to discover that the line had disconnected.

The smell of pine needles used to be one of Doriann's favorite scents. She would pick them from the tree outside their apartment, and rub them between her fingers. Sometimes she'd even placed crushed needles beneath her pillow so she could imagine she was sleeping in a tree house, or camping out in the woods on a fishing expedition with Grandpa.

As she huddled near the top of this tree, though, she wondered if she would ever love the smell of pine again. She hadn't realized, until she was up and settled on a branch she hoped was strong enough to hold her, that she could be stuck up here for a long time.

It was colder up here, and it was supposed to get

colder tonight. Would she be frosted over in the morning, along with the trees and crops?

Footsteps . . . the sound of shoes scrabbling over the rocky creek bed below.

Her nose itched, then tickled, then before she could stop herself, she sneezed. Froze. Listened.

The footsteps stopped.

Please, God, please, God, please, God, please!

She squeezed the branch and took slow, silent breaths.

A rustle of leaves.

Doriann closed her eyes tightly, pressed her lips together and waited.

More footsteps. And then heavy breathing.

She couldn't help it. She peered down through the thickly covered branches of the tree.

Clancy had light brown hair, and he wore a black-and-red plaid shirt. The black-red-brown pattern blurred beneath her. All he had to do was look up. The least sound from her, the slightest movement, and she could be captured again . . . or die.

Good thing he didn't have a gun.

He passed beneath the tree, then out of her sight. She listened to his footsteps disappear into the woods, brush rustling every so often until all she heard was her own breathing and the trickle of a thin stream along the creek bed.

Too, too close.

She couldn't see anything from this tree trunk,

just green needles in every direction, and other treetops, a small cliff above the dry creek. . . .

She studied the cliff more closely. A crevice halfway up the side of the rocky wall looked big enough for somebody to hide for a while, almost like a small cave.

She'd already fallen asleep outside the barn, and couldn't take the chance she'd fall from this height. Also, it would be colder up here in the tree than down on the ground. She would wait for a few minutes, until she was sure he wouldn't hear her, then climb down. There were better places to hide, and if possible, she might even find the river and start following it to River Dance.

Chapter Twenty-One

Tyrell ran his hand gently along a grapevine. The air was about fifteen degrees colder than when he had left for the clinic, but the weather could change at any time. He didn't want to ruin a single one of these expensive bales unless it was necessary.

"Clouds are still covering the sky," Daniel said, joining Tyrell at the end of the row.

Tyrell pointed to the western horizon. "But they're moving out. You can see sunlight spreading toward us. I figure by nightfall the sky will be clear. We'll get our frost. Below freezing temperatures."

"It's so unusual for this time of year."

Tyrell gave his brother a humorless grin. "This is Missouri. Expect the unusual."

"That's why I'm not a farmer. You always did like to gamble."

"I've never gambled in my life."

"Maybe not on the riverboats, but you gamble, just like Dad. How much does this ranch stand to lose if the freeze happens?"

"Hard to tell. We'll see the impact on the vines and trees for years to come."

"And yet you'll keep doing it," Daniel said, shaking his head. "Just like Dad."

"He did okay, didn't he? He has no outstanding debts, and he has enough to retire comfortably, and soon."

"He worked his tail off to get it all done."

They were both silent for a moment, and Tyrell wondered if Daniel had the same thought he did. Dad could have died today. What if he still didn't make it? Then there would be no retirement.

"He taught me as much as, or more than, I learned in college," Tyrell said. "He thought this freeze could hit after the unusually warm March we had." The sunshine and seventy-degree weather had coaxed the shoots out early. Right now, he could knock into one of those shoots accidentally, and it would fall off.

Tyrell studied a row of Vignoles vines. "You're right, life is a gamble. That's one reason Dad diversified years ago. The cattle aren't going to freeze.

And besides, stressed vines often make the best wine."

"That's an interesting thought, Tyrell, but a stressed Dad doesn't make for good healing. The guys are wanting to know if we should do something about the fruit trees down around the lower forty."

"No. Let's stop here. There's no guarantee we'll save the crops anyway, and we need to save a few more bales for the cattle. We could lose the grass for a while."

"Great attitude, there, brother."

"I'm not being pessimistic, I'm just saying—"

Tyrell's cell phone beeped. Caller ID showed it was their sister Renee.

"Tyrell?" Though not as characteristically serene as her twin, Renee nevertheless knew how to keep her cool most of the time. She didn't sound cool now. She sounded as if she'd been running. "Mark and Heather have an FBI agent at their place. They got a call just now. A motorist reported seeing an old brown pickup suddenly leave the right lane of eastbound I-70 and bounce down an embankment. It matches the description of the vehicle driven by the abductors."

Tyrell felt his gut clench. "Where on I-70?"

"Just east of Columbia. It's estimated that this happened about the same time the all points bulletin was issued on the truck." She paused for breath. "There was a report of a stolen vehicle that matches the truck's description. Want to know where from?"

He really didn't. "Where?"

"Swope Park area. And that truck had a scanner. Which means the kidnappers were probably listening to the scanner when the bulletin went out. That's likely why they stole that particular vehicle. Tyrell, this is . . . this is—"

"Take another breath, sis. Are the authorities focusing their search in the direction the truck went over the embankment?"

"Yes. The area south of I-70 should be crawling with police or FBI by now."

Tyrell handed Daniel his fuel can. "Renee, have you heard if anyone is searching the section of Mark Twain National Forest near Columbia?"

"No one has said."

"I have some friends in the forestry department up there. I think I'll give them a call." In fact, he could think of quite a few people he could call in this part of the state, all of whom would be eager to hunt for a brown pickup carrying a terrified eleven-year-old. "How are Mark and Heather holding up?"

"Not the best." Renee paused, took yet another audible breath as if to steady her runaway thoughts. "Heather's blaming herself, and the worry about Dad is putting everybody here over the edge."

Tyrell glanced at his brother. "Daniel says she's alive."

He caught his brother's approving gaze as he sensed the flare of hope those words gave his sister.

"He did, really?" she asked. "I mean, he's not just saying that?"

"I don't think so."

"Is he there?"

"Standing beside me."

"May I talk with him?"

Tyrell handed his phone to Daniel, and turned to gaze out across the rows of gray-brown vines, barely clothed with shoots of new green.

Tyrell had lived through some bad times, but he'd never had this much worry gnawing at his gut. As he listened to Daniel reassuring their sister, he tried hard to let his brother's words give him comfort.

It didn't work.

Chapter Twenty-Two

Ruth Lawrence taped a makeshift sign to the broken window of the front door and turned back to Jama, hands on hips. "No more patients. It's way past normal office hours, anyway."

Jama nodded. She had called Zelda Benedict and had her drive their final patient to the E.R. in Hermann.

"I'm sure no one else will come through that door," Jama said.

"Applicants only."

"How many more do you expect?"

"Two." Ruth straightened an already perfectly straight stack of periodicals and walked to the reception window, her brisk footsteps squeaking across the polished wood floor.

Jama followed her. "Is there any reason to interview more? I thought you'd made your decisions."

"We have no idea if Zelda or Chelsea will work out for us. I need more possibilities on file, just in case."

Jama studied her director. The telephone answering system had been switched on—it had taken them thirty minutes to decipher the directions and set up the recorded announcement. The task had focused Jama's mind and reduced her stress workload, but this left her more time to worry about Doriann.

Ruth's movements were erratic. She didn't seem able to sit in one place for long. She continually tugged at her braid, and several strands of wavy hair had escaped the weave.

Jama wondered if this increased agitation had begun after her husband's call.

Ruth caught Jama watching her. "What?"

"I didn't say anything."

"You're thinking something."

"Last I checked, it wasn't necessary for a woman to tell her boss every thought on her mind."

Ruth fidgeted once more with a strand of her

hair, then yanked the clasp away and fingered out the weave, allowing her dark brown hair to fall in waves over her shoulders.

It was then that Jama saw Ruth's vulnerability. Her posture revealed worry and traces of sadness. *That poor woman,* Eric had said.

"Are you okay?" Jama asked.

Ruth raised her eyebrows. "Of course."

"Really? Because it seems to me that you've been a little more fretful since the call from Tanzania." It wouldn't hurt to get the subject out in the open. Why ignore it?

Jama, mind your own business. You don't want anybody digging into your past.

"I've noticed that you and Zelda both have over-active imaginations," Ruth said.

Jama shrugged. Her cell phone rang. She tapped her Bluetooth. It was Tyrell.

"Jama, there's been some news."

She froze at the sound of his voice.

"The FBI believe the kidnappers are headed south from I-70."

"How do they know?"

"Reports about the vehicle. It left the interstate just past Columbia."

"You mean they could be headed in this direction?"

"It's possible. I'm calling everyone I know in the area to be on the lookout for a brown pickup truck."

"What can I do to help?"

"Right now there's nothing to do."

"I'll be working here a little longer, then I'll drive back to Columbia tonight. Call me if you hear anything?"

"I'll call." She heard the tremor in his voice.

When she disconnected, she was shaking.

"And you?" Ruth asked.

Jama looked up to find her director still standing in the same spot. "Me?"

"You asked if I was okay. I'm asking you the same. You're obviously not—"

"The kidnappers have been spotted, and are still in central Missouri."

"No ransom note, no calls of any kind?"

Jama shook her head.

Ruth sank down beside Jama with a heavy sigh. For a moment, she said nothing. Her hands were clasped tightly in her lap, head bowed. She stared at the floor with such intensity, Jama knew she was seeing something besides wood grain.

"There's no way to give someone comfort at a time like this," Ruth said at last.

Jama shook her head.

"I know this has been a difficult day for you."

Jama shrugged. What an understatement. "I can't imagine what's going to happen next. I can't even comprehend how people can be so evil." And yet Jama knew she was also guilty.

"Don't even try to comprehend it," Ruth said, her

voice gentle with compassion. "Just take it a moment at a time. Then when you get through that, take it an hour, a day, a week at a time."

Jama shivered. She couldn't face the thought that Doriann might simply disappear for good, and yet that was a frightening possibility. To never know what happened to her.

"It took a lot of effort to return to work today," Jama said. "It took even more effort to stay here. But now I'm afraid to leave and go home, which is silly. I just feel a need to be doing something."

"You are doing something," Ruth said. Compassion no longer threaded through her voice. The abrupt, dispassionate director had returned. "You're seeing to the health of a community. It's an important role. You can't do anything to help your niece right now, but you can help others." Ruth gathered her hair into its clasp as she stood and returned to her office, firmly ending any further conversation.

Jama watched her go.

That poor woman . . .

Lost. Doriann stumbled and fell to her knees in a pile of leaves, and was tempted to lie down in them. She didn't know where she was. She'd wandered in these woods for what felt like hours and hadn't found the river, the road or the Katy Trail. Retracing her steps would be like following the strands of a spiderweb.

She knew she'd passed a couple of trees at least three times, and she didn't know how to keep that from happening again. She'd found herself at a dry creek bed twice, but because she didn't know which way to follow it, she didn't try. Now she wished she had.

She shivered, hugging her arms tightly to her stomach. She'd tried to tell herself it could be worse. Clancy could've caught her. Deb could be with Clancy. It could be warm enough for snakes. Clancy could be killing someone right now, instead of chasing one fast, smart girl through the woods.

Yes, it could've been worse.

Doriann's face and hands hurt where the branches had scratched her, and she was hungry . . . so hungry. She wished she hadn't stopped to drink creek water, because it had only made her colder.

She closed her eyes and scrunched herself into a tight ball. It was one of the ways Aunt Renee said to avoid hypothermia. It didn't work. Doriann needed to move. That would be best.

Was Clancy lost in the woods, too? Before she'd been able to climb down from the tree, she'd heard him calling to her. He'd called softly at first, assuring her that all was well, and that he had just been trying to scare her, because little girls shouldn't be wandering around alone in a dangerous place like Kansas City. Then in the next second he'd screamed at her about all the things he'd do to her when he caught her. She hadn't come down from the tree until his voice fell silent.

She looked up into the sky, which was still cloudy above her. She could see a patch of blue near the horizon, but no sun, so she couldn't tell which horizon she was looking at.

If that was the western sky, it meant the clouds were clearing. That meant it could get colder. She couldn't keep going all night long just to stay warm.

But what else could she do?

Chapter Twenty-Three

Jama stretched in her chair, arching her back and rubbing her eyes. She was tired, and the words on the computer screen blurred more and more often. The later the afternoon grew, the less able she was to keep Doriann from her thoughts. And Tyrell. And Monty.

She heard a car door closing and looked outside to see a young woman pushing a wheelchair up the ramp to the front porch.

In the wheelchair was Jama's beloved old friend and the retired school coach, Ted Claybaugh.

The woman paused outside the door, looking at the sign Ruth had placed there. She said something to Ted, who replied gruffly. The woman shrugged, opened the door and backed inside with the wheel-chair.

"I'm sorry, Dr. Keith," she called over her shoulder. "Mr. Claybaugh insisted on being brought here."

Jama stepped into the waiting room and greeted her grizzled old friend with a hug. "Ted, I knew you'd be in charge of that nursing home by now."

The longtime widower grunted and shook his head, but there was the light of humor in his gray eyes. "I had to get my bluff in on them soon as I walked in the door." Gone was the former deep bass boom of his voice.

"You're not walking today? What's the deal?" Jama knew it was the nursing-home rules that anyone taken to a medical facility must be safely transported, but she also knew Ted would have walked, anyway, had he felt able.

"I thought I'd fake chest pain so I could come see my favorite student."

"Are you really faking?" She glanced at the aide. The woman shook her head.

"Tell you what, Ted," Jama said. "Why don't you let me get some vitals since you're here?"

"Guess you could. I should have the right to observe your skills, bedside manner, all that, while you work me up."

"It won't be much of a workup," she warned.

After falling for the third time on the front steps of his home a few months ago, Ted had checked himself into the nursing home, despite the protest of his son and daughter. He'd told them he'd never been a burden to anyone, and he wasn't about to start now.

"He's been complaining of chest pains since this morning," the aide said. "They've been getting worse, according to the pain scale."

"Since this morning?" Jama exclaimed. "Why wasn't his physician called?"

"I thought it was indigestion," Ted said. "We had chili last night for dinner, and Shirley Watts always puts too many beans and onions in it."

Jama led the way to a treatment room. "Most recent vitals?" She avoided glancing into her director's office. She could expect Ruth's displeasure to radiate into the hallway.

"I have them charted here." The aide handed Jama a sheet. Ted's temperature was elevated by a degree, his pulse a little fast and his respiratory rate a bit too rapid.

"So, Ted, what does the pain feel like?" Jama asked, pulling the blood pressure cuff around his arm.

He peered over his glasses at her. "It hurts."

Jama rolled her eyes at him. "Describe the pain to me. Is it dull, or throbbing, or sharp and piercing?"

He suddenly winced, bending forward. Beads of sweat formed on his forehead as his skin paled. "I'd say sharp."

"Where is it?"

He pointed toward his left lower chest.

Her concern increased a notch. This could be several conditions. Indigestion did not explain the fever, neither would simple pleurisy. If he had a left lower lobe pneumonia, it could hurt like the dickens. She should have sent him on to the nearest medical facility as soon as he'd been rolled in the door, but she hadn't expected his problem to be so serious.

"Takes your breath away?" she asked.

"Not for long." His grimace relaxed, and color returned to his face. "They never last long."

Jama tugged the stethoscope from her neck, pumped the pressure cuff, then released it. Not much change in his blood pressure. She pressed the bell of her stethoscope over his chest and watched his face as she listened to his heart. With the elevated temperature and sharp pains, it could be a simple respiratory chest pain due to his fever, but the fever wasn't that high. Still, she'd like to know where it originated.

"So tell me what you're thinking," he said before she could remove the bell of her scope from his chest, the boom of his voice returning via her earpieces.

"I'm not thinking yet."

"Sure you are, you're just not ready to tell anybody about it."

She straightened, then listened to his back. "Breathe for me."

"I haven't stopped breathing all day."

"Deeper."

He did as she said.

She couldn't tell much by the sound.

"Will I live?"

"That depends." She wrapped the stethoscope back around her neck.

"On what?"

"If you're talking about another ninety years, maybe not. I'd feel better if I could do more thorough testing, but we don't have the personnel for it right now, and as much as I learned in med school, I wasn't taught how to operate a lab or take X-rays. I'd like to send you to another facility—"

"When will this place be up and running?"

"Next week."

"I'll be back when you're up to speed," he told her.

"I don't think you should wait," Jama warned. "You could have a serious problem, and if it isn't caught in time—"

"I know, I know, it could kill me." Ted's weathered face broke into a smile that shot Jama's mind back to a time in the classroom, when she'd answered a question especially well. "Something's going to get me sooner or later, Jama Sue. Who wants to live forever?"

"Depends on the alternative."

"I've got a good one. It comes with a street of gold."

"Well, I'm going to do all I can to make sure you

don't hit the pearly gates prematurely. They might not have your mansion ready."

"Do what you need to, but just remember you're not God."

"I bet you're really popular with your regular doctor."

"I'm having my records transferred here next week. You're my doctor now."

Again, Jama was struck by the enormity of what she was doing. Physicians were discouraged from treating family members, and Ted felt like family to her, as had so many people in this town when she was growing up.

"I made that decision when you entered medical school." He grimaced. Obviously, the pain had returned.

Jama gave in and hooked him up to an EKG machine. In fifteen seconds, she saw the display on the monitor, which didn't show any significant problem for someone his age. Still, with anything less than a perfect EKG, she could not totally dismiss the possibility that the pain was coming from his heart.

She was wishing for a good phlebotomist and lab tech when Ruth stepped to the doorway of the exam room.

"Dr. Keith, would you mind introducing me to our patient?" Ruth asked.

"Ted Claybaugh," Jama said, "meet Dr. Ruth Lawrence. She's the director of the clinic."

Ted nodded.

"Mr. Claybaugh," Ruth said, "you need to go elsewhere for treatment."

Jama bit down on her tongue to keep from saying something she would regret.

Ted looked at Jama. "I don't care if she's the President of the United States, Jama Sue, if you've been away long enough to forget about the stubbornness of the Claybaughs, then you've been gone too long." He sounded as if he was addressing a football team after a fumble.

Ruth crossed her arms over her chest and took a step closer to Ted. It appeared to Jama that in Tanzania, bedside manner had not been high on the list of priorities.

Jama gestured to Ted. "Dr. Lawrence, meet our former teacher and football coach, who controls this town and everyone in it."

"He can call me Ruth." She approached Ted's side. "Very pleased to meet you, *Doctor* Claybaugh," she said dryly.

Jama was surprised to detect a glint of gentle humor in her director's eyes, though she couldn't be sure.

Their patient raised his thinning gray eyebrows. "You can call me Ted." He didn't break Ruth's stare.

"Ted." The gentleness of Ruth's expression expanded into her voice. "As Jama has already explained, it is unfortunate that we don't have the personnel we need to give you a proper medical workup today. The few tests we can do would not qualify as standard of care."

"And as I have already told Jama, I'm not too concerned about—" He winced again.

Ruth looked at the chart the aide had brought in. "Ted, you have every right to go to whomever you please for your medical care, and we would be thrilled to have you as our patient as soon as we're open for business."

"Thank you. That's what I intend to do."

"I understand that you mean to wait until Jama is able to take your case, but that wouldn't be wise."

"I'll take responsibility for that."

"Consider our position here," Ruth said. "The future of this clinic depends on a strong flow of new patients. For that to happen, we need to keep a flawless reputation. How do you think our clinic's reputation would fare if we tried to treat you today and something went wrong? Or if we sent you away without treatment, and you grew worse?"

"I would never blame this clinic for anything."

"If there is truly something wrong with you—and it appears that there may be—then that may no longer be up to you."

He studied her for a moment. "Nobody in my family would dream of suing this clinic."

"Symptoms suggest you could have a blood clot in a lung," Ruth stated flatly. "Left untreated, that could be fatal."

Jama bit her tongue. Those symptoms could mean anything at this point. These were scare tactics, pure and simple.

Ruth continued. "Word would get out about it. People don't want to go to a clinic where the patients die because the doctors misdiagnose."

Ted frowned and looked down at his hands for a moment, then looked at Jama. "Your director's been around the block a few times, hasn't she? Handled a few crotchety old men."

Jama grinned at him. She had worked with other arrogant doctors during her residencies. From what the mayor had said earlier in the day, and from Ruth's response to her husband's call today, it sounded as if she might be going through a divorce. Jama might be hard to get along with, herself, under the same circumstances.

Of course, she was dealing with comparable circumstances—actually, even worse circumstances. So maybe she was overly sensitive today, as well.

Give it a better try, Jama.

"I've got a lot of pride in this town," Ted said. "And we can't have something going wrong for this clinic before it even gets up and running. So I guess I'd better do what the doctor orders," Ted said.

Jama felt a rush of relief, though she wasn't ready to thank Ruth for bursting in and commandeering the patient. "Your family doctor is Stewart in Fulton, isn't he?"

Ted nodded.

"I'll call him and let him know you're on your way to the E.R."

Jama walked beside Ted's wheelchair out the door, hugged him goodbye and returned to her own office. She would call Ted's physician, and give her erratic emotions time to settle before facing Ruth.

How she missed her old relationship with Tyrell at times like these. In the past few months, she'd become accustomed to calling him to talk about whatever was on her mind. He'd always listened.

Why had he gone and blown it all by asking her to marry him?

Chapter Twenty-Four

Tyrell's crew had the hay bales set and ready to light as soon as the temperature dropped far enough on the large thermometer mounted on the side of the nearest shed. He also had a cord of firewood scheduled for delivery any minute. The crew had stacked limbs for bonfires down by the peach and apple trees.

There was something about dependence on God's mercy for a livelihood that made a man realize just how puny he was in the scheme of the universe. And yet, God still showed that mercy.

Tyrell's cell phone beeped yet again.

As he flipped open the phone, a truck entered the

property through the front gate a quarter mile from the house. The wood was arriving.

"Me again," Renee's voice informed him over the airwave. "You made a bunch of phone calls this afternoon, didn't you?"

"Everybody in my book."

"Calls have been coming in fast and furious. There are reports of a brown pickup speeding southeast of Columbia on H Highway near the Mark Twain National Forest, and one report of a truck with the same description headed east on Highway 94."

He felt a flare of hope. "That sounds as if the truck's headed toward River Dance."

"That's what I think, too," Renee said, "but why?"

"If they're on their way to St. Louis, 94 is a good route to take to be less visible than on the interstate. Old farm trucks are common place in this area." And Tyrell knew a lot of old farmers along the highway who could be on the lookout for that pickup.

"Do you think Doriann could have somehow convinced her abductors to drive to River Dance?" Renee asked.

"An eleven-year-old girl is not likely to convince these people of anything." Tyrell waved to the driver of the wood truck to pull around to the back of the house. "Just because several people spotted a brown truck on 94 doesn't mean it's the truck driven by Doriann's abductors." Although that was exactly what Tyrell hoped. "That kind of thinking could mess up an FBI operation."

"Obviously, it isn't going to mess up this one. No one is listening to me."

He heard the frustration in her voice. "Don't feel bad. Police get faulty tips all the time."

"Three of them? All in the same area? And don't forget the truck was spotted leaving I-70 suddenly."

"Wasn't that because of information the abductors might have heard over the scanner?"

"Merely supposition. Believe me, I know how capable Doriann is of making up very believable stories, and nobody knows if that truck was headed to St. Louis."

"I understand from the news reports that's where these people came from in the first place."

"Well, maybe not both of them."

"What do you mean?" Tyrell asked.

"Description of the woman with him has changed."

"You mean there may be three killers?"

"It's possible, Tyrell."

"That wasn't reported on the news."

"It isn't something the FBI wants to reveal yet. I've learned these agents do what they want when they want, and nobody changes their minds."

"If the reported sighting was of the right truck, and if Doriann has actually been abducted—which is something we still can't be positive about at this point—then the FBI will need to be prepared."

There was a pause, and he thought he heard a quick intake of breath. "You do at least think it's possible they're coming in your direction, then."

"It's possible." It was also possible, though not probable, that they could actually be coming to River Dance for some reason, as Renee suggested. But to think an eleven-year-old could convince them to come here? Not a reasonable idea.

"What if the captors know about Doriann's ties to River Dance?" Renee asked. "This could be an intentional plan then, not just an escape from the interstate."

"You're jumping to conclusions again." Tyrell circled the house to meet the delivery vehicle, where he found Daniel and the hired crew already unloading the wood.

"Okay, you agree with me, then," Renee said. "They're probably headed toward River Dance."

"I didn't say that. Don't put words in—"

"I need to have another talk with the agent at Mark and Heather's place. Maybe he'll listen this time."

"Does he have an alpha-male complex?"

"That could be a problem."

"Then have Mark mention it to him."

"Okay," Renee said, "here's another concern. After the initial calls about the truck, there have been no reports of a sighting for a few hours."

"Have any other cars been reported stolen in this area?"

"You're suggesting the kidnappers might have ditched the truck?"

Tyrell closed his eyes as the scent of freshly plowed earth settled over him. "I can't say what I think right now. I can't predict what killers will do. I do know you need to keep Heather from panicking. And don't panic, yourself. Keep your wild ideas to yourself or talk to me, not Heather."

"You think my ideas are wild, you try coming up with some, yourself. And how am I supposed to keep Heather from freaking? She's teetering on the edge already."

"How's that?"

"She expects to hear at any time that her daughter is dead."

Tyrell sank down on the top step of the back porch. "She can't lose hope."

"Convince her of that. I've told her Daniel says everything is okay."

"Daniel didn't say that," Tyrell reminded his sister. "All he said was that he knew Doriann was still alive at the time we spoke."

"See what I mean? How am I supposed to encourage Heather when even Daniel can't give us complete reassurance?"

"You could remind her that God is in control no matter what, and that God does hear our prayers."

There was a soft sigh over the line. "I want to get

out there and do something to help bring her back."

"I understand, Renee. It's cruel to expect Doriann's family to sit by and do nothing, and yet I know there's little else that can be done right now."

She was silent, and Tyrell recognized a frustration in her that matched his own.

"How can I have hope that Doriann will be safe through this when God hasn't made that promise?" Renee asked. "We can't expect our loved one to come through this alive, when the loved ones of millions around the world are lost every day, believers and unbelievers alike. We can have faith in God, but we can't have faith in our own personal safety, or in the safety of our children."

Tyrell could empathize with her. He remembered a scene in *The Lion, the Witch and the Wardrobe*, where Mr. Beaver emphasized that God was not safe, but He was always good.

What good could come of Doriann's capture?

Tyrell wanted to jump into his car and drive to the last place the stolen pickup had been seen, then track it from there. But he couldn't do it. He wanted to rescue Doriann. As Renee had said, they had received no promises that the situation would end as the family desperately prayed it would.

"We can't see the big picture from where we stand," he told her.

"What does that mean?"

"It means that this life isn't the big picture. Eternity is."

"Okay, I want you to stop talking like that right now. You're as bad as Heather. You're implying Doriann could die."

"Haven't you said the same thing in so many words?"

"But I didn't want you to agree with me, Tyrell." There were tears in her voice now.

"I've simply said that if her life does end on this earth, the time we'll be separated from her will seem like a blip in the screen compared to the eternity we'll spend with her."

This observation silenced Renee for a long moment, except for sniffing. Then she said, "I've got a call coming in. It's probably Mom."

"Keep me posted."

"I'll let you know if I hear more, but, Tyrell, please don't say anything to Mom about—"

"It's what she told me after Amy's death. Think about it, Renee. Our faith lies in God's ability to guide us into eternity."

He said goodbye and disconnected, praying he'd said the right thing.

Chapter Twenty-Five

Doriann plunged into the shadowed safety of a hollow in the rocks above the dry creek bed. If she used her imagination, she might believe it was a cave. She and Uncle Tyrell had gone spelunking in a wild cave two years ago, and Doriann had loved it, even when she almost sat on a bat. Caves were places to hide, and she needed to hide.

She wished now that she had not received her earlier wish—that Clancy would shut up and stop calling to her through the woods. His voice had creeped her out, but at least she'd known where he was.

Now he said nothing, and the only way she knew he was still searching for her was when she caught sight of his shadow in the woods, or heard the rustle of leaves, or the sound of footsteps on rocks.

But she knew something he didn't know. These rocky creeks, where boulders sometimes split the streams in half, could be wild when storms flooded the area. And then they would carve out very handy overhangs in the rock cliffs above the water. Great places to hide.

So far, she had found a couple of places that might work for a hiding place in a pinch. But she was afraid that a pinch might become more dangerous. She didn't like what she'd seen so far. Downstream a little farther, maybe she would find what she needed.

Doriann scuttled along the solid rock bank of the creek, glad for the silence of her jogging shoes on the smooth surface. She came to a notch high in the bank, peered over it and saw a path. Judging by the dark, flat splotches on the ground, she knew cattle had made this trail, and had used it recently.

After listening again for any sound from Clancy,

and hearing nothing, she climbed the bank, followed the trail through a thicket of raspberry
briars, and her jacket caught on one of the sharp
thorns. She ripped it loose and stumbled backward.
She fell hard on her rear.

In that instant, two things happened. She realized
she was warm from the exertion of walking—exertion?—*yes, dummy, of course that's the word.* And
she realized, as she looked around and discovered
she was in a clearing, she knew where she was for
the first time in hours.

It was a bad place to be. The gray-red barn huddled in the middle of the field, and now that she
knew where the cracks were in the walls, she could
feel those cracks turning into eyes and watching
her from inside.

Who watched her from the barn? Deb? *Has
Clancy followed me through these woods and
driven me back to this place the way Grandpa
drives his cattle into a pen for shipment to be
butchered?*

She looked behind her, stopped moving. Stopped
breathing. No sound. Not even a bird sang, and no
leaves rustled. She studied the clearing for a
moment. Someone could jump on her from any
direction. She looked up into the trees. No one.

Okay, then. What next?

Even though she didn't know how she'd gotten
here this time, she could remember how she'd
gotten here the first time, when she was following

Clancy and Deb, because they'd followed an old, overgrown tractor path.

She recognized the cracks and holes in the side of the barn. It was where she had fallen asleep waiting for Clancy and Deb to crash. This meant the entrance they had taken to this clearing was on the other side of the field. All she had to do was cross the field and go south—she knew which direction she was facing now, because they'd come straight north from the river.

At least, she thought that was right. It was the way the sun had looked when she followed them, before the clouds covered up everything.

She zipped her jacket and pulled the hood over her head, glad now that she'd fallen down that muddy bank. It occurred to her that she wouldn't have needed the camouflage if she'd worn her green jacket today.

Aunt Renee said people should pray before each big decision, and even pray before they got up in the morning to make good decisions all day long. Doriann had never thought that meant she should pray about what clothes to put on each morning. Didn't a girl get to have a say in *anything?*

She decided not to cross the field directly, but to skirt the edge of the woods. No sound came from the barn, and nothing moved.

As Doriann ran from tree to tree, pausing to hide for a moment behind each thick trunk and listen for anyone's approach, she thought about Deb.

She had yelled at Clancy in the barn. He'd hit her, and then for a few minutes, she hadn't said anything. She'd sounded strange when she did speak again.

Halfway around the field, Doriann was still thinking about that slurred voice. And she couldn't help wondering . . .

And that was stupid, because Deb might not be a killer like Clancy, but she was a kidnapper.

Doriann, being the child of two doctors, knew a little about medicine. Mom and Dad didn't get home much, but when they did, they talked a lot about their work, and Doriann had soaked up medical information. That was why she knew Deb could be in trouble.

Doriann had just reached the place where she had followed Clancy and Deb into the clearing the first time, when her dumb conscience wouldn't let her go farther.

Aunt Renee always said that the enemy you see today could be a brother or sister in Christ tomorrow, because with God, all things were possible.

I wonder how close Aunt Renee would get to that barn. If she was the one who'd been grabbed from the sidewalk and shoved into a truck, she might not be so fast to make friends then.

According to the things she'd heard from Mom and Dad, it was possible Deb could have a concussion. Clancy had smacked her so hard, she'd had slurred speech afterward. Someone with a concussion shouldn't be left alone.

Aunt Renee said that even the most evil people in the world had souls, and only God could tell who would and who would not choose life with Him.

Doriann groaned. "God, do I have to?"

She stared at the barn, listened again for sinister sounds in the woods. Nothing.

She stepped into the clearing and walked toward the barn.

Tyrell waited long enough for Renee to have laid bare her deepest worries to their mother over the phone, then he called the hospital and asked for Fran Mercer to be paged.

Mom answered in less than a minute, which meant she had been waiting for his call. She knew him well.

"First of all, how's Dad?" he asked.

"He's awake and feeling feisty enough to start asking why I'm hanging around. He wants to go home in the morning and check on the crops."

"Tell him I'm taking good care of the ranch, and I hope you've convinced him that coming home tomorrow isn't possible."

"Dr. George will talk to him later. Right now I'm more worried about my kids. Renee told me about her conversation with you."

"Oh? The whole conversation?"

"That's right. I finagled it out of her. She isn't

handling this crisis well. She thinks that you think Doriann won't make it out of this alive."

"That isn't what I said."

"I explained that to her."

"Thank you."

"But she's teetering right now, Tyrell. Don't take away what hope she has."

Tyrell was silent. He couldn't help wondering if there would be any hope. What were Doriann's chances?

Apparently, Fran Mercer read her son's mind. "I believe in miracles. If there's a possibility that Doriann's been taken to River Dance, then I can't help feeling that is something to give us hope, for whatever reason it's happening. I think you could help."

"In what way?"

"I need you out there looking for her."

"I'm not an FBI agent, Mom, and they aren't going to let a private citizen interfere in their investigation."

"You know central Missouri better than any FBI agent alive, and you know the people who live here. You know where all the hidden roads are, you've helped find the pot fields and the meth labs, you've hunted, fished, tracked right alongside your father all your life. If your father was able, he'd be out there looking for that truck."

"The time I spent on meth lab busts was for the police, not the Feds. They won't allow—"

"I'm not saying you should ask permission."

Tyrell frowned. His law-abiding mother was suggesting—

"You wouldn't want the FBI to allow you access to the investigation, even if they would allow it," Mom said. "If you were working under the authority of the federal police, then they would be liable for any mistakes you might make. It could jeopardize evidence."

Wow, Mom. "And you know this because . . . ?"

"I read. You should try it more often. I've told Renee to have a talk with one of the agents working with Heather and Mark, explain about all the experience you've had. That way, in case they do happen across you in the course of searching for my granddaughter, they might suddenly develop a case of specified blindness, but under no circumstances should any of you request special permission to work with them."

"Mom, I'm not a professional tracker."

"You're better than anybody I've ever known, except maybe Jama."

Now, that smarted. Mom really thought Jama was the better tracker?

"She has that typical female ability to see the big picture, whereas you have a gift of focus," Mom explained.

"Can't see the forest for the trees?" Dad had told him that before.

"The two of you make a great team."

"You can't expect me to drag Jama into a dangerous situation like this, and even if certain agents might be persuaded to turn a blind eye to a lone man searching for his niece, they're not going to allow a couple of us—"

"Last I looked, this is a free country, and they can't place crime scene tape around the whole Missouri River Valley. If a private citizen wants to drive Highway 94, nobody's going to stop him."

Tyrell sighed. He got the message.

"Honey," Mom said, "this is Doriann we're talking about. Now, I have the utmost respect for these specialized, brilliant, dedicated agents, but they don't know Doriann, they don't know you, and they don't know the lay of the land. They may not think they need our help, but if they receive it, that gives Doriann better odds. Right now, if I were a betting woman, I'd be betting on you."

"Renee's behind this."

"Yes, and I'm behind her. You've already made some calls. Make some more."

"But we don't even know—"

"Tyrell."

"Yes, Mother. I'll call everyone I know, although I'm pretty sure the local grapevine will have alerted anyone who has a telephone or computer."

"Good. It may not make any difference, but you'll feel better if you do. Now let's talk about your sisters," Mom said.

"I know this is rough on them."

"Renee was up late last night with Ajay because he was running a fever, then the baby woke her early this morning. She was so tired she fell asleep for a few minutes late this afternoon. She told me that when she woke up, she heard Doriann's voice in her head, a carryover from a dream. Doriann was yelling at Ajay for getting into her things, and then seconds later she was laughing at something the baby did."

Tyrell could imagine his niece's voice, her laughter. He recalled the last time she'd gone fishing with him, and the day she'd visited him at work, riding with him on the tractor to inspect a stand of corn or row of soybeans. Her questions were exhausting. Her vitality and fascination made his job much more fun than usual.

His memories caused his vision to blur. He blinked hard and cleared his throat. "I think I'll take a drive while there's still light to see."

"Good. One more thing. I'm worried about Renee. Mark and Heather sound better to me on the phone than Renee does."

"She's tired. The nightmare looms larger."

"I know Renee's kids drive Doriann nuts some-times, but they love her, and she loves them. Renee mentioned she felt she should have spent more time with Doriann one-on-one, but—"

"Mom, she isn't Doriann's—"

"She thinks that if she'd disciplined her own

children a little more, Doriann wouldn't have skipped out today."

"That's ridiculous. Renee does everything right. She spends more time with Doriann than Mark and Heather do." Homeschooling her own children plus her strong-willed niece was a heavy load.

Too late, he heard the heaviness of his mother's sudden silence, and he realized his last words had revealed his thoughts far too clearly. Mom had easily picked up on them.

"Tyrell—"

"Sorry. Forget I said that. Mark and Heather had no way of knowing that on this particular day, some crazy people were going to abduct their daughter."

"We just need to focus on getting Doriann home," Mom said. "Mark and Heather don't need the guilt, either. If the worst should happen and we don't get Doriann back, Mark and Heather are going to be—"

"I would never lay the blame on them."

"But you already have, don't you see? Mark and Heather know you disapprove of their casual parenting attitudes. Your attitude and words have shown that clearly in the past."

Tyrell closed his eyes at the sharpness in her words. They dug deeply.

The soft breeze from the north cooled the perspiration on his neck and face, and he caught a spicy floral scent in the air. A killing frost would destroy the blooms that produced that fragrance. At this moment, it felt as if death hovered, ready to swoop down and destroy everything in its path, both human and plant.

"I'm sorry," Mom said. "We shouldn't fight about the small things, we should stick together and support one another through this."

"I didn't realize we were fighting."

"It's going to be dark before long."

"I know. Just keep Dad happy and clueless as much as you can." Tyrell paused, then said, "And tell him I love him, okay? I'll do anything I can."

If he only knew what to do. Two weeks ago, he'd have been on the phone to Jama as soon as he'd disconnected. It wasn't as if he'd made a habit of calling to tell her his worries. He just called to hear her voice. The comfort of her presence, even over the telephone, had meant so much. Right now, he needed so badly to call her.

Why had he allowed this trouble to come between them? Why hadn't he realized that a marriage proposal would frighten her away, and threaten their wonderful friendship?

The eldest Mercer son needed a few lessons in empathy.

Chapter Twenty-Six

Doriann peeked into the barn from a crack between two ragged boards. She couldn't see much. Especially, she couldn't see Deb where she'd been before.

That could mean anything. Maybe Deb had followed Clancy from the barn, or moved to a softer spot to sleep.

But it did mean she'd moved, right? And that meant she could move, and so she wasn't hurt that badly.

Right?

Doriann turned and looked around the field, listening. An airplane flew overhead. The breeze rustled the treetops, but she heard nothing unusual, in the barn or out.

She was about to leave when she checked the interior of the barn once more, and noticed the tiny purple square of her cell phone on the dirt floor, next to where Deb had lain snoring earlier. It was probably where Clancy had dropped it after scrolling through Doriann's pictures and making fun of her family and friends.

If she could reach it without getting caught, this could be a way out of this crazy mess, after all.

She needed that cell phone.

With a final, long look around the field and into the woods, she crept to the broken barn door, which hung from one hinge against the siding. She waited a few seconds for her eyes to adjust to the darkness inside, surprised that, in spite of the holes in the roof and the cracked boards, the interior was too dark to see clearly.

There was only enough light for her to see the central portion of the barn. She saw no human forms. There were some square shapes in the darkest corner, probably old-fashioned, small hay bales, and she couldn't tell if anyone might be lurking near them.

But she entered, slow and silent, barely touching her arm against the rough wood of the dangling door. The inside of the barn smelled old and moldy, like the wine cellars in River Dance. She was within a step of her phone when she heard something outside . . . the brush of pant legs against each other? The swish of an arm against a bush?

Doriann grabbed the phone from the floor, raking dirt beneath her fingernails. She slid the phone into her pocket as she rushed toward the hay bales in the far corner. Her toe caught on something and she pitched forward.

She landed face-first in a bale of mildewed, smelly hay that muffled her grunt of surprise.

Another sound—whispers, soft chuckles, more whispers—reached her from the doorway, and she looked over her shoulder to see Clancy standing there.

God, help! She froze as his head turned in her

direction. It would take a few seconds for his eyes to adjust. He wouldn't see her until—

He turned away suddenly, as if startled, and looked back out the door. Doriann hurried behind the hay bale, stepping high to keep from tripping again. He hadn't seen her.

But as soon as she landed, she heard what had startled him. The baying of a hound. Before she could focus on that familiar hunting call, Clancy came running toward her, tripped and fell flat in the same spot where she had fallen. Under the noise of his scramble to get back on his feet, she scrunched more deeply between two bales of hay, trying hard not to sneeze.

Any second, he would find her, and she would be dead.

He stumbled against the hay bale to her left, and lay there panting. Only a bale of hay separated her from a killer.

Jama strolled through the quiet clinic as the long light of dusk slanted through the front windows. Evening was falling; she and Ruth had so much left to do. Meds needed to be ordered, supplies purchased, filing systems set up on the computer. Though the new personnel Ruth hired would take care of the office work, Jama and Ruth would both have to be competent with the system. Cross-training in a small clinic was vital.

Jama had given herself a long, silent lecture

about her resentment of Ruth's behavior with Ted.

Yes, this day had seemed to be derived from one of Jama's worst nightmares, and she knew that she would be understandably tense, but still she felt as if she'd been treated like a med student.

Ruth sat at the computer beside the reception desk, entering a list of meds on an order form.

"What you did was unkind," Jama said.

Ruth looked up at her. "What?"

"You were unkind with Ted."

"I didn't hear any complaints from the patient."

"He wouldn't complain. You handled him nicely, but you didn't give me the chance to do it myself in my own way."

Ruth perused the computer screen, punched Send, then swiveled to face Jama. "Don't be a prima donna. You joked with him about pearly gates when he needed immediate medical attention that we couldn't give."

"I was checking his vitals. I was attempting to gently guide him, and you loaded him with guilt."

"I saw the EKG reading. Mr. Claybaugh needed to be taken to another facility immediately."

"I do know how to read an EKG monitor, Ruth. Just because my bedside style is different from yours doesn't mean I can't handle patients." Jama heard the snap of her words, and looked away from Ruth's stolid stare. This was her director. She needed to remember that. *Be gentle with her.*

Ruth tossed a hanging file folder to the desk. She leaned back in the chair and looked at Jama. "Is this the way it's going to be for the next two years?" She shoved the other office chair toward Jama. Its wheels whispered along the polished wood floor.

Jama grabbed the chair and looked at it, then at Ruth.

"Sit down and stop towering over me," Ruth said.

Jama sat.

"Did you talk to your resident trainers the way you've been talking to me today?"

"I spoke up when I needed to, but I didn't feel the need to do so often. I was treated with respect, because until two weeks ago, I was chief resident in my hospital's family health program. I realize you're my director, but I had thought there might be a spirit of mutual cooperation. I expected to be treated the way I treated my med students and other residents. With *respect.*"

For the next moment, the only sound in the room was the soft hum of the computerized medication dispenser.

"You might eventually have convinced Mr. Claybaugh to leave," Ruth said quietly, "but it was easier for me. Nobody knows me. I don't have history with any of the patients, and none of them have their bluff on me."

"Ted didn't have—"

"Jama, you've got to learn how to take charge of a situation. You are responsible for the health of the patients who come in here."

"I know how to—"

"You have lives in your hands, and you can never forget the heavy responsibility of this job." Ruth returned her attention to the computer.

Frustrated, Jama stood up and pushed the chair back to its place. She turned to walk toward her office.

"If you think your friendship with these people is going to cause a problem, it would be better if you let me know that now," Ruth said over her shoulder.

Jama stopped. "And then what?"

"What I'm asking is whether or not you feel you need remedial help while working with family and friends. This is a close-knit community, and it's understandable that you might have some difficulty separating official responsibilities from friendships. It's why doctors are discouraged from treating family members. Just work on it, will you?"

Ruth stood up and held her hand out to Jama. In it was a silver key. "This is to protect the rest of our windows. It could save you a bundle of money." She turned and walked away.

Jama watched her retreating back. Ruth had a habit of getting the last word. Two years would be an eternity.

Doriann lay scrunched between the bales of hay. Clancy was in some kind of whacked-out frenzy, whispering questions to himself so softly that she could make out only a few words, then answering himself and giggling. Like a girl. Aunt Renee had never mentioned any drug reactions like these. Maybe he wasn't on drugs. Maybe he was just psycho.

Covering her nose with the sleeve of her jacket so she wouldn't have to smell his breath, Doriann closed her eyes and listened. . . .

"Whad'ya think of your perfect legal system now, Dr. Moore? You think they'll find your kid in the Mighty Mo?"

Doriann frowned. Who was Dr. Moore?

Soft laughter. "All you rich doctors who look down your noses at the rest of the world . . . you let her suffer! You could've kept her from suffering. You weren't the one who heard her screams. What'll you do when they dredge your kid from the river? Then you'll know what suffering is."

Doriann felt a little thrill of hope. He thought she might be in the river? He was confusing Dad with somebody else, but maybe this meant he wouldn't expect to see her hiding from him the next bale over. If she stayed very quiet and still, maybe he would leave before she sneezed or—

"Deb!"

The shout startled Doriann so badly she squealed and nearly wet her pants again.

"Hey, that you, Deb?" There was movement, and Doriann knew he was raising his head to look. He expected to see Deb.

Some kind of desperation took control of Doriann's brain. She couldn't decide what to do.

"Deb?" The voice was directly above her.

He couldn't see Doriann, but she could see his dark shape clearly.

He reached out. She braced herself. He was going to grab her.

But just before he touched her, the hound outside started baying again. The howl was closer now, really close, and Clancy swore, a long string of curses.

He leaped up, then jumped toward Doriann. She stifled a scream. As she tried to crawl away, she was grabbed from behind—not by Clancy, because he was still in front of her.

Something clammy and soft clamped over her mouth—someone's hand—and before she realized it she was rolling onto her back—onto a human body!—then back onto the floor. Rough hands shoved her away so hard she rolled and slammed into something hard.

She found herself in a stall, where she saw light coming through a hole in the outer wall of the barn. She remembered seeing a spot that looked as if a big animal had kicked out the wood. It was large enough for an eleven-year-old girl to crawl through.

She didn't look back. She was outside before she heard a voice in the barn.

"What's all the yelling about? I'm trying to sleep in here."

Doriann stood staring at the side of the barn. Deb?

The hound had run into the forest, the echo of his hunting yowl refracting through the trees. Refracting? Yes, that was the word.

While Deb scolded Clancy for being afraid of a little ol' hound dog, Doriann used the cover of her voice to run full tilt toward the trees.

Though she didn't hear the sound of anyone coming after her, she plunged into the darkening forest as the baying of the hound echoed through the trees around her.

Chapter Twenty-Seven

Tyrell issued final instructions and left the ranch in Daniel's care. He climbed into his freshly serviced Durango and was buckling his seat belt when his cell phone—nearly out of juice—beeped at him. Renee again.

"They've found it!" she cried.

His stomach clenched at her words, and then the tone of her voice registered. For the first time in hours, he heard hope. But he also heard dread, and a contagious urgency.

"Tyrell, they found the truck that was stolen ear-lier this morning in Kansas City. The old brown truck. They found it!"

"Who found it? Where?"

"You know Andy Griswold, Dad's buddy who lets you guys hunt on his land, west of River Dance?"

"Andy found the truck?"

"In that swamp near the road. The license plates matched. Now tell me, why would someone who knows he's in deep trouble with the law not change the plates if he wanted to get away with his crime?"

"Stupid? High on drugs? Was anybody found at the—"

"It was empty, but the Feds are on their way there now."

"How many agents are coming?"

"Not sure, but, Tyrell, you know that place so well. If Dad were able, he would be out there in—"

"I'm on my way."

"I love you, big brother."

"Then you can bail me out of jail."

He disconnected, leaned his head back against the headrest as he considered what might be hap-pening. How he wished he could talk to Jama.

Jama's cell phone call tone rang from her pocket as she began to organize the new desk in her new office. She'd never had her own office before.

The call was from her foster sister, Renee Abramovitz. "Jama, how are your tracking skills now?" were Renee's first words, no greeting in the mezzo-soprano voice.

"My what?"

"Remember that trick Dad used to teach you and Tyrell on his hunting trips? Actually, he tried to teach all of us, but you and Tyrell were the only ones who caught on."

Okay, something was definitely wrong with her. "Renee, are you okay? I know this awful ordeal with Doriann—"

"Listen to me! She's there, Jama. Near you, near River Dance. That's where the Feds think she is. What I need you to do is meet up with Tyrell, get out there before a whole squad of strangers can mess up the tracks, and work with Tyrell to find out where—"

"Hold it. Why do the Feds think Doriann's in River Dance, specifically? And if the Feds are coming—"

Renee sighed. "Tyrell hasn't kept you in the loop today, has he?"

"He didn't tell me she was in River Dance."

"He's probably calling everyone he knows from Columbia to St. Louis."

"So what's up?"

"You remember that swamp just off the road west of town on Highway 94? It's where sopho-mores dunk all the freshmen during initiation."

"Okay, I remember." When Jama and Amy had

238

been initiated, they'd been expected to find their way home in the dark without flashlights. But the sophomores hadn't counted on Jama's navigational skills to lead them to Andy Griswold's house.

"A brown truck was found in that swamp today, and the license plate numbers matched the vehicle we suspect was used to abduct Doriann."

Jama felt suddenly sick. "Has the swamp been dredged?"

"Andy saw recent tracks leading from the swamp. There was no one in the truck. He checked. That means Doriann could be someplace between Andy's place and River Dance."

"Renee, that's dozens of square miles of forest—"

"Which means you'd better hop to it. Do you have your hiking boots and jeans?"

"Not on me," Jama said dryly.

"Do you have clothes at the ranch?"

"No." Jama had given all but a few of her clothes to a homeless shelter after Amy's death. She'd cleaned out her closet at the ranch house, but she decided not to remind Renee about that.

"Then you'll have to make do with some of Amy's things," Renee said. "Mom's still storing all of it in the attic at the ranch, and if I remember right, you and Amy wear the same size shoe. You can use her hiking boots."

Jama hesitated. Renee's anxiety could be affecting her judgment. Was this expedition sanctioned by the FBI? Renee had always been the most excitable of the Mercer clan; as a child, she'd screamed at scary stories before they even got scary, she'd laughed more loudly and talked faster than her twin in a bid for attention.

It was Renee who had been the holdout in the family when Jama became a foster sister. Though Renee had accepted Jama as Amy's friend for so many years, Jama became a threat to Renee's place in the family when she joined it. Jama got the attention, for a while, because of her father's death, her rebellion and Fran Mercer's compassion. It was months before young Renee thawed enough to welcome Jama to the fold, though her twin, Heather, had embraced Jama from the beginning.

"Jama, we need you and Tyrell out there looking for Doriann before the place is overrun by people who don't know the area like you do."

"Where's Tyrell?"

"On his way to pick you up as we speak."

"So he's agreed to this crazy plan?"

"Crazy? Jama, Doriann's life is at stake. You're the only person I know who's better at tracking than Tyrell."

Jama continued to ponder this deluge of information.

"Hey!" Renee said. "Are you listening to me? You've got to get moving now!"

"Andy did see footprints coming out of the swamp?" Jama had known the place well at one time . . . many years ago. "Nobody was in the truck?"

"No, but one set of prints leading away from there was small. That's got to mean Doriann's still able to walk on her own."

"If those are Doriann's footprints. Are you sure you aren't jumping to—"

"No, I'm not," Renee retorted. "It's got to be her."

Jama was once again alarmed by the edgy sound of Renee's voice. With all the pressure she'd been under today . . .

"Look," Jama said, "it's been months since I've hiked, longer than that since I've done any tracking."

"Dad always said you were a natural, that you were born to it. Don't give the Feds time to trample the site, Jama."

"Are dogs being brought in?"

"Of course," Renee snapped, "but it'll be a few hours before Search and Rescue can get here. A young couple went missing two nights ago over the state line in Kansas, and I suspect they might have been victims of these same killers. Come on, Jama, why are you stalling?"

Jama sighed and cast her gaze to the ceiling. Tyrell was no pushover, and Renee said he was on his way through town. He was agreeing to this aggressive plan. He had more sense than to allow his excitable younger sister to browbeat him into anything. After all, he was the eldest, pragmatic beyond bearing sometimes.

"It would be crazy to wait," Renee said. "Every

moment that passes means more danger to Doriann. You're right there. Utilize your skills."

"Okay," Jama said at last. She heard Renee's soft sigh of relief. "I won't take time to suit up."

"Do you have a flashlight?"

"Several good ones in my car. You know the Mercer men all give them for Christmas and birthdays."

"Dress warm."

"You're sure Tyrell is picking me up?"

"He'll be there shortly."

"Which means you were pretty confident you could maneuver me into this, or you haven't told him yet, and you're going to call him and browbeat him into picking me up."

"This is the right thing to do. It's our best option."

"It's foolhardy."

"You've played the fool a few times, Jama. It won't hurt you to do it one more time."

Jama scowled at that uncalled-for remark. "It's also dangerous."

"Which is why I'm calling. Tyrell wouldn't dream of asking you to do this. But you know how to take care of yourself. You took that self-defense class. In fact, didn't you teach self-defense for a while?"

Jama closed her eyes and thought of Amy, who had talked her into taking that first class. Amy, her best friend in the world. If Jama could do something to help make up for this family's loss, then shouldn't she do it?

Or am I being a little overconfident? What makes me think I can do something the FBI can't, just because Renee wants me to?

On the other hand, the FBI may not have enough personnel for a thorough search.

Renee was right. The more time that passed, the higher the risk to Doriann.

"I can drive to Andy's," Jama said.

"His place is going to be overrun with cars before long, and the fewer civilian vehicles on the property, the better."

"In other words, this is a covert operation." Jama's unease mounted, but nothing about this day was comfortable.

"Tyrell will be there. Be ready." Renee disconnected, and Jama sat staring at the cell phone in her hand.

She couldn't tell if her racing heart was from fear, or excitement that she might actually be able to help find Doriann, or from trepidation about spending still more time with Tyrell.

Doriann took precedence. Her safety was top priority. Jama would do this for her.

Tyrell was driving through downtown River Dance—total distance, four blocks—when he received yet another call from his sister.

"You need to stop at the clinic and pick up Jama."

Why was he not surprised? "No."

"She's agreed to help search."

"It's dangerous out there. We don't have any idea where these killers might be."

"You're right, and Doriann's out there with them somewhere. Jama's an adult with self-defense training, Doriann's a helpless child. Jama's waiting for you at the clinic, because I told her you would pick her up."

In spite of his doubts about Renee's plan, he found himself automatically turning toward the clinic when he reached River Street. "Since when did you become the head of this family?"

"You try homeschooling four strong-willed children and caring for a baby, while helping your husband with his landscaping business."

"I don't have a husband. Come to think of it, I don't have children."

"Stop fooling around. You're picking Jama up, aren't you? She'll be out there tracking, anyway, she might as well be under your watchful eye."

He pulled into the clinic parking lot and saw Jama waiting beside her car, wearing a pea-green army coat over navy-blue scrubs. She still wore her bright white, thick-soled shoes, which would be caked with mud by the end of the night . . . whenever that end may come.

She was in the passenger seat before he could get out and open the door for her.

"I'm in, Renee," she called loudly enough for Renee to hear.

"Then my work is done," Renee said. "Call me as soon as—"

"My cell phone's out of juice," Tyrell said. "I'll call you when I can." He flipped his phone shut and tossed it into the console.

Jama reached for it, pulled an electronic charger from one of the many pockets in her coat and plugged it into Tyrell's phone. "It'll be recharged by the time we reach the trailhead. It's a good thing I talked Monty into the family plan when I changed phone companies. Your phone's compatible with mine and Monty's. Now that Fran's agreed to get a cell—"

"Wait a minute, which trailhead?"

"Well, okay, it's not an official trailhead, but you know where the Katy Trail comes closest to the road without actually crossing it, about a hundred and fifty feet east of Andy's swamp?"

"Sure. There's an open field and a creek where we used to have bonfires."

"It's the best place for you to park."

He thought about that for a moment, realized she was right and grunted. So now, not only was she a better tracker than him, she was also a better strategist.

"It'll be dark soon," she said.

"I brought plenty of flashlights."

Jama turned around to study the contents of his backseat. He studied her.

Jama Keith had outgrown the awkward adolescent stage at about the age of thirteen, and from then on had grown more beautiful every year. Her hair, long and golden, her body with appealing curves, her face, oval with a firm-but-feminine chin. Her cheeks right now were flushed with excitement.

Tyrell's parents had always warned their children—all of whom were considered attractive by their peers—that good looks could be the bane of a person's life. Jama had struggled with that in high school. She had the attention of lots of guys, with her beauty and her free spirit. After her father's death, the free spirit had become outright rebellion, and it had taken over her whole life for a while.

Tyrell still wondered if that rebel had been completely tamed. He thought he still caught glimpses of that facet of her personality from time to time, and he hoped that aspect of her wouldn't completely go away.

She turned to him, nodding with approval. "Good backpack." She patted one of her pockets. "I brought mace and I'm packing my piece."

"Uh . . ."

"Brought my pistol. Don't worry, I have a license to carry."

He blinked as he turned onto Highway 94 and headed west. "You never mentioned it before."

"I guess the subject never came up."

"Really? You have a license to carry, and you never thought to mention it to me?"

"I've had it for a couple of years, so I guess I just tend to take it for granted."

"You just up and decided to get a gun license one day?"

Jama sighed. "A fellow resident was raped in her apartment building one night. She needed moral support afterward, and I thought if she had a way to protect herself, she'd feel safer. So I taught her some moves, and while we were practicing we decided we couldn't be too careful in the city. Monty had already taught me how to shoot. I taught her, and we got our licenses."

"You didn't tell any of us what you were doing?"

Jama looked at him. "Tyrell, my friend never reported the rape. She didn't want anybody to know, and I promised her I'd keep her confidence. We didn't deliberately conceal what we were doing, but we didn't advertise it, either."

"You didn't report—"

"How about you? You're carrying, aren't you?"

"Of course." He was still trying to wrap his mind around the life she had apparently lived, the experiences she'd had, without sharing it with the Mercer family. He felt a sense of loss. What else had she never told him?

"Have you been to target practice lately?" she asked.

He grimaced. "Maybe a few months ago."

"Bull's-eye every time?"

"No. You?"

"Not *every* time."

He shot her a glance. She was serious.

"We're going to do this," Jama said. "For Doriann."

"For Doriann."

Chapter Twenty-Eight

I am not lost. I'm not. Got to be going the right direction. And Deb isn't a killer. She saved me from Clancy.

As Doriann thought about it, she remembered that something had pushed her in the rump when she was climbing out the back window of the truck. Deb? It had seemed accidental at the time, but maybe not.

And it was Deb who had thrown herself in front of Doriann when they ran off the road . . . to keep Doriann from flying through the windshield head-first?

Okay, but what was up with this?

Doriann was tired of thinking about it. She was so tired she could barely stand. She'd run so fast and so hard to get away from Clancy, her clothes were wet with sweat. As the air temperature dropped, she could almost feel the wet clothing crackle with ice.

But that had to be her imagination. And besides, she had her cell phone now. She could call for help as soon as she was sure Clancy wouldn't reach out from behind a tree and grab her.

With another glance behind her and into the deepening forest shadows, she squatted between the needle-heavy branches of a juniper tree and opened her cell phone.

It didn't light up.

She pressed the power button. She remembered using it only once since charging it last. Nothing happened. She pressed again. It still wouldn't come on. Nothing.

Clancy. He'd done it on purpose. He'd run down the battery on her phone because he was an evil, wicked man!

She'd been depending on this phone to get her out of here. But now? She was stuck here.

She was lost!

She'd never been afraid of the dark. She'd never actually been afraid of much of anything. Why should she be? Aunt Renee and Mom and Dad and her grandparents and uncles had always told her that Jesus would always take care of her. And she believed that. But as the light disappeared from the sky, she felt very afraid. She'd been afraid a lot of times today.

Closing her eyes, she inhaled deeply, trying to calm herself the way Aunt Renee had taught her.

It didn't work. Instead, she thought about how the trees had grabbed the hobbits in *The Lord of the Rings* and dragged them beneath heavy roots.

Heart thumping, Doriann wriggled from the juniper's clutches and stumbled over a root as she rushed away from the tree limbs. In the growing darkness, she couldn't avoid the limbs so easily.

As she continued to wander in the forest alone, every movement, every rustle of a leaf, every echo from her own footsteps made her heart scramble around in her chest like a squirrel in a live trap.

She felt awful, suddenly, for telling those scary stories to her cousins. How could she have been so mean?

It seemed as if, all at once, God had decided she would pay for her actions. She saw now how it felt to be afraid, the way Ajay was afraid when she told him a story about the shadow monsters that paced the hallways at night, ready to pounce on him when he got up to go to the bathroom.

He'd wet the bed last week. Aunt Renee had been so mad. Doriann had been ashamed of herself, and she'd tried to be nicer to Ajay. After all, he was younger than she was. She should know better. Even if he did pull her hair and sneak food off her plate when Aunt Renee wasn't looking.

Today, Doriann was finding out what happened when she lied and disobeyed her parents. She had even discovered why she shouldn't drink coffee. As Aunt Renee had warned, it made Doriann hyper, which had made her more afraid with Clancy and Deb. It had also made her wet herself today—which would have made Ajay laugh.

If she ever saw Mom and Dad and Aunt Renee again, she would apologize. She'd never been very good at saying sorry. That was another thing she needed to work on. She would try to apologize for something every day for the rest of her life. Especially to God.

She looked up and saw a streak of deep purple and blue through the lacy-black branches of the trees. For a moment, she forgot everything else. Her mouth fell open. She caught her breath. Sunset. In the west.

It was beautiful, like a special gift, a reminder from God that He was still there. Doriann had always loved sunrises and sunsets, and when Mom and Dad were home she dragged them out onto the balcony of their apartment and made them watch the sun go down.

This was the best one ever.

"Thank You, God," she whispered, speaking aloud for the first time in hours.

Now she knew to keep walking the way she had been going. It was south, and that would take her to the river. If only Clancy hadn't been chasing her again when she came to the Katy Trail. But, as Aunt Renee always said, "if only" is for dummies. One was never to say "if only," but she was supposed to say, "next time."

The next time Doriann was running from a psycho drugged killer, she would pay more attention to the direction she ran, and she would stay as close as possible to the road, or the trail, and not get lost in the endless woods.

She had just come to a dry creek bed, determined to push through these woods as fast as possible and get to the river before it was too dark to see, when she heard a noise behind her.

Footsteps. Again.

But she wouldn't panic and lose her way again. Instead, she studied the high cliff bank on the other side of the creek. She'd been here already this afternoon. She recognized the dark hole that was an entrance to a tiny cave.

Clancy would expect her to go south—if his drug-cooked brain was working. He didn't know about the little hidden crevices in the rocky cliffs along this part of the river valley—she hoped. And better than hiding in a tree, she could hide in one of the little crevices. Some of them were actually tubes, with two openings, so if he did come looking for her, she could crawl out on the other side.

She turned and looked over her shoulder, but saw no shadows move in the darkening woods. Had she really heard a footstep, or had it been a squirrel jumping from tree to tree? Or a raccoon or possum looking for dinner?

It didn't matter. She wouldn't try to make it to the river now. Instead, she crossed the dry creek bed while she could still see well enough to use the large, flat rocks to cross on tiptoe. Silently.

When no one came after her, she stepped into one of the cavelike shadows and crawled inside.

Later tonight, when she'd had some rest, if the moon was bright enough, she would climb back down to the creek bed and follow it to the river.

If she didn't freeze to death first.

Jama felt suddenly pumped. This was the real thing. They were going to do this—plunge into the woods and look for Doriann. Tonight could be the night she'd be able to put her defense training, her target practice, her tracking—everything—to good use.

The stress with Ruth Lawrence rolled off Jama's shoulders like rain rolling off her warm, lined jacket. Why worry about the small stuff? Life was at stake here. There were more important matters at hand.

"Is anybody else invited to the hunting party?" she asked Tyrell.

"Just us, I hope." His full, deep voice sounded calm. "At least until we've exhausted all opportunities to follow whatever tracks we find."

"By then, the FBI will be there," Jama said. "It seems to me that we could use more help, not that the FBI would take my advice."

Tyrell looked at her askance. "Who else did you plan to invite to the hunting party?"

"Oh, I don't know. Everybody in River Dance, perhaps? Comb the woods?"

"Not in this case. If the townsfolk messed up a valuable lead, it would not be helpful."

"Sure, hold them off until we've done all the tracking we can, but there's safety in numbers."

"Not going to happen. Daniel and the guys on watch at the ranch all volunteered to come with me. I had to nearly wrestle them to make them stay at the ranch. Right now, the fewer people trampling the evidence, the better. You and I are taking a huge risk right now."

"That's what I told Renee, but would she listen?"

"I doubt it."

"She's all gung ho about this. Thinks we can round up the bad guys and safely rescue Doriann before the Feds even arrive."

"And now she has you thinking it," Tyrell said.

"You bet. Renee should be a motivational speaker."

"She doesn't understand the seriousness of the Feds," Tyrell said. "When they're after two of their top-ten wanted—which may turn out to be three— they're not going to take kindly to any interference."

"Which is what I implied to Renee before she browbeat me into submission."

"It's her way."

His earlier words finally registered. "Three kidnappers?"

"I've been on my cell a lot this afternoon. It seems the two suspects stopped for gasoline halfway between KC and Columbia, and the cashier remembered some things." He slowed for a fox squirrel that danced in the middle of the road before choosing a direction to dart for escape. "The female suspect sighted today doesn't match the description of the woman who was implicated with the man earlier."

"Women change their appearance all the time," Jama said. "If she knew she was wanted by the FBI, she could have done a lot to change her looks."

"True. No one seems to know what happened to the other female."

"What was the description of the female today?"

"Skinny, rough-looking woman with stringy blond hair."

"Well, that narrows it down," Jama said dryly.

"I think Renee said the first woman was described as petite, with short black hair. A woman could get a stringy blond wig, but she can't easily change her height."

Jama thought about that for a minute as she studied the curving, hilly road that disappeared into the deepening forest shadows. She slid her window down, sniffed the air, stiff with cold and wood smoke.

"But the descriptions can be subject to interpretation, depending on who's doing the describing," she said.

He glanced over at Jama and gave her one of those deep, thoughtful looks that had always made her melt. "I've always loved your logical mind."

She melted more than expected.

Reminding herself that shared danger made for heightened emotions, and forbidden fruit always seemed sweeter, she avoided that deep, bottomless gaze. She slowed her suddenly erratic breathing and studied the shadowed indentations of the winding countryside.

"Almost there," she said.

She could see from the corner of her eye when he returned his complete attention to the road.

"We haven't even begun the trip." His voice was soft, quiet and filtered down over her like the warmth of a sauna.

"What?"

He signaled and turned into the grassy drive that led to the creek where River Dance high-school classes had held their bonfires and parties since the inception of the town. "We have a lot of talking to do, and a lot of time to do it tonight."

"We have to focus on the job at hand," she said.

"Of course we do, but to work well together, good communication is vital."

"Silence is vital to keep from giving away our location, Tyrell."

She heard his chuckle as he parked, and it irritated her.

"I don't see anything humorous about tonight," she said.

He opened the door, and she caught sight of his

face in the overhead light. She saw the evidence of hours of agonizing worry, of hard work and struggle in the vineyard trying to save the future of the ranch.

She regretted snapping at him. Why was she so prickly? She understood Tyrell's heart. As he had done earlier today, as he had always done during tense situations, he took the edge off his own tension, and attempted to lighten the mood for those around him, with humor, with redirection, even when his own heart wasn't in it. Even when his heart was breaking.

It was a sharp reminder about why she loved him so, about why this was so hard. If only . . .

Her foster sister Renee loved to read. One day, when Renee was hiking the perimeter of the Mercer Ranch, she had stumbled upon an old dumping ground, which included the shell of an old car. In that car she had discovered a treasure of well-preserved Reader's Digest magazines dating back dozens of years.

For weeks afterward, she spouted little tidbits of wisdom she had learned from her forays to the stack of tomes she'd hauled to the house. "Never complain about 'if only,'" she'd said often. "Just plan on what you'll do better next time."

Then Jama had reminded Renee that Fran had always said the same thing with different words.

As Jama stepped from the SUV, she glanced again at Tyrell, his firm chin with the deep cleft,

257

straight, dark eyebrows. Recalled the touch of his lips on hers, the feel of his arms around her.

If only . . .

There would be no "next time."

Chapter Twenty-Nine

Tyrell watched as Jama circled the SUV to join him. Even in the pea-green jacket, she looked great. He forced himself to look away. A man had no business thinking about something that might never happen, especially at a time like this.

And yet he hadn't given up hope. He wouldn't. She was here with him now, wasn't she? Which was something that had him thinking hard and long on his way here. First, of course, he needed to remember that he was a man, not a boy who felt threatened because a woman exceeded him in certain abilities, like tracking and strategizing.

His second thought had been that he hated dragging Jama into danger. He told himself that the only reason he'd driven to the clinic was because he knew if Jama decided to do something, she'd do it with or without him. And he'd rather be with her, watching out for her safety.

To be honest, though, he knew he'd decided to get her partly because of Renee's passionate belief that he and Jama had a chance to rescue Doriann, and partly because of the irresistible draw Jama held for him. He wanted to be where she was.

Simple. That hadn't changed in years, he'd just become more honest with himself about it.

Now his gaze rested on her as she stood beside him.

"Remember the first day we met?" she asked.

He tugged his pack from the backseat of the truck and slung the hefty nylon straps over his shoulders. He tried to get his mind around her question as he focused on the job at hand. Not an easy task.

"Why don't you remind me?" he asked.

"I was seven."

He thought a moment, nodded, reached inside the Durango for a couple of flashlights in the netting behind the front seat. "You had the biggest, most beautiful blue eyes."

"Blue-green."

"You can tell your story, and I'll tell mine. I remember they were blue. They've just changed color."

"Tyrell, eye color doesn't change. Mine has always been—"

"They looked like the ocean, and they were as filled with salty water." Tears, dripping down a pale, frightened face. Even at that age, his protective instincts had flared. "You had hair so blond it was white."

"You were eleven, playing fetch with your dog on the front lawn when Amy and I came walking up."

Oh, yes, he remembered. While Amy went

tearing through the house, then out to the garden, searching for Mom to come and make everything better for Jama, Tyrell had decided he would rush to the rescue.

"You introduced me to your dog," she said.

"Gladys."

"And I told you that was a weird name for a dog, while I wiped my nose on my sleeve."

"I don't remember the nose wiping." He closed the door, handed her a bottle of water and stepped ahead of her to follow the narrow path that led to the Katy Trail just over the rocky rise pelted with cedar trees. "What I remember is a pretty little girl, lost and scared, who spoke her mind about everything." He loved that she still spoke her mind.

She also still looked lost and scared more often than Tyrell wanted to see. When a man loved a woman, he liked to think he could make all her fears go away. For some reason, Tyrell seemed to have escalated Jama's fears with his proposal. Not a good omen for a relationship, but he'd beaten that horse to death. Time to get past it.

Jama fell into step behind him, and he could tell by her footsteps that she was once again focused on their mission. He could feel her wariness.

He glanced over his shoulder, and saw her gaze darting toward the trees, the road, the bridge over the creek. She shivered.

"Cold?" he asked.

Her spine stiffened. "Not in this coat. It's double-lined."

"Remember the game we played that afternoon we met?" Tyrell asked.

She skipped up to walk beside him. He stepped aside on the narrow trail, made sure she was walking on the actual beaten path so she wouldn't trip in those shoes—should've grabbed some of Amy's hiking boots from the attic. But then, how was he supposed to know he'd be picking up Jama?

"You're doing it again right now," she said. "Using your distraction technique."

"Isn't that what doctors do with little kids when they're scared?"

"Sure, but I'm not a little kid."

"But it still works, right?"

She allowed her silence to tell him that it did.

"I've forgotten what I called the game that day," he said.

"I Spy. You had Gladys sit beside me on the porch steps, and then you sat on my other side."

He remembered. He'd put his arm around her shoulders and told her about a game Gladys loved to play. He would name a landmark, and she would go to it and bark. Gladys was some smart dog. Of course, "fence," "tree" and "grapevine" were easy commands for a dog with such a large vocabulary.

"Your arm felt so good around me," she said quietly. "I didn't want you to move away."

As if he would have. But she couldn't have known that then. Did she know it now?

That night, when Mom had taken Jama back to her parents, Dad had helped Tyrell to understand what Jama was enduring with her mother's rejection.

He smiled, remembering seven-year-old Jama's outspokenness.

"Now *you're* doing it again, sweetheart," he said, trying to imitate his father's favorite actor. Bogart.

Jama stumbled, nearly fell. Tyrell caught her by the elbow, then drew her close to his side, once again feeling his protective instincts rise.

"What am I doing?"

"You're falling under my spell," he said, then chuckled softly.

The white of her teeth flashed in the growing dusk. "You big goof." But her tone told him she didn't think he was goofy at all.

What was it, Jama? What went wrong between us? How can anything be wrong when we're so good together like this?

He glanced through the trees to their left, and saw the barest reflection of the waning sunset over the river. "I spy something ever-changing but never-changing."

She frowned, then looked around. It took only a few seconds for her to tune in to his wavelength. "The water particles are never the same from second to second, but the river is always there."

262

"You got it."

The light slowly disappeared, and Jama fell behind him again, which allowed him access to the trail once more. Smart woman. She knew how easily a rock could blend into the ground and trip a person when the shadows melded into blackness.

"You seemed so grown-up to me back then," she said. Her voice was soft, thoughtful.

"And I don't now?" he teased.

"Well . . ." There was a smile in her voice. He loved that sound.

"That's the curse of the birth order, oldest sibling and all," he said.

She didn't reply, and a companionable silence stretched and grew between them as they reached the Katy Trail.

Every time Jama stepped on this trail, she felt as if she was a part of history, connected to the many others who walked or biked this rails-to-trails state park that stretched more than two hundred miles across Missouri.

It reminded her of the moment she'd stepped from her car this morning and her hometown had enveloped her in a magical sense of connection and nostalgia. But the day's events had shocked her back to the cold reality of the present. There was never a way to go back.

She and Tyrell walked less than a quarter mile before he pointed to a diverging trail that led to

Highway 94. They took it. At the road, Tyrell pointed to tire marks on the pavement that led to the other side, where something large had obviously torn through brush and rammed into a sapling before continuing down to the swamp.

Jama's shoe squished into mud. She peered into the swamp, studying the square shape of a pickup's cab—the only part of the vehicle above water.

"I wonder when the search-and-rescue dogs will get here," she said.

"No telling."

Without another word, Jama and Tyrell skirted the swamp counterclockwise. The powerful beam of Tyrell's flashlight showed multiple footprints in the mud. Disturbing the evidence as little as possible, they continued slowly along the swamp's edge.

Jama focused on the ground in front of her, on the swish of the underbrush against the material of her scrubs—the air had more of a bite to it now that the sun was almost gone. She was glad she had worn this coat and her thick wool socks for extra cushioning.

"I see something." Tyrell aimed his flashlight at a thorn tree and illuminated a small piece of purple cloth caught by a long, wicked-looking barb.

"It looks like cloth from the hooded jacket Doriann got for Christmas." Jama reached for it, but Tyrell touched her arm.

"Leave that for the FBI," he said. He aimed his

light at the ground, revealing three sets of foot-steps, a single set curving one way, two other sets veering in a slightly different direction.

Jama rushed forward, following the single set of prints that came from a smaller shoe. "Tyrell, you know what this means?"

"I'm not ready to jump to conclusions."

"It looks like Doriann escaped from the truck and the swamp first, and ran away from her captors. They came after her, but must not have seen where she went. They followed a different path."

"How can you tell she got out first?" he asked. "What if the kidnappers saved their own hides first and ran away, leaving Doriann to drown?"

Jama gave him a long look. "That's the wrong attitude, you know?"

"They're killers, Jama. And on drugs."

"Do you think these people would go to all the trouble to abduct Doriann specifically, because she's Mark Streeter's daughter, then just leave her?"

"In a situation like this, they would think of themselves first. Why don't you follow the one set of tracks, I'll follow the others. That may help us determine if Doriann got away. Try not to leave your own trail."

"Of course, I'm watching my steps." She pulled out her own flashlight and made her way forward. She moved slowly, methodically. Doriann had obviously headed in the direction of the river.

Excitement made Jama clumsy, and she nearly stepped off the side of a steep, washed-out mud bank. A ledge crumbled beneath her feet, and she scrambled backward to more solid ground. As she straightened, she saw evidence that Doriann might have done the same with less fortunate results. Small shoeprints told the tale from the bottom of a collapsed slope of loose mud and earth.

But then, it appeared that the girl had climbed back up the steep slope. Using more caution this time, Jama continued to follow the tracks, and ended up standing beside Tyrell.

"Um, I think we have a problem here," Jama said.

He studied the tracks, frowning. "I don't get this. They turned around at this point. Two larger sets of prints, probably a man and a woman. Had to be the kidnappers, right? There are indentations in the mud that might indicate a fall." He gestured to a place where someone's hands and knees might have landed in the soft earth.

"Or someone was knocked down," Jama said.

"So they stopped looking for Doriann at this point?"

"But why?"

"I don't know. Maybe they heard someone coming and were afraid they would get caught, so they got out of the area."

"But, Tyrell," Jama said, stooping more closely to study the prints, "it appears as if our little spitfire followed them."

Chapter Thirty

Doriann scrunched onto her side in a ball, wishing she could feel safe in this tiny cave above the creek. Unfortunately, her teeth chattered so hard she could probably be heard all the way to River Dance.

There were lots of dry, crackly leaves on the floor of the cave that rustled when she moved, so she tried to stay still. The leaves had either been washed here with flooding, or had been carried by some animal for a bed. From the smell, Doriann figured it was an animal that had never been potty trained, but she didn't care much right now. Leaves were warmer and softer than rock.

As the darkness deepened in her hiding space, her fear returned. She couldn't breathe very deeply, no matter how hard she tried.

Pray, Doriann, pray.

"Oh, God, please send someone besides evil Clancy to find me," she whispered. "And would You warm up the weather tonight? That way, Grandpa and Grandma's crops won't be ruined, and the killers will live to be arrested and justice will be done, and I won't freeze to death out here. You know how that would break Aunt Renee's heart . . . and Mom's. And Dad's."

Doriann realized that she mustn't fall asleep. She'd read stories about people falling asleep and never waking up, freezing to death. They lost consciousness and just drifted off.

And so she prayed harder, calling to her mind everybody she'd ever known. She prayed for Aunt Renee, who had her hands full with so many things in her life right now, and sometimes threatened that she was "going to lose it!"

She prayed for Mom and Dad to make it through their residency training so they would stop fighting so much, and be home more and get the jobs of their dreams—but only if that meant they could be home more often.

Was that selfish? Yeah, probably.

She prayed for more patience with her cousins, and for Grandma to get flowers for Mother's Day again this year, because last year she was so happy to get them she cried.

She prayed for God to forgive her for being such an ornery kid.

And as she prayed, she realized that she was thinking of reasons to keep praying, because she discovered that she felt closer to God. Safer. It made the fear go away for a little while.

"And, God, please help me forgive my enemies . . . You know who they are . . . because Aunt Renee says I have to before You'll answer me. I'm sorry I don't feel very forgiving right now, but I'm willing to try if You'll help me."

She was so sorry she'd decided to try to follow Clancy and Deb in the first place. She'd be halfway home by now if she hadn't. Funny how things looked a lot more possible in the daylight, when at night they seemed so crazy.

As she struggled to stay awake, she thought she heard voices. She held her breath. The rustle of the wind? Birds? Coyotes?

No, not animals. They were human voices, softly whispering. A man and a woman.

Suddenly, Doriann was wide-awake again. Clancy and Deb?

Tyrell signaled for Jama to wait at the last sighting of Doriann's tracks. He then went ahead to search for the next track. He found two sets of larger prints, but not Doriann's. His first objective was to find his niece and get her to safety. Her prints were vital. The Feds could deal with the abductors.

"Branch to your left," Jama said softly, aiming her flashlight at a stand of cedar saplings.

There was a small, broken branch on the nearest sapling, and behind it her flashlight illuminated a muddy patch with the imprint of what looked to be Doriann's shoes all over it.

"Was it her?" Jama asked.

"I think so."

"Any other tracks?"

"Not that I can tell. If she was following them, she could have stepped back here to hide." But he still couldn't understand why his niece would follow her abductors. It made no sense. Did she have some kind of superhero complex? He knew Renee had a way of making people believe they were stronger, wiser, smarter than they actually were, but what on earth could his sister have taught Doriann that would make the girl think she was capable of taking on two criminals?

He searched for more tracks, and finally found a partial at the far edge of the little copse of cedars. The girl still seemed to be following her abductors.

Jama was staring off into the forest, to the other side of the track, her flashlight aimed in that direction. "Over here," he called to her in a whisper.

Jama hesitated, then joined him, stepping carefully in an obvious effort to avoid making her own tracks.

"I don't get it," Jama said.

"We don't have to get it, we just need to get Doriann."

"And fast, from the looks of it."

"We can't rush this or we may lose her trail. Just keep your light steady and keep trying not to disturb any evidence."

The larger tracks were straightforward, following an old lane that led to a field up ahead. Tyrell knew this place. It belonged to a friendly neighbor of Andy Griswold's. The field ahead was Andy's.

The smaller prints did not follow a straight path, but darted behind bushes and trees along the way.

The mud was soft, and that path wasn't hard to follow.

He glanced at Jama in the dim glow of their flashlights. So many mysteries hovered around her, even though they had known each other for most of their lives.

"You never let anyone know where you went after Amy died." Tyrell kept his voice gentle.

Jama's steps faltered briefly. "No."

"Why?"

She didn't reply. It was the first time he'd ever asked her this question. He'd steered clear of the subject after Amy's death, but now, in this crisis, the time seemed appropriate to raise such a touchy topic.

"I called Monty and Fran from time to time and let them know I was okay."

"But you never told them where you were."

"That's because I was an adult, and they respected my privacy too much to press the issue."

"Are you saying I'm not respecting your privacy?"

"Well?" Her voice let him know he'd hit the mark. "Had you or your brother and sisters known where I was, you might have come barreling across country to find me and drag me back."

"Is that a problem?"

No answer.

"Really? You went across country?"

"Yes."

271

"Where?"

"Maybe I shouldn't tell you. I might want to disappear there again someday." There was a teasing note in her voice.

Tyrell was not amused. "Even after you returned, you hardly ever visited."

"Yes, I did."

"Twice a year?"

"I came more than that. Just because you didn't see me doesn't mean I didn't come. You weren't exactly a permanent fixture around here back then. You were living your own life in another town."

They paused at a barbed-wire fence. The tracks led through it. Another little fluff of purple showed them Doriann did not emerge on the other side unscathed.

Tyrell held the wires apart for Jama, and she stepped through. They were entering Andy's property again.

"You disappeared for six months after Amy died." Tyrell joined Jama on the other side. "Then you avoided us afterward. I know you were hurting, dealing with survivor's guilt, whatever, but families stick together. You didn't have to withdraw like that."

"You don't know what I had to do, Tyrell. You may not know me as well as you think you do." Still looking at him, she stepped into mud. "Oops, I've left a track."

"It's hard not to in this open field."

She turned off her flashlight, and Tyrell immediately knew why. She was feeling exposed.

"Tyrell, after all this time, why are you suddenly blasting me like this?"

"I'm not blasting you, I'm just trying to figure out why you did what you did."

"Perhaps you could trust me to be mature enough to know what I needed to do for myself and not pull the big brother act." She turned on her flashlight again.

"Count on it, Jama, being your big brother is about the furthest thing from my mind." For a few moments, they searched side by side in the dark, their beams skimming, stopping, focusing, then passing on while he smarted at her words.

"I never wanted to hurt Monty and Fran," she said at last. "I never meant to. I think I made that clear to them. We all deal with grief in our own ways. Don't castigate me for mine."

Her voice echoed too loudly from the trees that surrounded this field. He shushed her. Her movements stilled for several seconds.

"Okay," he soothed. "You're right. I'm an interfering lummox."

"I didn't mean that, Tyrell. I just—"

"I've known you for most of your life, and though I realize it's impossible for one person to truly know another, I did think I was pretty tuned in to everything about you. You're a puzzle to me, but I used to think I at least had all the pieces. I've discovered lately that I don't."

She stopped then, and raised her flashlight to illuminate their faces. "What if you find those pieces and they don't fit into the picture you have in your mind for me? What will you do then?"

"There will always be room for me to make new discoveries about you, Jama. That's how it should be."

Why did he see such doubt in her eyes?

Chapter Thirty-One

Jama felt herself melting again. Tyrell's words touched her, even though he'd spoken them without the knowledge of what he could learn about her—and what it could mean. The truth . . . the missing piece of that puzzle could destroy them. It could destroy everything, her whole life. How selfish was she for withholding it? Didn't all the Mercers deserve to know? And didn't she deserve whatever happened after they discovered the truth?

"Where did you go?" Once again, he stepped forward slowly, cautiously.

"Utah."

He said nothing, but she could sense his surprise. She studied the sizable perimeter of his flashlight beam, took a step, waited for him to join her, and studied the next patch of well-lit ground. Renee was right. The tracking skills had come back easily.

"What did you do in Utah?" Tyrell asked.

She took another step, and waited again for him to follow. She saw a small indentation in the grass, some bruised blades. Perhaps the result of a child's footprint? Jama shook her flashlight, frustrated that it didn't have the power of Tyrell's.

She pointed. "Do you see—"

"Yes, I do. Look for more prints."

They bent over and searched, slowly and methodically, and Jama wondered if Tyrell was as aware of her warmth beside him as she was of his warmth, his presence, his scent, the very feel of his movements, almost in tandem with hers.

"It's amazing how cheaply a person can live if they have to," she said.

"I know. I learned that when I was doing mission work abroad. How did you live in Utah? You couldn't have practiced medicine there."

"I could have gotten a license if I'd wanted to."

"You're saying you didn't want to practice? As a fourth-year surgical resident, you must have qualified for some kind of work in the medical field."

She had no answer for him, because she didn't really know, herself. It probably had to do with not feeling worthy of the profession she had worked so hard to join. She followed the pattern of Doriann's steps. It was slower going here in the grass.

"What did you do?" he asked.

"I worked odd jobs when I needed cash. I washed dishes at a restaurant for a week, and I was a file clerk in a temporary position."

This took some time for him to contemplate. "Where did you live?" His voice was different. More somber.

"In my car. In Amy's old tent. I hiked and camped. I stayed in Canyonlands National Park and along the Colorado and Green rivers for nearly four months. I was in The Maze for two. I ate a lot of beans and rice, dried fruit, nuts."

She felt his attention riveting on her instead of the task at hand.

"Watch what you're doing," she said. "We're looking for Doriann, remember."

For several long moments, they searched in silence, found more signs of footprints, continued forward.

"You lived in the wild?" he asked at last.

"I didn't live in the wild, I lived in a tent and a car."

"I remember the tent. I got it for Amy as a college graduation gift. I got you a down comforter, because it was more your style."

"Well, I guess you don't know everything, then. The tent was just big enough for two, lightweight and strong. Amy and I took it when we hiked the Grand Canyon that summer before we started med school."

"You borrowed my car for the trip."

"We discovered in med school that we probably should have been studying and working, not hiking, but I'm so glad now that we did it that way."

"It was Amy who loved to camp out. You hated it," Tyrell said.

That used to be true. "I remember those nights in the Canyon. We had nothing but our sleeping bags and the tent floor between us and the hard ground."

"So you did it for Amy."

"She was always teaching me to try new things," Jama said. "Camping was one. I came to like it."

"Enough to do it for months? By yourself? Alone in the wilderness?"

She didn't answer.

He stopped walking. "You camped out all those months to punish yourself for your best friend's death."

Jama looked toward his dark form. Why had he brought up the subject tonight of all nights, after all these years of avoidance?

"But there's more to it than that," he said. "Isn't there?"

Time for a safer subject. "Amy taught me to see camping out as an opportunity to be surrounded by God's sanctuary, instead of buildings erected by human hands. The Canyon was a good school, but I didn't learn the deepest truth until I was alone in the silence of Utah."

They searched the circumference of the area

where they found the last track, then picked up the trail again.

"What was the deepest truth?" he asked.

"That I will never have all the answers, no matter how much I study and learn, and no matter how long I live. That I will always fail if I try to do the right thing in my own power. That God is bigger than I ever imagined. It took the trip to Utah, all that time alone, to show me that I need God in my life."

Jama slowed at a pile of last year's leaves that had most likely washed across the field during last fall's flood. No form of an eleven-year-old.

The stillness of the night was intensified because the cold had silenced the spring peepers—the frogs Jama loved to listen to in the evenings when she was growing up.

Tyrell's flashlight flickered, and he jiggled it. The battery was getting low. Jama knew he carried spares in his backpack.

"For the past four and a half years," he said, "everything connected to Amy's death has been a forbidden subject between us, and I don't feel comfortable with forbidden subjects."

"Meaning you have to knock down any wall that gets in your way."

"It's a caveman thing. I wouldn't expect you to understand it."

"Forbidden subjects are a Jama Keith thing, and *you* obviously don't understand *that*."

"Believe me, I've been trying. Tell me, Jama, is it just me, or do you push everyone away like this?"

The tone of his voice stung more than his question. How badly had she hurt him by trying to not hurt him worse . . . or herself . . . or the friendship they had shared for so long?

"We weren't going to do this," she said softly.

"I never promised that."

"You're right. I'm sorry."

She turned just in time to see the muzzle of a rifle planted in front of her face, heard the metallic cocking of the gun. She looked at Tyrell and froze.

Chapter Thirty-Two

Teeth chattering . . . icicles forming in her brain . . . frost must be settling down from the sky. Snuffling . . . movement . . . rustling . . .

Doriann jerked awake, cried out, braced herself. He'd found her!

Something touched her face—something cold. She swallowed a scream and scrambled away, tried to stand and run, hit her head on the roof of the cave and fell back into the smelly leaves.

She heard a whimper and grew still. That wasn't Clancy. It wasn't Deb. Something soft and fuzzy touched her nose. And then something warm and slimy rubbed over her chin, flicking her lower lip with a familiar smell. Dog breath.

Dog breath!

A loud hound howl filled the cave.

Doriann gasped, choked on the smell. "Humphrey?"

Another howl.

Doriann reached out and felt his long, floppy-soft ears, his long snout, and even smiled when he licked her face again and again. "It's you, Humphrey!"

She started to cry, and buried her face against his soft fur, and held his warm, wriggling body in her arms. She felt as if she could almost reach out and touch God's hand, it was that close. He really was watching over her!

She sniffed and wiped her face with her sleeve. "It was you I saw on the road, wasn't it, Humphrey? And it was your howling that scared Clancy." More answers to prayer she didn't know to pray.

She realized that if she hadn't grabbed the steering wheel when she did, Humphrey would be injured or dead now, and not warming her up in this cave.

Of course, she also realized that she probably wouldn't be here, either.

Or maybe she would.

He nudged against her arm, his way of asking to be petted. She flung her arms around him again and cried harder. Jesus had sent a piece of home to her here in the forest in the dark, in the middle of danger.

Humphrey nestled closer, nuzzling under her arm, panting dog breath all around her. He lay down beside her. She wiped tears away again so they wouldn't freeze on her face.

This was why Humphrey was a wandering dog. Because God knew that someday, this dog would need to wander here and find a freezing kid in the middle of a killing frost. His warmth seeped through her, and comfort surrounded her. She let herself drift. This time she could fall asleep without being afraid that she'd freeze to death.

Agent Sydloski's face was gold-and-black granite in the glow from the dashboard lights of his agency car. "This won't happen again."

Jama looked at Tyrell's silhouette from her position in the middle of the backseat. His face was carefully expressionless.

The agent looked at Tyrell, jaw protruding. "Right?"

"You think we want to risk jail time?" Tyrell asked, and Jama wondered if the agent realized Tyrell was avoiding a direct answer.

The agent turned in his seat, making eye contact with Jama. "You do realize, don't you, that there are armed and dangerous killers in the vicinity? You two may be the best marksmen in the state, but there's a man out there who's already proven he's not only capable of killing, but is happy to do so. You two have strict orders to get into your vehicle and remove yourselves from the blockaded area. I will receive a call when you have passed the eastern roadblock, and if I do not receive that call within the next ten minutes, we will come looking for you, and you will be taken into protective custody."

"No need to come looking for us." Tyrell pointed to the gravel exit, directing Agent Sydloski to turn into the creekside area where his SUV was parked. "But you have to understand that there was no roadblock when we arrived. You should reserve your surveillance for the killers."

Agent Sydloski parked in front of Tyrell's vehicle. "Our job is to protect United States citizens. Your best chance of seeing your niece alive again is to let us do that job and not distract us from our objective. Go home and stay out of our investigation."

With a final thanks for the lift—Jama could hear nothing but respect in his tone—Tyrell climbed from the car, opened the door for Jama and gave a half salute to Sydloski as he escorted Jama to the passenger door of the Durango.

"You knew it could happen," Tyrell said as she slid inside.

"They didn't have to be so rude."

"It's the FBI, Jama. You just don't smart off to a federal agent." He closed the door, walked around the front, got in, his profile outlined by the lights from the agent's car. When the SUV's engine was running, the agent pulled back onto the highway. The man drove slowly away, making it obvious that he was still watching for Tyrell and Jama to leave.

"I didn't smart off," she said at last. "I simply explained that we saw no roadblock. You told him the same thing."

"Not with your flair," he said dryly as he pulled onto Highway 94 and headed toward River Dance.

"How were we supposed to know this section of the Katy Trail and the road were cordoned off?"

"If we hadn't entered by an alternate trail we would have been warned away. You should be glad we got to keep our pistols."

"Why did we?"

"Renee probably paved the way for us. Having our permits probably made an impression, as well."

"Slow down," Jama said.

"Excuse me? I'm not stopping. We could still be thrown into jail."

"I didn't tell you to stop, I told you to slow down. We could get ticketed for speeding, couldn't we?"

He released pressure from the accelerator. Jama smiled to herself.

"I wasn't breaking any speed limits," he said. "Why slow down?"

"I want to check the river."

"For what? I'm pretty sure there hasn't been any flooding since we saw it at dusk."

They saw the promised roadblock up ahead, and a deputy sheriff stepped out, waved them down, hand on his weapon.

"Okay, this is too weird," Jama said. "That can't be Tim Holloway. I graduated with him."

"He's back in River Dance, was sworn in as deputy a few months ago."

"This isn't right. He couldn't hit a single target in school to save his life. What's he doing with a gun?"

Tyrell shushed her.

Tim beamed a bright light through the windshield at them, recognized them both, then waved them through with his old, crooked smile.

"He's going to get himself killed if he doesn't know what he's doing," Jama said.

"He knows how to handle a gun now. He joined the Coast Guard after graduation. Spent ten years out in San Diego and got tired of the overcrowding and high cost of living."

"Oh. Guess I've been out of the loop for a while."

Tyrell shot her a look. "You think?"

"I should know better than anybody that people can change."

"Sure they do. And sometimes it takes a lot of tries to get it right. Remember Carla Haines? We thought she'd be a doctor or attorney, maybe run for office someday. Who would believe she would drop out of college her first year, lose her scholarship and become a professional dancer in Vegas?"

"Don't forget Mark Richland," Jama said. "I went steady with him for two weeks in eighth grade. He goofed off all through school, totaled two cars, barely graduated, and was told he'd never amount to anything. Now he has his own business with five hundred employees."

"People falter," Tyrell said. "That doesn't mean they've failed. It just means they've learned from their mistakes."

She caught sight of the bridge over Fern Creek. They were nearing the river. "You know the boat landing at Carson's Crossing?"

He didn't answer.

She looked at him, and saw the suspicion on his face. "We're out of the blockaded area," she said.

"And you're reminding me about this because . . . ?"

"When we saw that first broken branch, after it became obvious Doriann was following her abductors?"

"Yes?"

"I thought I saw those same small shoeprints aimed in the other direction, toward the river, cutting through the woods almost willy-nilly. I told myself at the time that it had to be a simple case of Doriann attempting to find a better place to hide as she followed them."

"Why didn't you say anything about it then?"

"You found more tracks going the other way, which seemed to confirm my reasoning."

"And you knew I wouldn't agree to our going separate directions."

"Exactly, but now it appears I might have been wrong."

"Why? The tracks obviously led to the barn, where the Feds had found abundant evidence that Doriann and her captors had been there."

"Okay, but isn't it possible we could have missed a separate set of tracks that led away from the barn? She wasn't there, and she must have gone somewhere."

"So you're saying she would have tried to return to the river."

"The shoeprint I saw was dug deeply into the mud, as if she'd been running. There were leaves scattered, also as if someone had run through them."

He looked at her.

"Maybe she was caught tailing her captors," Jama suggested. "Maybe she stepped on something like a limb or rustling leaves, and they heard her and made chase?"

"That's possible."

"And she's a smart girl. She would know she could follow the river to safety eventually."

"We didn't see any other shoeprints coming from the opposite direction."

"We weren't looking," she said. "Think about it, Tyrell. We were focused on those particular prints, headed that particular way. It's the same reason I didn't seriously consider following tracks headed any other direction, because those tracks kept going north from the river. We both know that other people follow that old tractor path, and so we weren't expecting anything else."

Tyrell braked at a low spot in the road and turned right. The tires shifted onto gravel that popped and crackled in the cold evening stillness. The SUV's headlights plunged into fog that blanketed the great river.

Tyrell eased to the very edge of the concrete ramp and parked, switching off the headlights.

"I blew it," she said. "I should have mentioned the tracks to you the first time I saw them."

"You did fine."

"But no Doriann."

"What's on your mind, Jama?"

"We start from here and follow the river west, the direction Doriann might be coming from."

"We should notify the FBI of our suspicions—"

"They're covering the blockaded area, and with only a skeleton crew." Jama said. "I mean, my goodness, Tim Holloway's been pressed into service. There's no way the FBI will be able to cover the acreage that needs to be covered. We've still got our guns, we know how to shoot, and we're already here. What's a little jail risk when Doriann's life is on the line?"

Tyrell put the truck back into gear and reversed.

"What are you doing?"

"If we're going to do this, we can't park in plain sight." He shifted and eased the vehicle into the deep shadows to the right of the boat ramp, where a path led from the Katy Trail to the river's edge. He parked behind a stand of cedars. "They can't see this from the road."

"How do you know?"

He looked at her and grinned. "It was a favorite parking spot when we were in high school. Don't tell me you never—"

"No, I never."

His grin widened. "Good for you."

"Don't act so surprised. The rumors of my adolescent crimes have been hugely exaggerated."

"So you weren't the one charged with vandalism for climbing Mr. Earle's prized dogwood on the school grounds."

"I'm just saying—"

"You're saying you never went parking here," Tyrell said.

"Never."

"Amy didn't—"

"Amy was too busy working her way to valedictorian to mess around with messing around. So . . . who'd you go parking with?" Jama asked.

"Why are you asking?"

"I bet it was with Patty Miller."

"You'd lose that bet."

"Sandra Green?"

"There's nothing wrong with parking at the river

and watching the moon float between clouds as you talk and dream and share a kiss or two."

A kiss or two? "Aha! So it was Sandra?" Jama felt a sting of unwarranted jealousy. "Did that often, did you?"

His gaze on her was teasing. "A gentleman doesn't kiss and tell. Don't you wish it had been with you?"

She glared at him as he opened his door and got out.

If only . . .

Chapter Thirty-Three

In spite of Jama's vigorous insistence that they could find Doriann on their own, Tyrell did not agree. He wasn't nearly as supportive of this action as he led her to believe. Although he felt fairly certain, as Jama did, that the FBI had not extended their search boundaries this far, he also knew the agents had surveillance equipment that could do the work of a hundred men. But like Jama, he couldn't just give up searching for Doriann.

And so he called Agent Sydloski on his cell phone, and told him about Jama's speculation that Doriann had fled the barn and headed to the river. To Tyrell's surprise, the agent seemed grateful for the input, but also adamant that Tyrell and Jama not get involved.

Not that the feeble warning was going to stop Tyrell from walking the river's edge.

"Keep your light aimed directly at the ground in front of you," he told Jama after he disconnected the call.

"Okay, sorry, I wasn't thinking. I thought I heard something in the trees."

"Like what?"

"Oh, I don't know . . . wind? Air movement that could keep the frost from settling? Maybe signal a change in weather?"

"Don't I wish. Then we wouldn't be burning hundreds of dollars worth of good hay to save the crops."

"Okay, not wind. Maybe that surveillance equipment you've been telling me about, placed in the treetops by the FBI to monitor all movement on the ground. The agents would have checked to see if the abductors managed to escape via the river, wouldn't they?"

Tyrell looked out across the pockets of dense fog across the waterway. "Yes, but something tells me the kidnappers couldn't have gotten far without a boat, and considering the accident that landed them here in the first place, I doubt they came prepared. What you're hearing is Fern Creek trickling into the river a few yards ahead."

Jama walked a few feet to his right, silent for the moment. They crossed the creek, then moved closer together as the tree line encroached over the riverbank.

His attention returned to the fog. "I see something that reminds me of a jewelry store."

He heard a soft intake of breath beside him, and he wondered if she was thinking about the ring he had wanted to give her. He could see only her dark silhouette. The rhythmic swish of her jacket whispered a soft and steady pulse into the air.

"The gemstones in the sky?" she asked. "The pearl of the moon and the sparkle of the stars?"

"Wrong. Jama, you're getting rusty at this game."

"Then the onyx glow of the moon's reflection on the water."

"That's a nice thought," he said. "Much nicer than what I was thinking, actually, but not as fitting, because the moon isn't reflecting on the water, it's reflecting on the fog."

"I see some clear spots out there now."

"I'm looking at the fog, Jama."

"Okay, why would fog remind you of a jewelry store?"

"Don't you think it looks like the cotton the jeweler layers into the boxes?"

"They don't do that in jewelry stores. They do it in department stores for costume jewelry. The expensive stuff comes in fancy boxes with velvet linings."

"Oh." He studied the fog again. "Then try this. Looking out across the river, seeing the patches of fog interspersed with patches of blackness, I'm reminded of the patches of darkness I sense in you."

Her steps slowed, then sped up. "Nice segue, Mercer."

He followed her.

"I have a new job," she said. "Secure for two years, at least. I know the people, so I don't have to settle in with new patients. Maybe I'm more conscious of my high-school years now because there are so many people to remind me about them, but it isn't something I've agonized over all this time. If anything, it's a triumph, because given my school record, who would have expected me to come back and work in River Dance as a doctor someday?"

"Yet you seem unhappy about being here."

"Maybe things are uncomfortable with my new supervisor, but that can happen anywhere."

Tyrell misstepped in the darkness, landed into water up to his calf with a splash, and stumbled out. "Would you slow down a little?"

"Sorry."

"So you and Dr. Lawrence weren't able to work things out today after you returned?"

"Define what you mean by working things out. Nobody told me she was a missionary who had left her mission in Africa, and apparently her husband, as well."

Tyrell nearly stepped into another spot of water. "She told you this?"

"Keep your voice down. Eric told me."

"Eric?"

Jama explained what she had learned about Ruth today. "She must have contacted Eric Thompson about a job when she left Tanzania."

"A missionary? Really?"

"My thoughts exactly. Eric told me not to ask her about it, which probably means I shouldn't be discussing it with you, either, but since almost everybody in River Dance will probably know her whole life history within the next month or so, I doubt I'm breaking any sacred trust."

"Why would she leave her husband and their mission?"

"I don't know. It isn't as if we share confidences. I'm surprised every time we exchange a civil word with each other."

"She's obviously under a lot of stress, which can make some people unpleasant, and prone to building barriers for protection."

Silence for a few steps, then Jama asked, "Have I been mean to you?"

He hesitated, thinking of the safest reply to that. "There are other behaviors that can suggest an emotional wound."

"This is interesting, Tyrell, listening to you philosophizing tonight."

"Are you making fun of me?"

"Not much."

"You are. Maybe that's to distract me from

developing another theory. Is there someone else you've been seeing since our breakup? Because that would provide a whole 'nother reason for this not-getting-married position of yours."

Jama hesitated, and Tyrell felt a twinge of dismay. Maybe he shouldn't have introduced the subject. He didn't want to know.

And yet, he had to know. "Jama?"

Her steps slowed, and then she stopped. Her breath sent puffs of mist in the air as she looked up at him. "You don't get it, do you?"

He braced himself.

"Tyrell, don't get a big head or anything, but there's never really been anyone but you."

He realized he'd stopped breathing. He started again. "Don't kid me."

She took a step closer to him. "You wanted honesty?"

"That's what I wanted."

"Then you got it."

"Then I don't understand why—"

"Now is not the time to get into it. Aren't we looking for Doriann?"

"You and I both know that even if she is following the river, she won't have gotten this far."

"We need to keep going, anyway. The sooner we find her, the sooner we can get her warm and safe. Let's go."

"Wait."

"Tyrell, don't—"

"The fog." He pointed to the river, where whirls of mist floated in tufts across the lake. "You were right about the patches of water. It's moving. That means—"

"It means we might have been granted a reprieve from the freeze. The crops may be safe."

"It's possible."

"Monty will be relieved."

Tyrell resumed the trek along the river's edge. They still hadn't accomplished their most important goal tonight.

Chapter Thirty-Four

Whispers awakened Doriann. She opened her eyes to feel the warmth of Humphrey pressed against her belly and the hardness of the cave floor against her right side. Her fingers tingled because the dog lay across her arm.

Where had the whispers come from? Had she had a bad dream?

But the voices continued. She blinked in the darkness, then froze. He'd found her?

She craned her neck, trying to see out of the mouth of the little cave. No light except for one patch of starlight through the treetops. But the stars seemed to blink on and off, on and off as she watched. Airplane?

No, the moonlight showed her the swaying branch of a tree.

Moving. Wind.

Humphrey whined and sat up, then grunted when he bumped his head against the cave ceiling.

The whispers weren't coming from human voices, but from the leaves in the trees, rustling in the wind.

Doriann rolled onto her stomach and inched her way forward until she could stick her head out of the cave and look around. She realized she wasn't frozen to death.

Though Humphrey no longer huddled close, she didn't feel as cold as she had. Could the weather be changing? The best she could tell, this wind was from the south.

Granddad and Uncle Tyrell would be so relieved!

She shook her right arm to get some feeling back into it, scooting closer to the edge of the cave mouth. She listened. Definitely. Not much, but it was there. She felt it on her face, heard it in the trees, smelled smoke from somewhere, which meant that smell needed to be carried by the wind.

She climbed from the cave and sat for a minute, dangling her legs over the ledge. "Thanks, God."

A girl never realized how much she could appreciate warm clothes and a warm home when she didn't have either.

She remembered a verse Aunt Renee read to them just the other day about the trees singing. That's what Doriann believed was happening here. The trees sang with the warm wind. This forest was singing because the frost was being melted away, saving the leaves and shoots and shrubs and blooms.

Doriann wanted to sing with them!

A cold, wet nose touched her cheek, and she giggled softly. Humphrey responded by licking her chin and thumping the sides of the cave with his tail.

And then he jumped down from the rocky outcropping of the cave and turned to look at her, whining.

"What is it, Humphrey?" she whispered.

His throat made a squeaky sound, as though he were fretful about something, then he took off at a trot down the dry creek bed.

Doriann started to call him back, but then she heard something else over the wind: the voice of a man.

The day's terror returned through her whole body with a jolt. Humphrey bayed ahead of her, and the man's voice came again from behind. Far behind.

Clancy was afraid of Humphrey. Doriann had seen that in the barn. He would stay away from the dog if he could.

Humphrey howled again—a hound on the hunt. The man fell silent. Good. This would be the protection she needed from that goon. And Humphrey was going toward the river—the way Doriann needed to go. He might even lead her all the way home.

She scrambled down from the rock ledge and followed Humphrey by the light of the moon.

The blanket of fog across the water continued to swirl in eerie shapes as the clear, star-studded sky hovered above. Tyrell was hungry after scrambling around in the forest and along the riverbank for hours. Why hadn't he packed some food?

He'd heard no complaint from Jama. In fact, for the past mile or so, he'd heard little of anything except a brief comment now and then about a possible tricky step over the rocks.

"We can see the lights of River Dance from here," he said as they reached a bend in the river.

Jama stopped and turned, close enough for him to feel the warm mist of her breath against his skin.

"I think we're about halfway back to the area where we saw Doriann's tracks." Jama unzipped her coat. "I wonder how far she made it."

Her flashlight dimmed, and she shook it. "When the store opens in the morning, I want to buy a flashlight like yours. This thing's been giving me fits all night."

He pulled more batteries from his pack and gave them to her, then watched her, holding his beam on her hands as she worked. He loved those hands, the compassionate care he had seen them convey to those who needed a healing touch. Like her, they were strong, gentle and sure.

He'd been unable to stop thinking about her flight after Amy's death. "Why Utah?"

She looked up at him, squinting in the light, then shrugged and returned her attention to the battery. "Amy and I drove through there on our way to the Grand Canyon. It was so wide-open and wild. We stopped at a few of the trailheads and talked about returning someday. But someday never came."

"So you went there to feel close to Amy?"

Jama shoved the spent, rechargeable battery into her pocket. "Lead the way."

He did. "You didn't answer my question."

Silence.

Time to drop that topic. "Where would you be if you didn't have the obligation of your loan here in River Dance?" he asked. Something told him she wouldn't be anywhere near here.

"I haven't thought about it." She sounded relieved for the subject change, and perhaps just a little apprehensive that he might lead the conversation back.

"Just off the top of your head," he said. "Where would you be?"

There was silence again, but this time he could tell she was running the question through her mind.

"I don't think it's healthy to dream about what might have been."

"Is there a place you'd like to go after your two-year debt is paid in River Dance?"

"Maybe to Hideaway. It's a place down in

southern Missouri. I hear they're looking for doctors."

Tyrell felt a sharp pang of disappointment, but he knew he'd asked for it. What had he expected? That she would suddenly proclaim her undying devotion to him, tell him she wanted to be wherever he was?

"Do you know someone there?" he asked.

"Charla Dunlap, the lady who sold her land to the town for the River Dance clinic, was originally from there. She returned, after all these years, to work at a boys' ranch. It sounds like a neat place, isolated from the rest of the world, where a boat is the fastest transportation to the neighboring towns."

"River Dance is pretty isolated."

There was a soft whisper of laughter. "I'm not isolated here. I'm surrounded."

"You want to hide away?"

"I just told you I liked the idea of the place." Jama sounded irritated. "Don't keep trying to psychoanalyze me."

She was quiet for a moment, then she asked, "Where would you be?"

"Here."

Their footsteps moved in tandem for long moments.

"You've always loved working the land," she said.

He thought about his concerns earlier today. "I

have, but it doesn't consume me the way it's always consumed my father."

"Monty does a great job of balancing his work on the ranch with his family time. He had to work hard to support a family of seven . . . and eight, when they brought me in from the cold."

"I'm just saying that there are now modern ways to handle the ranch that my father didn't have when I was growing up. There is more efficient equipment, which is expensive, but worth the cost when it comes to spending time with loved ones."

Again, a long stretch of silence except for the gentle wash of the mass of river to their left, and the sound of their footsteps on gravel.

"All I'm saying, Jama, is that I would want to spend more time with my wife and family than Dad was able to do."

"Your father is one of the most loving, responsible, good men in the world."

"I think so, too."

He heard her steps slow behind him, and he tried to match his steps with hers, hoping she wouldn't retreat back into her silence.

"You didn't do anything wrong, Tyrell. Nothing at all."

He turned to look at her, took a step closer to her, until he could almost feel her warmth. "Then I don't understand why we aren't engaged now, because there is nothing about you I don't love."

"You don't know everything." She touched his

arm. "Look, I'm sorry if I made you feel responsible for this. It's me, not you."

And then she did retreat into silence. Minutes later, they heard the baying of a hound through the darkness. A few seconds after that, Tyrell's phone rang, and he flipped it open.

"This is Agent Sydloski," came the curt baritone voice.

"Yes?"

"I understand you passed the roadblock in good time, but we've heard from the sheriff that your vehicle has not been seen in River Dance, and that Dr. Keith's car is still in the clinic parking lot."

Great. They'd been caught. The sheriff's office had one holding cell at the edge of town. Tyrell had seen it once on a class field trip.

"Surveillance equipment has picked up a couple of familiar voices," said Agent Sydloski. "Apparently some people are walking west along the Missouri River."

"You don't say."

"If those people do not return to River Dance immediately, there will be a warrant issued for their arrest."

"Understood."

The connection ended.

Tyrell folded his phone and returned it to his pocket. "It's time to go home, Jama."

Chapter Thirty-Five

Doriann smelled the river seconds before she saw it—tiny waves moving in the moonlight beneath heavy splotches of fog. She stopped, surprised that it was so close.

She still heard the man's voice behind her in the woods. So Clancy was either with Deb, or he was still crazy and talking to himself. He didn't sound angry now, but the voice was too distant to tell what he said.

She hurried after Humphrey, who chuffed and whined, his nose to the ground. Barely a hundred feet downriver rose high cliffs. Humphrey started climbing, and Doriann followed. The trees grew thickly here, and she ran into a low limb. It smacked her in the forehead. She stumbled on a rock and fell hard on her rear.

"Slow down, Humphrey! I can't keep up."

Still whining, he came back and licked her. Then he stopped and sniffed the air. Whined some more. By the time Doriann was back on her feet, he was on his way back down the way they had come. He didn't howl. He whined, that squeaky-scared sound in his throat.

"That's the wrong way," she said. "Come on."

He didn't come.

She continued climbing without him. He'd prob-ably smelled a rabbit or squirrel. One time he'd led her to a tree where a mama raccoon and three babies huddled in the limbs, looking down at them. And one time a skunk—

"Uh-oh." She stopped and sniffed. Okay, no skunk. "Come here, Humphrey," she whispered as she continued the climb.

He came slowly, as if she were dragging him with a rope. He continued to whine.

Sweat dripped down Doriann's forehead by the time she reached the top of the cliffs and started down the other side. Halfway down, she heard a thunk-thunk-thunk below in the darkness. It blended with Humphrey's squeak-chuff, squeak-chuff.

Doriann stopped. The wind cooled the sweat on her face, chilling her.

She wished she'd found the Katy Trail, or even Highway 94. The riverbank wasn't made for walking. And her feet hurt. She had worn her best walking shoes, but after so much running and walking, even they rubbed in places they'd never rubbed before.

Humphrey bayed suddenly, and she gasped. Humphrey's baying was beginning to drive her nuts. How much noise was a girl supposed to take?

The thunk came again, and she finally peered over the cliff's edge to the water below. In the light of the moon, she saw the outline of a small boat dock. She thought she could make out a little rowboat in the water. The thumping was probably the boat hitting the dock with the motion of the water.

She hadn't seen a lot of boats docked on the river or permanent storage. Grandpa said that the current was strong enough that if a boat came loose from the mooring, it could get swept downriver all the way to the Gulf of Mexico.

The thunk grew louder as Doriann stumbled down the side of the cliff. Some of Grandpa's friends along the river had boats. Grandpa had taken her out on the river a few times, and though they were usually on motorboats, he'd taught her how to paddle a canoe.

She heard the voice behind her again, getting closer.

If she could paddle a canoe, she could row a boat, right? She could get to River Dance if she could avoid the old stumps and snags in places along the shoreline. Out in the middle of the river, she could avoid those and make good time.

She climbed down to the little wooden dock, stepped onto it and studied the rowboat. Two paddles. It was small for such a big river, but if she could stay near the bank, she'd get to River Dance a lot faster.

She'd gone on float trips down the Gasconade. She could do this. She reached down to release the rowboat. The rope was stiff and tight around the post, and she had to work at it.

Humphrey growled. Doriann jerked around, startled. The dog stood in the moonlight, his back to her as he looked into the dark woods.

Some bushes at the edge of the river shifted, rustling from something more solid than the breeze.

And then a shadow rose from the brush, black and menacing. "Hey, little Dori."

Clancy!

Humphrey snarled and lunged. Doriann screamed.

Jama followed Tyrell through the gurgling waters of Fern Creek. Her shoes would take days to dry out, and she'd probably never get them clean enough to wear to the clinic again.

Tyrell stopped and turned around. "Did you hear something?"

"Like what?"

He took a few steps toward her. "I don't know. It sounded like a mix between a dog's bark and a scream."

She heard it, too. "Coyotes."

He stood looking upriver for a few seconds, then turned back. "You're probably right, but what if it isn't?"

She listened again. Nothing. "If the FBI picked up our voices, they're sure to pick up the sound we heard. They'll know if it's coyotes or not."

Doriann shoved at the rope as Humphrey tangled with Clancy. The rope caught on a jagged edge of wood. Humphrey yelped with pain, but when

Doriann turned around to look, he was attacking Clancy again.

The rope came off, but the current of the river pulled it out of Doriann's hand. Humphrey yelped. She grabbed at the rope, but the rowboat disappeared beneath the dock. She ran to the other side and watched for it to float out.

She looked over her shoulder. "Humphrey, come!"

Clancy came instead. Fast. Humphrey was faster. He grabbed Clancy's leg and tugged, snarling like a Doberman. Doriann had never seen him so ferocious before.

The boat came out from beneath the dock. Doriann sat on the edge of the rough wood and slid down until her feet touched the boat bottom. "Humphrey! Hurry!" The boat rocked beneath her. She grabbed the edge of the dock. But the boat kept going. She couldn't hold on.

"Humphrey!"

Clancy reached for her. She grabbed an oar, tried to knock him away. He jerked it from her hands. She lost her balance. She saw the water rising to meet her.

Humphrey attacked Clancy again as Doriann dropped to her knees and grabbed the sides of the boat. It rocked from side to side. "Humphrey!"

Something flew toward her and she screamed. It hit the water beside her and sprayed her face. The oar. It broke the surface and bobbed. Clancy had thrown it at her. She reached for it, couldn't get it.

The current of the river swirled it away as it turned her in circles.

There was another cry as the dock, the dog and the monster disappeared into darkness and fog.

"Humphrey!"

Chapter Thirty-Six

The digital clock in Tyrell's truck read nearly midnight. Jama stared at the reflection of headlights against the layers of fog across the road. They entered the outskirts of River Dance. Five blocks to the clinic.

Tell him.

But it would be so difficult to face him—to face all the Mercers—day after day, so nearby.

Do it anyway. He deserves to know. Jama was ashamed of the way she'd treated Tyrell. He believed he had done something wrong, that he lacked something to make her happy. He deserved better.

"Slow down," she said.

From the corner of her eye, she saw him glance at her. "We're done for the night, Jama. There'll be a heap of trouble if we go back out—"

"Do you want to know why I can't marry you?"

The speedometer dropped to twenty.

"Okay, maybe you'd better park somewhere."

"We were parked in the perfect spot before we left the river."

"I wouldn't want to spoil all your great memories of that place," she said dryly.

He didn't stop. He drove to the clinic in silence, parked beside her car, turned off the engine and switched off the lights.

The clinic was dark, and Jama wondered when Ruth had left. Across the street, Zelda's lights were still on. Maybe she'd fallen asleep without turning them off. She never stayed up after the ten-o'clock news.

"Let's talk, Jama." Tyrell's voice was gentle, filled with warmth.

Jama turned to him, glad it was too dark for him to see her expression clearly. He could always read her so well. "You took me by surprise two weeks ago."

He hesitated. "I was so sure . . . just so sure."

"I'm sorry. I should have picked up on the clues."

"If I've rushed you, I'm sorry. You may not be ready yet, and if—"

"Don't apologize and make me feel any worse than I do right now."

"What could you feel bad about?"

Jama closed her eyes and braced herself. "I killed your sister."

One ghost after another formed in front of Doriann, then disappeared as the boat plunged through it. She didn't know where she was, how far she'd floated or how much time had passed.

"Humphrey," she whispered. She couldn't cry again; she was already damp enough. But she felt the warmth of tears in her eyes, anyway, felt them drip down her face, then chill in the wind.

It was colder on the water, and the fog dampened everything on her so that the wind froze her all the way to the bone. She kept trying again to steer the boat to the left, but she had discovered that a rowboat didn't steer the same as a canoe. She needed two oars.

Why had she shoved the oar at Clancy? He couldn't have gotten to her unless he'd tried to jump into the boat with her.

Something else rammed the side of the boat, and she cried out. She almost expected Clancy to come bursting from the water and grab her.

Again, she shoved the oar into the water to her right. Again, the boat turned in a circle. She was definitely doing something wrong.

If she kept turning in circles she was going to throw up. She pulled the oar into the boat and huddled in the middle, arms wrapped around herself. She was too tired and scared to do anything but shiver and cry.

But then a sound reached her. For a moment, she imagined one of the ghosts in the water had found a voice and howled at her. Or maybe it was the wind howling through the trees. It suddenly felt strong enough.

But the sound grew louder. Clearer. It came from the left riverbank. It wasn't the howl of the wind.

It was the baying of Humphrey.

He was following her! Doriann's best friend was following her. "Thanks, God."

A long, hunting-dog howl surrounded her. She'd gotten this far. She'd escaped the FBI's most wanted killers. She'd made it through the freeze. She could get to shore.

She picked up the oar again, determined to do it this time. It could work like a canoe paddle, only she'd have to do short strokes from side to side, then place the oar only halfway into the water to point the boat the way it needed to go.

She shoved forward. Yes!

But something went wrong. The oar struck a solid object hard. A limb? A log? The impact hurt her hands. She tried to hold on. The oar was wrenched from her. She scrambled to the side, reached out and tried to grab for it. She couldn't. It floated from sight beneath another ghostly wraith of fog as the boat spun once more in the water.

Tyrell felt as if the temperature in the SUV had suddenly dropped below freezing. He knew Jama couldn't mean what she was saying.

He looked across the seat at her. With no dash lights, the only illumination was from an amber security lamp above the clinic that cast only minimal light into the parking lot. Her head was bowed, and he couldn't tell if her eyes were closed.

"Tell me more, sweetheart. You can't stop there."

She jammed her hands inside her jacket pockets.

"Are you cold?" He reached for the keys in the ignition.

"No, don't. I'm not cold, I'm just . . . I'm not that kind of cold."

"Do you have a key to the clinic yet? We could go inside where we can be more comfort—"

"No. I've put this off for four and a half years, and nothing's going to make this comfortable."

"Okay, then. Let's talk." He wanted to take her hand, to wrap his arms around her and hold her. Yet he knew she wouldn't let him, and besides, a chill had begun to rise inside him, too.

"Before I go on, I want to say that I love you, Tyrell. I love your family, your mom and dad, all of you. I can make no excuses for what I've done. I've convinced myself all these years that I could never tell you or your family about this because I didn't want to hurt you more than you've already been hurt."

"I know you wouldn't do anything intentionally—"

"Please, just listen. Don't try to excuse my way out of it. There's no excuse for what I did. It's because of this change in me—it's because of Christ—that I've come to this point."

"Then why don't you tell me the point?"

"In the past few years I guess you might say I've

grown. You know. As a believer. Recently I read a passage in Proverbs that made me rethink everything in my life. It said, 'The Lord detests lying lips, but He delights in men who are truthful.' It struck me hard. I've had lying lips. Deception is a lie, whether you speak it or not.

"And then just a few days before you asked me to marry you, I had read, 'A wife of noble character is her husband's crown, but a disgraceful wife is like decay in his bones.' I would be a decay in your bones if I marry you with a lie hanging over our heads."

"Jama, you're stalling."

"I know, but I've got to work my way up to this, okay? I just need you to understand . . . Oh, Tyrell, I need you to see."

"You know I will."

"Don't say what you don't know to be true." She laid her head back against the seat and took a deep breath. "Amy and I both worked the day before Christmas, but I got off at two in the afternoon. She got called to assist in an intricate surgery and realized she was going to be there for several more hours. After working a twenty-four-hour shift already, she was dead tired, and asked me to drop the car off to get the brakes checked because she was worried about them. Then we both agreed that I'd go to our apartment and get some sleep, so I'd be fresh to drive to River Dance for the holiday.

"Amy knew better than to drive when she was

sleep deprived. We were determined to get home—
Fran had told us she would have our favorite dishes
prepared and waiting."

"I remember," Tyrell said. "Mom decided on
nontraditional Christmas fare that year. She prepared a favorite dish of every person coming to
dinner. You would have had your favorite meat
loaf, and Amy her crème brûlée. I still wanted
turkey and pumpkin pie. I think Heather went with
devil's food cake, and Renee with angel food. Dad
his chicken and dumplings."

"Comfort food," Jama said.

He heard the irony in her voice.

"We all knew you had a hard time at Christmas,"
Tyrell said. Not only had her mother left on
Christmas Eve, but a week before Jama's fifteenth
Christmas, her father was killed.

"You saved my father's life today, Jama, and you
risked your own life, and possibly risked jail time,
to help look for Doriann." Now he was stalling.

"Would you just listen to me? You're not going
to be able to excuse this away so easily. As I was
walking out of the hospital that day, some of the
other residents invited me to a Christmas Eve party
at the chief surgical resident's house. There was
going to be great food and lots to drink. I declined.
But as I was walking out to the parking lot, I will
never forget what I saw."

A pause. Tyrell waited.

"There was a little blond-haired girl, about eight,

being wheeled to the entrance. She'd probably had her tonsils removed or something. She looked healthy and happy. She had balloons tied to her chair, and her mother walked beside the wheelchair, laughing and talking about what they were going to do when they got home." Another silence. "When they reached the car outside, while others loaded the flowers and balloons, the mother knelt in front of her daughter, kissed her tenderly on the forehead and then gathered her into a tight hug."

Jama looked out the window, then raised a finger to draw a circle on the film of fog that had formed there from her breath. "I couldn't look away from the expression of love on that mother's face for her little girl." Her voice trembled. She turned back to Tyrell. "I decided I was hungry, and the party had already begun—we had to take our celebrations when we could get them.

"I couldn't stand being alone right then, so I went to the party after all, thinking I could get some food, visit with friends for a few minutes, then get the brakes checked and still have time to sleep.

"Not only was there food, there was champagne punch, eggnog, mixed drinks of all kinds. So I had an eggnog."

"You've always loved that stuff."

"This brew was made with spiced rum, and it was delicious. But I should have known better."

He waited.

"That one drink didn't help me forget. It just

made me depressed. So I had another cup to take the edge off, and then some champagne punch. Then I realized I hadn't eaten."

"You drank on an empty stomach."

"I got snockered, but I still maintained my equilibrium. I visited with colleagues and other staff, people I seldom had a chance to talk with. It felt so good being surrounded by people who understood the pressure of the job, the stress of holding a life in my hands every time I picked up a scalpel.

"I was still at the party hours later, had just swallowed another eggnog, when Amy called me on my cell to come and get her. I was surprised by the time. I remember that. We had already packed for the trip. You were coming home that year, and you'd been gone for so long.

"I used mouthwash, brushed my teeth, stuck two sticks of gum into my mouth, pretty sure I'd covered any smell on my breath. And then I drove to the hospital and picked up Amy."

Tyrell closed his eyes. "You weren't driving when the car ran off the road."

"No. As soon as Amy got into the car, she asked if I'd had the brakes checked. I told her they were fine. I didn't tell her I hadn't gotten them checked, and she didn't push it. I kept telling myself I could do it, that I could drive, I wasn't too inebriated, and the brakes were fine. She always did tend to worry too much.

"We were well past the suburbs of St. Louis, with

Amy sleeping beside me, when she woke up suddenly and sniffed the air."

Jama glanced toward him.

"And then what happened?" His voice didn't sound right in his own ears.

"I'm sorry, Tyrell. You'll never know how sorry."

"What happened?" He hated the hard edge in his voice.

"She was so mad that night." Jama's voice trembled, grew softer. "She was going to turn us around and drive us straight back to the apartment, but I begged her to continue on to River Dance. I'd already gotten us that far, and it was only a little over an hour home, and I kept reminding her you would be there this year. Either way, she would have to drive. So she went on."

"You could have slept in the car," Tyrell said.

Jama was silent for a moment, obviously retreating from his anger.

"I'm sorry," he said. "You have to understand I'm just living this for the first time."

"We could have done a lot of things differently," Jama said. "We could have stopped at a bed-and-breakfast we had just passed. But I was so eager to get to River Dance, and I'd handled the traffic in St. Louis just fine." Jama bowed her head and rubbed her face with her fingertips. He knew she was exhausted physically and emotionally.

She looked at him again. "All I could think about was seeing you. We only had twenty-four hours off. She did it for me, Tyrell. She knew how I felt about you even then."

"The brakes?"

"I've always wondered about that. The police report stated that there were no skid marks on the road where we went off. I never knew if that was because Amy fell asleep and never woke up, or if the brakes failed to work, because I was asleep, too."

She fell silent except for the shivering. He could think of nothing to say to make it easier for her.

In spite of every promise he had given Jama, Tyrell couldn't deny his anger. Then grief hit him afresh. His beloved sister had died a senseless death. And the woman he loved with all his heart had been the cause. He felt as if he'd been punched in the gut.

He started the engine and turned on the heater.

"I couldn't bear to lose the only family I had," she said quietly.

"But you distanced yourself from us. And by not telling us, you lost the support you could have had from family."

Jama looked at him. "What would I have lost if I'd admitted what I did?"

He was silent. What could he say? He needed time to digest this.

"I couldn't face it," she said. "When I came back from Utah, I visited as often as I could, and told myself that brief connection was enough."

"And then we started dating," he said, still regretting the vehemence in his voice. Still unable to do anything about it. All this time, he'd been so sure they could work through any problem, as long as she felt safe enough to share it with him. But right now she couldn't possibly feel safe.

Neither did he.

"I had a life-changing turn-around in Utah," she said. "I came back a new person, and I knew it. But, Tyrell, I wasn't raised in a Christian home as you were. It took me some time after becoming a believer to grow and learn. I've been more and more convinced as time went on that I would have to tell the family my part in Amy's death. Those verses I just quoted to you made a huge impact on me. But it's been hard." Her voice caught. She took a deep breath.

"When you and I started spending more time together last year, it felt so right and good that I just allowed myself to enjoy it. I knew we were getting closer. I'd already loved you for so long that . . . I didn't think that . . .

"I kept telling myself there would be time. You'd never even hinted at marriage before."

It was getting hot inside, so Tyrell switched the motor off again. The silence surrounded him and pressed him down. He could think of nothing to say.

Chapter Thirty-Seven

It was the silence that hurt Jama the most. No matter how often she told herself she deserved Tyrell's response, no matter how many times she'd rehearsed this explanation in her mind, she hadn't prepared herself for the silence. Cold. Rejecting.

Some people thought she was tough. So many old friends had told her how proud they were of her. Hometown orphan who surprised everybody and did well. Strong, determined Jama Sue Keith.

But part of her wasn't strong at all. Part of her was still that little seven-year-old child pounding on the door, screaming for a mother who didn't want her. Would she always be outside?

Well? Didn't she deserve to be?

"When you proposed," she said after the silence became more than she could bear, "I was shocked. My time was up. I knew I couldn't live with my secret and live with you, but I'd always told myself there was time."

Now she wished it wasn't dark. She needed to see his expression.

"I also realized that, not only would I have to tell you, but by telling you, I'd also be telling the rest of the family."

"You think so little of me that you don't believe I can keep a confidence?" Still the roughness in his voice.

She winced, unable to bear much more. "I guess I had that coming. Look, we're both tired, and I've got a long drive to Columbia." She reached for the door handle.

He touched her arm, and she jerked.

"You're not driving back there tonight. You can stay at the ranch. I have my own apartment, and you can sleep in the house."

"I can't, Tyrell." She thought she'd be able to handle this, but—

"You can't? So you're going to risk having the Mercer family lose another loved one to sleep deprivation?"

She winced, realizing that, somewhere deep inside, she had held out hope that he would forgive her. Not that she expected marriage—she'd never been foolish enough to harbor that hope—but that somehow he might be able to give her absolution after all this time. She would rather sleep in her car than go back to the ranch with him like this.

She had placed him on too high a pedestal. He was bound to tumble off someday. But tonight of all times . . .

"Now you see why it wouldn't work for us." She grasped the latch and squeezed. She moved from his touch and stepped out. "I think the irresistible force just met the immovable object."

Before he could respond, she closed the door and stepped toward her car.

Someone was standing in the shadows beside the Subaru. She froze.

"It's me, Dr. Keith." Familiar voice. Zelda Benedict.

The rush of relief mingled with the pain, a shock to Jama's system. "Zelda, can't a couple have a little privacy—"

"I wasn't spying. Listen, did you ever get a key to the clinic? Eric hired somebody to replace the window, the young coot, and I don't want to be the next one to have to break out—"

"What's wrong?"

The passenger window of Tyrell's Durango slid down. "Jama?"

Jama closed her eyes briefly. No coldness now, just concern. Tyrell was back in character. How long would that last?

"Nothing," she said. "Go home. I'll stay with Zelda tonight."

"Sure thing," Zelda called to him, eyeing Jama in the dim glow of the security light. "Though I think a bath would be in order first. Clothes and all."

"Jama?" Tyrell asked, his voice softer now. "You're sure?"

"Of course," Jama said. "Get some sleep." Oh, yeah, as if.

Doriann felt a little ill. The boat kept turning in slow circles, and judging by the speed she was moving through the fog, she had to be going at least as fast as the tractor when Grandpa plowed. Probably faster. The Missouri River was higher than usual.

She had realized, far too late, that the man's voice she'd kept hearing behind her when she was on land wasn't Clancy. It couldn't have been, because Clancy leaped from the bushes at her only a few moments after she'd last heard the man in the distance.

Somebody else was out there, probably looking for her. FBI? She hoped they found Clancy.

"Jesus, if you'll just get me out of this, I'll never shove Ajay into the pool again, and . . ."

Doriann suddenly realized she'd been praying wrong all day. She'd been bargaining with God to get out of this horrible mess. Aunt Renee said not to bargain with God, because everything you had belonged to God anyway, so it was like offering a bribe to a person who had given you all your money to begin with.

"Well, then, God, I guess I'll just have to ask for mercy," Doriann said softly. That was what Mom said when she missed church Sunday after Sunday because of work.

She listened for the sound of Humphrey's howl, but she knew he couldn't have kept up with her. She thought again about the dog's attack on Clancy. And wow. Humphrey was afraid of everybody, but he'd charged a killer to defend her.

She thought about how she'd escaped the swamp, about Humphrey finding her in the cave and keeping her warm. She thought about reaching this boat at just the right time.

Maybe she was just a sassy kid who didn't mind her parents, but she knew what mercy looked like—a sunset. She knew what it smelled like, sometimes, too—swamp water and cow poop and dog breath. It felt like blisters on her feet, and a rough wooden boat beneath her bottom, and sweat frozen in her hair.

Now if God would just keep her from floating all the way to the Mississippi River, she'd be happy.

Zelda led Jama into her house, where the aroma of some kind of Southwestern dish filled the air. Jama remembered that Zelda had always loved spicy food, even though it gave her heartburn. She'd probably stop having heartburn if she stopped smoking a cigar every night, but she also probably knew that.

"You going to tell me why you need to get into the clinic?" Jama asked.

"I'll do better than that. I'm going to show you." Zelda led her down the hallway to the back bedroom. She turned and looked at Jama, and the lines of her face were more prominent than Jama had ever seen them, pulled down by some heavy sadness.

Opening the door, Zelda called out, "Debra? Honey, you need to wake up now."

Debra? Benedict? Zelda's granddaughter? Jama stepped into the room as Zelda switched on the overhead light. The smell of unwashed body and dirty socks wafted into the air.

The body in the bed was turned away from the door. Sharp, nearly fleshless shoulder blades were prominent beneath a floral blouse that was obviously Zelda's. From what Jama remembered of Debra—she was the age of the Mercer twins, several grades behind Jama in school—she had always preferred black T-shirts with skull and crossbones insignias and threadbare jeans, not fuchsia and orange and lime-green tropical pullovers.

The still form stirred only when Zelda placed a hand on her shoulder and gently nudged her.

"Turn over here and let the doctor take a look at you, hon. I want an expert opinion." Zelda motioned for Jama to join her at the twin-size bed.

Debra rolled over onto her back, and Jama was stunned by her appearance, as if a Halloween mask had been painted onto her face. Her eyes were barely visible from the swollen, discolored flesh around them. Her blond hair, fuzzy and damaged from what appeared to be too many applications of hair color, was matted with blood on the right side.

Debra looked up at Jama and nodded a greeting.

"Haven't seen you in years." Her gold-hazel eyes looked weary, as if she could barely keep them open. Her forehead—the only part of her face that wasn't swollen—had wrinkles. She wasn't even thirty.

"I've been keeping a close eye on her," Zelda said. "I'm afraid of a concussion, some broken ribs, maybe broken facial bones and soft tissue damage. She won't let me take her to a hospital. I've tried."

"I don't need a hospital. I'm tired, and I have a migraine. The swelling will go down." Debra grimaced, and Jama noted that she was missing a couple of teeth.

"You know what I think?" Zelda asked. "I think she's found herself another loser who takes his lack of manhood out on a defenseless woman."

Without asking permission, Zelda reached down and pulled up the shirt to reveal bruises over Debra's ribs. "She came in like this about an hour ago, won't tell me what really happened."

"I did tell you, Grandma, but you didn't believe me." Debra's voice had lowered and roughened over the years, and now it grated. "I was cycling the Katy and some idiot on an ATV ran me off the trail. There is not even supposed to be motorized stuff on that trail. Now my bike's in the river and I had to walk to town."

Jama caught a whiff of Debra's breath. It confirmed her suspicion, and she felt sick.

326

"Debra, you need a medical exam now," Jama said. "We can drive you to—"

"I'm not going anywhere. I've gotta sleep off this migraine first, okay? If I move, I'll throw up." Debra pulled the sheet up over her head, then turned her face to the wall with a grunt of pain. "Just let me sleep. It's not as bad as it looks."

Zelda crossed her arms. "Well, folderol. Jama, I know we can't force her to do anything she doesn't want to do unless we do an involuntary commitment, but can't you make her see reason?"

Jama studied the bony figure on the bed. "The nausea concerns me. Any signs of dizziness?"

"Leave me alone," Debra rasped. "It's the migraine. Stop talking about me like I'm not here."

"Could I at least give you a quick exam?" Jama asked.

"I'm great, okay? I couldn't've walked all the way here if I'd been dying, could I? I'll be up doing my daily run first thing in the morning if you'll just let me get some sleep!"

Jama studied the weak and helpless woman on the bed. Zelda was right, a man could have done this. It had been a hard thing to see over the years. Zelda's daughter had become involved with an older man. A drug pusher. She'd had two children by him, then died of an overdose when her kids were in their teens.

Zelda had done the best she could with her

327

grandchildren after that, but the legacy of addiction had left its mark on Debra.

Debra was once a beautiful girl, with straight, golden-brown hair and dimples in her cheeks. Jama remembered seeing her wave from the float at the homecoming parade as queen in her senior year—wearing a black dress, of course. This was barely a shell of the girl she'd once been.

Now she looked like death.

Chapter Thirty-Eight

Tyrell negotiated the private, quarter-mile drive to the house on automatic pilot. This lane had been lined with cars when he left. Now it was empty. All was quiet, except the storm taking place in his mind.

He parked in the circle drive instead of the garage. There was no reason for it, nothing he could do for Doriann now, but something kept him on the alert. He wanted to be able to get wherever he might be needed at a moment's notice.

He sat looking out over the shadowed rows that covered the hillside on which the house was built. He longed for a warm wind to blow away the chill in his heart, the same way the vines and trees had been saved.

Everything was shattering. Dad, the constant strong presence in Tyrell's life—who'd grounded him in the solid love for the land—lay helpless in a hospital bed. Doriann was still lost, and the family was forced to depend on strangers to find her.

And Jama. A deep sigh escaped Tyrell as he rested his forehead against the steering wheel. He felt as if she'd died. In essence, she had, since the image that he'd always carried of her in his heart had been destroyed with her confession. The Jama he knew would never have placed her best friend in a situation that might get her killed.

He remembered wondering earlier if the rebel still existed in Jama. And he'd hoped that, in some ways, it did.

"Welcome to reality, Mercer," he murmured. The picture of rebellion wasn't so appealing in a zoom shot.

Zelda had always been a determined lady, but as Jama stood beside her in the bedroom where Debra lay, she could feel defeat roll off the poor woman in waves.

"I'm sorry," Jama said. "We can't force Debra to do anything. I just hate to see that pretty face damaged. When the swelling goes down, we may see more problems than we can right now."

Zelda looked at Jama and shook her head. "You could show her some moves, Jama. Teach her how to fight back."

"If you two are going to keep talking like you don't believe me—"

"Sure, I could teach her," Jama said, "but right now she needs medical attention. Debra, if I could just check your vitals, your pulse—"

"No!" Debra growled.

"Okay, then, will you at least let me walk you across the street to the clinic in the morning? We can get some shots with our new X-ray machine, see if there's anything we need to be doing."

"I'll be there," Debra said. "Just please close the door behind you as you *leave.*"

Zelda turned to lead Jama down the hallway. The door remained open.

Jama cast a final glance back toward the bed, and felt a stirring of unease. She shook it off. Coincidences happened. Just because Zelda's rough-living granddaughter had arrived injured on the same night that a "skinny blond" member of a killing duo had been in an auto accident nearby, it didn't necessarily mean anything. It couldn't. Debra was no killer.

Jama remembered seeing Debra visit the lonely people in the nursing home—the ones no one else visited. She'd once nursed two baby orphan raccoons and then released them back into the wild.

Coincidence . . .

"Debra?" Jama said softly. "Which direction were you coming from on your bike?"

For a moment, Jama thought she wouldn't answer. Then she said, "From St. Charles."

That was the eastern trailhead. The truck had

been found in a swamp west of River Dance. Opposite directions. But then, wasn't that where someone would place herself if she were on the run from the FBI?

"Didn't you date Mark Streeter in high school?"

"Yeah. He dumped me for your foster sister. Now can I get some sleep?" The voice was sharper now.

"His little girl went missing today. It's believed she was abducted and brought to this area. I just thought that if you were on the Katy Trail for very many miles, you might have seen or heard something that could help us find her."

Debra lay still for a long moment, so still that she looked as if she had stopped breathing. Then she took a deep breath and turned over to look at Jama, pain evident on her swollen face. "She hasn't been found?"

"Not yet. I just came back from searching."

"If I'd seen a child in danger, don't you think I'd've done something to help her?" Debra snapped.

"Of course you would. Okay, Debra. Call us if you need anything." Jama retreated and followed Zelda, still uneasy, trying to remember where the Katy Trail from St. Charles came close enough to the Missouri River that Debra could be run off the road, fall hard enough for this much damage and lose her bike in the river. And then, of course, she would have to be close enough to walk here with her injuries.

"Let me get you something to sleep in," Zelda

told Jama. "I'll throw those clothes into the washer. I gather you didn't bring a change?"

"I'd planned to return to Columbia tonight." Jama felt a deep stab of pain as she thought about Tyrell, his anger. And once again, the loss.

They walked through the kitchen, and Zelda pulled a small casserole dish from the refrigerator. "Tortilla pie. You used to love this, didn't you?"

Jama had been hungry earlier, but her appetite had fled.

"When did you eat last?" Zelda asked.

"I had a late breakfast."

"You need to eat," Zelda commanded. "You can clean up in the hall bathroom. The bedroom across the hall from Debra is yours. I'll just take the unfolded laundry from the bed. That's my junk room. I seldom get many overnight visits."

"I could take the sofa."

"You'll take the bed. By the looks of it, you need as much rest as Debra does. I'll keep checking her tonight."

"I'll help. Set an alarm for me."

Zelda stuck the tortilla pie into the microwave, then turned around and pulled a kitchen chair away from the table. She sank down with obvious weariness. "You'll do no such thing, Jama Sue. You look bushed. You're sleeping, end of argument. Get washed, changed, and by then the food will be hot." She glanced down at Jama's shoes. "Those are a lost cause."

"They're my only ones. I'll try to scrub them up in the bathroom."

"Leave your muddy clothes in the hallway. I can stick them in the washer now, then dry them next time I check on Debra."

"You're too good to me."

Zelda gave Jama a long, sad look. "You feel like one of my own." She gazed down the hallway, sighed and looked back at Jama. "That would make me proud."

The tragedy in those words weighed Jama's heart with sympathy and blessed it with love. She carried that comfort with her as she washed . . . for a little while. But then she began to wonder how eager Zelda would be to embrace someone who had carelessly cost a bright, promising young surgeon her life.

After all the years of hard work in the field both at home and abroad, a few hours tramping through the woods would not typically faze Tyrell. He enjoyed the physical exercise. But tonight he felt as if he'd been climbing a mountain that couldn't be scaled. He ached as he stepped from the SUV and hauled his gear from the backseat.

Jama's confession had killed his appetite, but in the house he went through the motions of making himself a sandwich, heavy on the roast beef between thick slices of Mom's homemade, whole grain bread.

He remembered Jama's words about that long-ago Christmas dinner Mom had planned. Comfort food.

All of Jama's words continued to flow through his mind, like pieces of flaming confetti tossed into the air.

He had moved his things into the studio apartment above the garage, but tonight he felt as if that was too far away. It had no phone service yet, and if someone tried to call the house instead of his cell for some reason, he wanted to be here.

He carried his sandwich and a glass of milk to the breakfast bar, pulled out a stool and prayed. Mercers always said grace before meals, and though there were many times he'd forgotten over the years, in this house it was second nature.

It was brief. No words involved, not even silent ones. Just a need for connection. A call for help. An opening of his spirit to make way for the Holy Spirit to connect with him, to fill him, give him wisdom.

How could this happen? How could he have spent so much time with Jama and not sense she was withholding a secret so devastating?

No answer came from above.

He remembered the passages of scripture she had quoted to him—words she had memorized, obviously. Words that had moved her so profoundly that she changed the course of her life because of them.

She had given up a promise of life with the man she loved because of the guilt she carried.

Tyrell shoved the sandwich aside, placed the milk back into the fridge and found the family Bible. It had all the birth and death records of the Mercers, dating back to the early 1800s, written in Mom's neat script, which she had transferred from the huge old Bible handed down from generation to generation.

Holding this book comforted him. He opened it and saw the colored highlighting and underlinings on the pages, and in spite of everything that had happened today, he smiled. It was a study Bible, one Mom had purchased a few years ago, and which she and Dad had read through time after time, underlining different passages at different times, Mom in blue ink, Dad in yellow highlighter. Some verses were both underlined and highlighted.

Because of Jama's memorized passages, he carried the Bible to the kitchen table and found Proverbs. A book of wisdom. He could sure use some wisdom right now.

Chapter Thirty-Nine

Baying . . . in the darkness. Humphrey? Rocking. Doriann was rocking. She opened her eyes and still saw darkness, still felt the rocking. Then she felt the hardness against her side, heard a splash of water. She jerked awake then. She'd fallen asleep in the boat. Just curled up in the bottom and fallen asleep. For how long?

More baying. It wasn't a dream. She grabbed the sides of the boat and pulled herself up. Humphrey. It couldn't be him! She knew hunting dogs could run for miles . . . had seen them running back and forth, back and forth, eager for the hunt, sniffing the ground and howling with glee at a scent.

Lights onshore. Doriann caught her breath, and then cried out. How far had she floated? How long had she been sleeping? Could that be River Dance? She saw the outlines of buildings, those gold-yellow security lights, saw some windows with dim blue glow coming through them. Someone at home watching television.

"Hey!" she cried. "Hello, help! Somebody. Is anyone there? Help me!" And then, because it was louder than any other noise she could make, she just screamed and screamed. A little-girl scream that Aunt Renee said could peel the bark off a tree.

Humphrey howled and kept howling.

Somebody would have to hear her. They'd have to!

Jama sat at the kitchen table, hair dripping, toes freezing. The pajamas Zelda had given her were five inches too short and they hugged her a little snugly in some places, but they were flannel.

She cut a wedge from the tortilla casserole with the side of her fork, and transferred it to a small saucer.

The aroma of steaming cheese, chilies, beef and beans piqued her hunger. Zelda knew how to cook.

The first bite trailed heat down Jama's throat and warmed her stomach.

After quick instructions for Jama to make herself at home, Zelda had gone to bed. She had a rough night ahead of her, checking on Debra every hour for signs of concussion.

Jama had taken her third bite of casserole when a sound from somewhere outside puzzled her. There was a distant baying of a hound dog on the hunt, and then the piercing strum of a scream mingled with it. Like the sound earlier, when she and Tyrell were on the riverside. They'd decided the sound was coyotes at the time, but now she wasn't sure. Perhaps an animal being hunted? Trapped? She'd heard rabbits cry like little babies when caught by a cat.

She shivered. All the chaos of the day was catching up with her. She thought about the dogs that were supposed to arrive to help search for Doriann. Had they been brought in yet?

She took another bite of the food, washed it down with milk, then got up and covered the casserole. She would wait until it cooled further before replacing it in the fridge.

Overshadowing everything was the memory of Tyrell's angry voice. Regret filled her. Hunger abandoned her.

She should have told him long ago about her part

in Amy's death, but to have told him today of all days, with everything else hitting him, was the wrong timing. If he had suspected the kind of bomb she'd drop on him, he might not have pressed so hard for answers.

"Oh, Tyrell, I'm so sorry," she whispered. She sank back down at the table and buried her face in her hands.

"I'm sorry."

Tyrell paced across the living-room floor, listening to the squeak in one particular floorboard every seventh step. It was a large living room, in a large house, built by Tyrell's grandfather, Joseph Mercer, with the intention of filling its rooms with a large family.

Now it was empty and dark, lacking the comfort Tyrell had always found here.

He stepped to the wall of windows he and Daniel had helped Dad install twenty years ago. They overlooked the hillside of vines. The thermometer read forty degrees now, and though it was warmer than it had been, it was still too cold for a child to be out there alone.

He heard a creak of floorboards behind him. He stiffened. Before he could react, the lights came on. Daniel stood in the middle of the room, hair sticking out, wearing jeans with no shirt.

"Went upstairs to read. Must've fallen asleep," Daniel said.

"I didn't know you were here."

"I parked in the garage. I was just going to rest a few minutes, then change and check the temperature."

"It's fine."

"You're back."

"Jama and I were warned away twice by the Feds, threatened with arrest . . . We figured that was pushing it."

"Where's Jama?"

"Zelda Benedict's for the night." Tyrell heard the stiffness in his voice.

Daniel's gaze sharpened, and Tyrell knew he was about to ask questions.

The house phone rang and he answered eagerly, glancing at the caller ID. "Renee? Any news?"

"I thought you might have some for me." Her voice, typically vibrant with life and the type-A personality that drove her, had an unfamiliar edge to it. "I was clued in that you and Jama were ousted from the search."

"We avoided jail, obviously."

"Of course. Is Jama at the house with you?"

"Why?" Why, all of a sudden, was everybody so interested in Jama? He knew immediately that his recent thoughts colored his voice.

A pause.

He glanced at Daniel, saw the concern. "I'm sorry, Renee. It's been a long night."

"Getting longer." Still that edge.

"Something's up?"

"The agents found tracks all through the woods. They heard some kind of altercation a little over an hour ago, animal and human, probably a dog. Screaming. Maybe Doriann. Shouting. Maybe the kidnappers. There were signs of a struggle near a small boat dock owned by a local—"

"Wait. What time did they hear the commotion?" He recalled the sound he had heard as he and Jama returned to the Durango.

"It was about an hour and a half ago, maybe two. I'm not getting minute-by-minute reports. Why do you ask?"

Tyrell closed his eyes. "Jama and I might have heard the same commotion. We thought it was coyotes."

"Oh, Tyrell," Renee whispered.

Vexed that they might have been so close to Doriann and missed the chance to reach her, he stood and walked to the windows, glaring out into the darkness, toward the security lights of River Dance that did not make him feel secure.

"What are the Feds doing now? What else have they found?" he asked. "Are they any closer to finding these monsters?"

"They started interviewing local landowners and discovered there's a rowboat missing. Then they went farther downriver and discovered that there was also a fishing boat missing. There were drops of blood on the dock."

"No sign of anyone in the forest?"

"None yet."

"We know Doriann escaped them at one time. We could tell by the tracks we followed. Then, for some reason, she turned and followed her abductors." Now it sounded as if she had either been caught again, or she was being followed. And now she and her captors could be headed downriver, out of the vicinity. They could be anywhere.

"The hunt has expanded," Renee said. "Several law enforcement units have been called in."

That didn't comfort Tyrell. Doriann could be at the center of a maelstrom of danger.

"Where are you getting all this information?" he asked. "I know the federal agents aren't giving you a play-by-play."

"Remember my friend from school, Mona Johnson? She married Tim Holloway, who's been called to help secure the perimeter. He got the news from the sheriff, then told Mona, and she's called me three times with updates."

"Good. Keep me informed, and don't go telling anyone else about Tim's involvement, or he'll be in trouble. Want to talk to Daniel? He's here."

"First, I want to make sure you call Jama. She needs to know."

"Not tonight. She's probably asleep."

"She'll want to know, Tyrell. I can't believe you're trying to keep her out of the loop. I think—"

"Here's Daniel," Tyrell said, then swiftly handed

the cordless phone to his brother, and left. He took his sandwich and the family Bible to his apartment. Daniel was at the house to answer the phones. He would get Tyrell if there was any news. And Tyrell had his cell.

Ironic that he was being forced to wait and pray and contemplate at a time when he most needed to be doing something. He knew that the disasters of the day weren't happening simply to teach him how to do what had always been difficult for him—to wait. But the lesson was being learned, nonetheless.

He sat at the window overlooking River Dance. From here he would be able to see the top of the clinic roof during the winter months when the deciduous trees were bare. He could see the Show-Me River flowing into the Missouri during day-light, and if he opened his window, he knew he would be able to hear it.

He turned on the lamp beside his chair and opened the Bible. He selected an ink pen from the collection he kept in a coffee mug. It was a red pen. Appropriate, he thought. Tonight, he felt as if his own blood had been spilt.

He read for a while, then prayed, then read some more, with red pen in hand. He kept going as his eyelids grew heavy. He shared with God his agony over Doriann's abduction, his worry over his father, his pain and disillusionment with Jama. His anger.

Oh, the romance that had carried him these past few months, when he'd craved time with Jama. Since she was a resident in Springfield, only thirty minutes away from where he worked, they'd seen each other often. How right it had felt, and how sure he'd become that she was the woman he wanted to spend the rest of his life with.

That romantic, idyllic bubble had burst tonight, leaving a clearer view of the woman he'd thought he knew so well.

Driven to his knees, he felt his heart cry out to God as never before, and as he prayed, his past mistakes came to his mind—his outspoken judgment of Mark and Heather's parenting skills. How much blame did they lay on themselves because of his words?

He thought of the judgment Jama must have heard in his voice earlier tonight when he scolded her about Utah, about the times through his life that his words—his thoughtless attitude of judgment—had wounded others. And worse, some of his final words to Jama tonight had been harsh and wounding.

He laid it all bare to God. And then he continued to pray for mercy.

Doriann's throat hurt, and she'd lost the sound of Humphrey's howl. She couldn't scream anymore. She sat huddled in the center of the boat, freezing.

Aunt Renee was always reminding them not to

343

give up praying for something they really wanted— if they thought it was God's will. So was it God's will that Doriann get out of this river alive?

"Please, God, take care of me. I want to go home." She felt tears again, and sniffed to keep from crying, because that just made her colder.

This was the first time in Doriann's life that she was homesick. She loved to travel, to camp, see the country with her grandparents and vacation at their time-share. Once, she'd gone to England with Mom and Dad for a symposium. She loved adventure. But not now.

The boat bumped into something hard, jolting her. This was not the kind of traveling she liked. Oh, to be home listening to Mom and Dad talking about an exciting case, competing with each other over who had done the most surgeries that day, and who had engaged in the most compassionate doctor-patient heart-to-heart. They were really big on having a great bedside manner.

The boat bounced against something again, and then just sort of slid into some bushes. Leaves brushed across her face, and she jerked away with a cry. What now?

The boat turned again with the force of the river, but the clinging brush proved to be too much for the current. She had hit a shore of some kind.

She looked up to find trees hovering over her, the deep gloom of shadows and darkness. She'd landed somewhere. But where?

Chapter Forty

Jama was drying her hair with Zelda's blow-dryer in the bedroom when her cell phone rang. It was Renee. As Jama listened to the news from her foster sister, she felt a cold vise squeeze her.

"Doriann might be on a boat?" The screams. The howling. "And you said there was an animal involved?"

"And of course Tyrell didn't call and tell you. I told him to—"

"Renee, call the FBI. Tell them I think I heard her. It couldn't have been fifteen minutes ago. If she's on the river, she could be more than a mile away by now. They'll need to set up a barricade quickly. Meanwhile, do you know of anyone in River Dance with a boat?"

"Why?"

"Never mind." Disconnecting, Jama opened dresser drawers until she found some of Zelda's old scrubs. When she pulled them on, they were a little tight, but they'd have to do. Thank goodness Zelda hadn't washed the jacket. The gun was still in it, as well as Jama's flashlight.

She pulled on some dry socks, her wet shoes, and then rushed out of the room, nearly colliding with Zelda in the hallway.

"You still up?" Zelda asked sleepily. Then she

345

looked at Jama more closely. "Hey, what are you up to, young lady?"

"I think I heard Doriann just a few minutes ago," Jama told her. "Who has a motorboat on the water right now?"

"Water?"

"The river. I'll explain later. Do you know of any—"

"Sure. Phil Carraway's here for a week on a fishing trip. He's camping down by the river." Zelda gave directions. "He's got a bass boat with a trolling motor. Took me out on it the other day. So quiet, it wouldn't even scare the fish."

"Good. The FBI are on their way," Jama said as she headed for the door. "But this can't wait."

"Who's going with you? Did you call Tyrell?"

"No time."

Zelda followed her to the front porch. "Don't you dare go after them by yourself!"

"Tyrell is sure to know by now. I'm not leaving Doriann in danger any longer if I can stop it." She ran down the steps, across the flagstone path to the street, and kept running as she followed the directions Zelda had given her. She only wished she had the powerful beam of Tyrell's flashlight.

Tyrell stared at one passage that had been both highlighted and underlined. It would make sense that Mom and Dad would both be drawn to this particular set of words. "Have I now become your enemy by telling you the truth?"

Paul had some straight things to say to the Galatians.

He also had some good things to say to the Corinthians. "Love is patient, love is kind . . . keeps no record of wrongs."

And John's "Little children, let us not love with word or with tongue, but in deed and truth" really hit home.

He closed his eyes as those passages made him ache.

Who was he to judge? He'd always excused his self-righteous attitude with the birth order. The oldest did tend to take responsibility, to expect more from everyone, and tended to have difficulty forgiving.

Okay, maybe that wasn't specifically noted anywhere by the psychologists of the day, but it was an excuse he'd used more than once.

Sure, he was so good about excusing himself, but when it came to others, he tended to run out of excuses quickly.

He paged on through the Bible, but before he could read farther, Renee called again on his cell.

"I think Jama's up to something," she said. And then she explained.

He had his shoes on before she finished. "Did she tell you what she was doing?" But he already knew. "I'll talk to you later." He flipped off the phone, grabbed his jacket and ran out the door.

Doriann stood at the top of a rise and peered through the trees that surrounded her. There was water everywhere. She could see the moon reflecting from it.

She was on an island in the middle of the river! There were lights upriver, but no one would hear her tonight.

She sank to the ground on a pile of last year's leaves. "I'm never getting home."

It was a lot warmer here on land than it had been in the boat, and so she reached for some more leaves, gathering them around her like a blanket. If she could make it to morning, she could call to somebody passing by. "It'll be okay."

She had all the leaves around her, piled as high as possible, and then she curled herself into the middle of the mound. She closed her eyes and listened to her teeth chatter.

It was a few minutes before she heard another sound. She clenched her jaws and listened. An engine. The quiet hum of a motor.

She peered around the island until she saw a shape in the water. Long and dark. A boat pulling alongside her rowboat. No lights, no one talking.

Someone was coming for her. Someone who didn't want to be seen or heard.

The sound of feet jumping to shore . . . grunts of pain. Cussing. A man.

Clancy had found her.

Jama guided Phil Carraway's sleek new bass boat through the river of ink, his admonitions ringing in her ears about what he would do to her if she damaged his baby. She directed Phil's wonderful, big, bright searchlight across the surface of the water, and understood why the man felt such passion for the vessel—it handled like a dream.

"Doriann!" she called. It was likely that, if those had been Doriann's screams earlier, she would be much farther downriver by now, but after everything that had happened in the past seventeen hours, Jama wasn't discounting anything.

"Doriann!" Her voice echoed against the cliffs to her left.

She used only the quiet, electric trolling motor so she could hear any sounds over it. She didn't want to go too fast and miss something.

"Doriann!"

Silence, except for the soft hum of the motor . . . and then a sudden scream out of the darkness.

Ahead and to the right.

Jama switched on the gas-powered motor and ran it full tilt across the water in the direction of the scream.

Tyrell backed his father's boat and trailer down the ramp by the campground at the edge of town. It was tricky for one person to put a boat into the water, but it could be done with a long enough tether. He'd done it many times before.

He'd placed the boat and was parking the trailer when he heard shouting downriver. Jama calling his niece's name. Then he heard a scream. Then the sputter of an engine.

No time to use finesse. He grabbed the tether, jumped into the water, then into the boat and revved the motor.

Clancy's fingers dug into Doriann's arms. "How does it feel to live like us poor people, little rich kid? To be hunted like an animal?"

She screamed again. And she heard her name being called from somewhere across the river.

Clancy clamped his hand over her mouth. "Shut up."

She tried to break away, but his hold was like concrete. She couldn't budge his arms.

"Your daddy's going to know what it's like to lose somebody he loves." He was hurting her. "Privileged little girl. You don't even know what life's all about. You think you're better than us because your clothes are clean and you get three squares, live in a nice home. How'd you like to grow up without a daddy?"

His hand was cutting off Doriann's air. She kicked at him.

His grip grew tighter. "I'm not going to kill you

yet, little spoiled rich kid. You're still my ticket to freedom."

If he wasn't going to kill her, why wasn't he letting her breathe? *God? I'm sorry for everything I've ever done. Guess I'm going to see You in a few . . .*

She panicked, she fought. She thought she heard Humphrey again, and she saw a bright light in the trees. And then the roar in her ears grew louder.

The hand jerked, as if forced from her mouth. Clancy let her go, shoving her aside. She spun, landing on her belly in the leaves. She heard the breath go out of him.

He lurched forward and fell, trapping her beneath his leg. She reached out to grab a sapling and tried to pull herself out from under him. He was heavy.

His mouth started spewing dirty words again, and she could see him clearly because there was light. She saw Aunt Jama standing in the glow of the light, grabbing Clancy around the neck from behind and squeezing with her arm. He bucked and shoved Aunt Jama against a tree, breaking her hold. Then he turned on her. In the light, Doriann saw a knife flash in his hand. He raised it. Doriann screamed and lunged at his arm. She scraped the inside of his shin with her heel. Aunt Jama had taught her a few things.

He knocked her sideways with his elbow. Aunt Jama hit him again. He hit her back and knocked her down. She reached into her pocket, but he jumped on her. He grabbed her by the throat.

"No!" Doriann jumped onto his back and clutched him by the hair. She screamed into his ear, reached for his face and tried to poke him in the eyes. He knocked her off, elbow gouging into her stomach. She fell to the ground, trying to catch her breath.

Another roar from the water. Jama kicked up and broke Clancy's hold on her throat. She kicked him again and again.

He raised his knife and plunged it down, but a shadow flew at him and rammed him up and over. He hit the ground with a grunt. A big shape—a man—jumped on top of Clancy and shoved his shoulders backward into the leaf blanket Doriann had made.

Doriann recognized her uncle Tyrell's black hair and big shoulders in the bright light. She looked at Aunt Jama, who hadn't jumped back up the way Doriann expected her to.

"Doriann, are you okay?" Uncle Tyrell asked.

"I'm good, but Aunt Jama's not moving."

"I'm moving," Aunt Jama said quickly. "Just not very fast." She groaned and sat up.

Doriann scrambled to her side. Uncle Tyrell had Clancy under control. Doriann knew he would.

Aunt Jama was bleeding. Doriann gasped. Aunt Jama reached up and pressed her fingers against Doriann's lips.

"I'm okay, sweetheart," she said, then she pulled Doriann into her arms.

"I thought he'd killed you!" Then Doriann burst into tears.

Chapter Forty-One

Jama stood at the Dancing Waters Winery between Agents Sydloski and Bosch, who had escorted her from the island. Both men had fired questions at her all the way up the hill—and it had taken some time with the delay in securing Doriann's abductor for transport.

The chopping roar of rotor blades had silenced the questions at last, and Jama watched the jet-black FBI helicopter lift Tyrell and Doriann into the sky. The sound most likely awakened the whole town. There would be calls to the clinic tomorrow. Maybe even tonight.

Agent Sydloski took Jama by the elbow. "Are you sure you won't let us drive you to join them at St. Mary's? You need to have that wound looked at. That's quite a puncture."

"There's a lot of blood, but the cut isn't deep. There's a brand-new, state-of-the-art clinic just down the hill," she said. "I have my very own key to it. I also have a critical patient who needs my care, and there's no other physician who knows her case and can take care of her."

"We'll need to interview you and get a statement."

"Can it wait until I've seen to my patient, and myself, and had a few hours of sleep?"

Sydloski looked at Bosch. "We'll still be here in the morning."

Bosch nodded. "It can wait."

There would be a happy welcome for Tyrell and Doriann at the Jefferson City Hospital as soon as the helicopter touched down. Doriann would be thoroughly examined, treated, fed and debriefed. Jama had done a cursory exam, and found no obvious injuries. Jama had already told the agents everything she knew—which was very little that they hadn't already known.

In the excitement of the fight, the convergence of six agents onto the tiny island in a sudden hailstorm of light and sound, and the aftermath of the arrest, there had been no time for Jama to speak to Tyrell except to assure him she was okay.

"You and Mr. Mercer are two determined people," Agent Sydloski said.

Jama looked up at him. Doriann might be dead if Jama hadn't disobeyed orders. But it could have ended differently had Tyrell not arrived in time.

"Are you still looking for the accomplice?" she asked.

"The search dogs have arrived. We don't have a scent for them to follow, and there were multiple tracks through the woods. We'll still be in the area until we find her, but this partner was not the original woman who went on the killing spree with him. That woman was found dead three days ago."

"He killed his partner?" How chilling.

"The case is still under investigation." He checked out the blood on Jama's upper arm. "You're going to treat that yourself?"

"No problem. Look, I know Doriann's a brave kid, but everything that's happened to her is going to be a huge trauma for her."

"She'll receive the best of care, and I think she'll provide a lot of answers for us."

There was a sudden, loud baying of a hound behind them, and Jama turned to see Humphrey, Monty's hunting dog, running toward them up the hill. His tongue hung from his mouth. He was panting hard.

"Hey, boy." Jama knelt to pet him. "Didn't I see you out on the highway this morning?"

His body quivered. He was wet. When Jama ran her hand down his side, he winced and whined. He was spattered with drying mud.

"Easy, Humphrey. You look beat. You've covered some miles, haven't you?"

Agent Sydloski knelt beside her and smoothed the ruffled hair on the dog's head. "You know this animal?"

"He's one of the Mercers' hunting dogs. Doriann rescued him from a ditch a few years ago."

"We picked up sounds of a dog baying for miles along the river," Bosch told her. "It looked like a dog got a few bites at Doriann's attacker at one point."

In the glow from the security light in the parking lot, Jama raised Humphrey's snout and looked into the depths of his brown-black eyes. "Was that you I heard tonight, boy? Did you follow Doriann down the river? Are you a hero?"

"Looks like he could use a trip to the vet's office," Bosch said. "Is there one nearby?"

"Sure is. I'll walk him down to Dr. Witherspoon's house."

"Tell us where that is, and we'll take him," Sydloski said. "You need to get that wound taken care of."

Tyrell held his squirming niece on his lap, safely in his arms, and he had some serious doubts about being able to release her to the care of others once they landed.

"Wow, Uncle Tyrell, I've never flown in a helicopter before!" She leaned as far to the right as she could to look down at the retreating lights of River Dance. She waved, as if someone down there could see her through the mirrored black glass.

"Is Aunt Jama going to meet us at the hospital?"

"I don't know yet."

"Why couldn't she ride with us?"

Tyrell didn't know that, either. He'd been unable to wrest her away from the two agents who had hovered over her all the way from the island.

"Did you see what she did, Uncle Tyrell? Clancy had me in a stranglehold and I was going down, and she jumped him and knocked him over, and then he almost had her, and I used some of those moves she taught me, and we held him off long enough for you to come to the rescue."

She looked up at him, that little mud-streaked face, mud-caked hair, red-rimmed eyes. She gazed at him as if he were a superhero.

He smiled down at her, then pulled her into a tight hug. Though she'd been in tears on the island, she'd recovered quickly enough once the FBI personnel had begun to arrive. Since then, she'd been awed by the gear the agents wore, and asked question after question about their weapons and whether or not they wore earplugs when they shot, and whether or not they wore bulletproof vests. Once he managed to calm her excitement over riding in a genuine FBI helicopter, he checked her out, as Jama had done on the island. No blood on her clothing. He felt up and down her legs and arms. No wincing.

"Doriann, do you remember if you were unconscious at any time today?" Had they knocked her out?

"Yeah. I stayed up too late, and was sleepy. I'd never make a good private investigator, because I fell asleep right outside the barn where Clancy and Deb were hiding!"

"You followed them after the truck went into the swamp. Why?"

She looked up at him then, and her eyes grew somber. "It's what you would've done. You wouldn't have let them get away so they could kill more people or kidnap more little kids. Clancy had my cell phone, and I wanted it back. They were high on meth, and I heard Deb say they would have to crash soon. So I tried to wait until they crashed in the barn." She grimaced. "It didn't work, and Clancy almost caught me."

"Did they hit you or inject you with any needles?"

"No, but Deb smacked me in the face a couple of times, but then she protected me from Clancy later. Humphrey found me and kept me warm."

"Humphrey?"

"He's some good dog, isn't he, Uncle Tyrell?"

"He is."

"When are you and Aunt Jama getting married?"

Tyrell decided not to ask Doriann any more questions.

Jama let herself in through the front door of the clinic with her new key. The hinges didn't squeak; there was no noise at all. She removed her dirt-caked shoes before stepping inside.

She turned on the lights in the reception office.

The familiar quiet hum of the Pixus machine whispered from the far corner of the office. It would be moved to a more appropriate location as soon as there was opportunity to decide where that would be.

She entered the first exam room, with the minor meds treatment chair, switched on the light and gathered the supplies she would need to treat her arm. The clock on the wall registered three o'clock. She'd been up for nearly twenty-four hours—and most of those hours inundated with high drama and tension.

Residency had given her the mental and emotional resources to deal with day-to-day life-and-death issues with multiple patients, but nothing had prepared her for what she'd just endured.

She worried about how Doriann would handle everything that had happened to her. She'd been talkative and had interacted well with everyone after those first few moments on the island. When would the effects of the day hit her? Would she be scarred by this for the rest of her life?

Jama sank onto the chair and stared at the meds and instruments on the stainless steel tray table beside her. Tyrell . . .

She felt like crying. But Jama Keith never cried. Even when she'd been forced to make a life-or-death decision about a loved one. Even when she had a life-and-death struggle with a killer to save another loved one. Even when she was finally forced to confess her guilt about Amy's death.

But after all that time spent with Tyrell, his

promise that she could trust him *no matter what,* and now his response to the confession he had wrested out of her—who wouldn't lose a tear or two?

Or fifteen or twenty . . .

Tissues. There were no tissues in this whole stupid office. Jama sniffed and her nose ran, and she rushed into the bathroom at the end of the hall, belatedly remembering why she didn't cry. It was a messy business, and it wasted paper.

She was walking back from the bathroom, trying to blow her nose on a paper towel, making a mental note to purchase facial tissues, when she heard a soft thump. A whisper of movement behind one of the closed doors.

Silence. She waited. The accomplice?

She reached for her cell phone and was about to dial for help when there was another quiet movement, and she isolated the direction of the sound. It was behind Ruth's office door.

Oh, why call for help now? After everything else she'd done in the past few hours, was there anything she couldn't handle herself? She reached into the right pocket of her jacket and pulled out her pistol. She'd lugged the weapon around all night and hadn't used it yet.

She released the safety and reached for the doorknob. It was locked.

"Who's in there?" she demanded.

Another thump, and a grunt.

"I'm calling the police," Jama warned.

The knob clicked, twisted, and the door opened. Ruth Lawrence stood there barefoot, hair in her face, wearing her scrubs. Behind her lay a pallet on the floor.

"Don't shoot," Ruth said dryly, her voice filled with fatigue.

Chapter Forty-Two

Doriann was asleep in Tyrell's arms when the helicopter landed on the hospital helipad. He carried her inside without waking her. His mother stood just inside the entrance, and when she saw them, she burst into tears and ran to meet them.

"I knew you and Jama would do it," she whispered as she turned to walk with Tyrell and the two agents to an exam room. "Is she injured?"

"Not that we can tell. Jama checked her over at the site, and then I did a second check on the way here. How's Dad?"

"He's sleeping peacefully, doing great."

"Did he find out about Doriann?"

"Not a thing. Heather, Mark and Renee are on their way here." She looked into her granddaughter's sleeping face, then up at Tyrell. "Do you realize Jama had a hand in saving two of our beloved in less than twenty-four hours?"

He nodded. Yes, he knew. And then he thought of Amy, and he felt weary to the bone.

"Worked late?" Jama clicked her safety back in position and shoved the weapon into her pocket.

"I decided to save on gasoline." Ruth watched the gun enter the pocket, swallowed, looked back up at Jama.

"Then I guess it's a good thing our private facilities have a shower," Jama said. "Eric told me you're staying in Hermann."

"You carry that thing with you all the time?"

Jama patted her pocket. "I keep it locked in my car. I've been in places where one of these might have come in handy." Like tonight, if she'd had a chance to get it out of her pocket. There'd been no time.

Ruth glanced down at Jama's clothing. "You look awful."

"It's been a long day. Doriann is safe, one of the kidnappers is in the custody of the FBI, and—"

"And you were involved in the apprehension?" Ruth asked, nodding toward the bloody sleeve of Jama's jacket.

"I had backup. Tyrell arrived in time to keep me alive, and then the FBI came to haul away everyone but me."

"How did you rate a stay here?"

"I have a patient at Zelda's. Her granddaughter will need some attention first thing in the morning."

"I heard the activity, especially the chopper."

Ruth reached out and tugged on Jama's sleeve. "Let's take a look at you."

Jama pulled off her jacket and allowed herself to be led back to the first treatment room. She sat down, leaned back and felt some of the adrenaline that had kept her going begin to drain from her. Someone else could take care of her arm. Someone else was taking care of Doriann, of Monty.

But Debra and her worried grandmother?

Nothing could be done for a patient who declined treatment. For the past couple of hours, a nagging suspicion had grown in Jama. She didn't want to think it through now.

"Any particular reason for the tears?" Ruth asked. "Or are you doing as I do, using them as a pressure valve release?"

Jama looked up at her director, surprised by this bit of personal sharing. She winced as Ruth probed the wound.

"An incident in my past has caught up with me," Jama said.

"Just one?" Ruth's voice held the same gentle kindness it had when she'd spoken of Doriann's abduction earlier today, and when she'd spoken with Ted. "I'm sorry that some of your troubles today came from me. I didn't stop to consider a few things." She probed the puncture deeply again.

This time Jama didn't wince. She knew the routine. A wound like hers had to be thoroughly irrigated and checked for foreign particles.

"What didn't you consider?" she asked Ruth.

"That the tales I heard about your youthful escapades might have little connection to the strong, capable and self-assured woman you've become."

Jama looked up into Ruth's golden-brown eyes. She wasn't being sarcastic. Wow. What kind of metamorphosis was this?

"You weren't the one who caused the trouble," Jama said, then thought about that. "Okay, *some* of my trouble might have come from wondering if I was going to be in conflict with you for the next two years."

"Which is still a possibility," Ruth assured her. "Three opinionated women working together may strike some sparks, but iron sharpens iron. I realize you've had a rough first day, but I called St. Mary's earlier, and your foster father is still doing very well. Is Doriann going to be okay?"

"You called?"

"Of course. I knew you'd be worried, and I noticed that you didn't receive a lot of updates this afternoon."

"That was kind of you."

Ruth gave a wry smile. "I can be that way on occasion. How's Doriann?"

"Physically, she looked good. There was no evidence that she was violated." For some reason, Jama couldn't stop thinking about Debra's injuries.

"So . . . back to you, then." Ruth examined an injury on Jama's forehead that Jama hadn't known was there. Ruth cleansed it and put ointment on it. "The tears?"

Jama hesitated, eyeing Ruth's wrinkled scrubs and bare feet again. "Do you really have a place to stay in Hermann?"

"Obviously not tonight."

"All the lodging full? That surprises me. This is so early in the tourist season. I'd think you could find some good deals."

"Not the kind of deal I'm going to need." Ruth's voice changed. She wouldn't meet Jama's gaze.

"Where's your car?" Jama asked. "It isn't in the parking lot."

"I pulled it behind the building so I wouldn't get any midnight drop-ins. Since your car's still out there, however, my efforts weren't much use."

"Where will you stay?" Jama asked.

"I'll stay in River Dance as soon as I find a place to rent."

"And until then?"

Ruth's eyebrows went up. "You're pretty good at changing the subject, aren't you?"

"So are you." Jama flexed her arm and stood up from the treatment chair. "If you need a place to stay—"

"I have a place to stay," Ruth said, finally meeting Jama's gaze. "It's right here until the city council coughs up my signing bonus."

"Missionaries don't make a lot of money," Jama said.

"No, and their accommodations are sometimes less comfortable than a pallet on the floor and a hot shower in a building that is warm when it's cold outside, and cool when the weather heats up."

"I know of fifty people here in River Dance who would gladly offer free room and board to a wandering missionary."

Ruth sighed and sank into the wheeled treatment stool; she gestured for Jama to take the other chair. This time Jama didn't hesitate. She was tired. All she wanted was to lie down and sleep. Even Ruth's pallet had looked good to her.

"Last night I slept in my car," Ruth said. "I showered at a campground with facilities. I'd have stayed in the car again tonight, but I couldn't resist the temptation to stretch out. I spent nearly all the money I had just to get here, and the car is the one my husband and I had in storage when we left for Africa." She sighed, as if that admission had taken great effort.

It also took Jama some effort not to show her astonishment. Why would Ruth be so desperate to leave her husband that she would place herself in this predicament?

But what surprised Jama the most was that Ruth had actually revealed so much. "Your personality sure changes after midnight," Jama told her.

Ruth smiled again, but it was a sad smile. And she looked tired, too. "You and I are both off duty and out of uniform. And you caught me with my guard down. Now, your turn."

Jama grimaced.

Ruth sat watching her. "Be glad you have a life to cry about. I'm in the process of rebuilding mine. And before you ask, don't."

Her words reminded Jama of Eric's allusion to some tragedy in Ruth's life.

Jama realized she'd been practicing Tyrell's habit of distraction because he was the last thing she wanted to think about right now.

Ruth sat back in her chair with a sigh. "I'm a doctor, Jama. I'm good at keeping confidences. You don't have to tell me anything you don't want to, but you know as well as I do that it does help to talk. Even to a stranger."

"It's funny, but when you aren't snapping at me, you remind me of someone I once knew."

"That wouldn't be Amy, would it?"

Jama narrowed her eyes. "Who's been talking?"

"Everybody in town, Jama." Ruth leaned forward, resting her elbows on her knees. "I've pieced together quite a story from the things I've heard about you. It's taken a few hours to sift through them, but I've finally managed to draw my own conclusions by watching you in action."

"And that conclusion would be?"

"You're loyal, you take bedside manner seriously, you do excellent suture repair, no matter what grade you got in sewing class in high school.

And you have a tender heart." Ruth grinned. "And you're argumentative, speak your mind and have a chip on your shoulder."

Jama thought it ironic that she had thought Ruth was the one with the chip. Maybe they both had one.

"Would you like me to tell you what I've heard?" Ruth asked.

"Were you told these things in confidence?"

"No. In fact, I have a feeling the people in this town want you to know how proud they are."

"I've failed so many."

"You don't know what failure is."

"You don't even know me."

"Well, we're going to have two years to change that," Ruth said. "I'm willing to listen now, if you're willing to talk."

Jama felt her resistance begin to crumble. It had been a long day, and she felt weary to the bone. And friendless, in spite of this warm gesture from Ruth.

Sharing with someone was somehow suddenly especially appealing. To her surprise, Jama heard herself telling about the night Amy died. A story she'd never told to anyone, and here she was relating it for the second time in a few hours.

Chapter Forty-Three

Tyrell watched through the window of the private ICU room, where Mark and Heather hovered at their daughter's bedside. After giving them a tearful and apologetic greeting, with a promise to never, ever, ever disobey them again, Doriann had begun to tell them about her harrowing experience. She hadn't shut up since.

Doriann had been examined to see if she had been sexually violated, and she had not. Tyrell wished the authorities would have just taken her word for it. Why inflict more anxiety on her when she'd been through so much?

Heather and Mark had been flown to St. Mary's hospital from Kansas City by the FBI. Tyrell was grateful for this, even though he knew the agents' reasoning was that a child could not be questioned without a parent present.

As he watched the Streeter family together, he thought about forgiveness. Doriann's actions yesterday morning had nearly cost her life, and Mark and Heather had been frantic. Yet when they arrived at the hospital, all was forgiven as soon as the parents saw their cherished child.

He could forgive Jama for her actions on the night of Amy's death. He knew he could. Her act was not intentional, and she had punished herself for it ever since.

What hurt him the most, after he'd had time to consider it, was that she didn't feel safe enough to tell him.

But why should she?

When he'd finally convinced her that she could trust him with anything, he'd responded to the truth with anger.

He professed to love her so much, and yet he sure hadn't loved her when she was most vulnerable.

Someone squeezed his arm. Mom. He looked down at her. Anyone meeting Fran Mercer for the first time was always surprised when her age was revealed. She could pass for a woman in her forties. No one believed she was sixty, but tonight they would.

"You need to get some rest, Mom."

"So does everyone else. Are those people going to keep Doriann up all night? She needs to sleep."

"She told me she slept for a while in a cave with Humphrey."

Mom looked up at him in surprise, and then a smile lit her eyes. "So it was Humphrey that Jama and I saw on the road. That's where he was going."

"Not possible. Doriann couldn't have even been there yet."

"All things are possible, honey."

He simply nodded.

Her hand tightened on his arm. "You're brooding."

He nodded again.

"Tyrell, you should be overjoyed. Your father and your niece are both out of danger, the frost didn't happen. Our family is still intact."

He nodded. "It's a little surreal to me right now."

"And you're thinking about Jama."

Of course. With everyone else out of danger, Jama was all he could think about.

Jama told Ruth everything, and Ruth gave her total attention. When Jama was finished, she sat back. Her hands were shaking.

"That's an awful thing for you to endure, Jama." Ruth's words were tender, as if she were talking with a child.

The gentle response soothed something deep inside Jama.

"It was awful for Amy," she said.

"It isn't awful for her now, from what you've told me," Ruth said. "You're the one suffering the most over this."

"Her family suffered the most."

"I know . . ." Ruth's voice faltered. "I know." She swallowed and sighed, looking down at her hands. "They still live with the grief, and they share it with each other. And you live with the grief plus the guilt. That's a heavy burden to bear alone all these years."

Jama stared at her. She understood.

"So you think you're the sole reason she died."

"My actions—"

"You're not God, Jama. Your actions might impact a lot of people throughout your life, but the consequences are controlled by God, not you. You made a good call with Amy's father in an emergency situation, and it appears you put your life on the line for Doriann. That's two lives your actions influenced in twenty-four hours. But God trumps your actions."

Jama cast her gaze to the ceiling. "Of course He does."

"Have you ever lost a patient under your care?"

"Yes."

"Have you ever made mistakes with patient care?"

"Yes, every resident does, but—"

"And you obviously didn't change professions because you made a mistake. You learned from it so it didn't happen again. So you're telling me that big hunk who came to the clinic this morning is the kind of man who will hold one bad decision against you for the rest of your life?"

"That bad decision killed—"

"No, your bad decision and her bad decision killed her. She didn't have to drive anywhere. You could have slept in the car right where you were." Ruth held her hands out to her sides. "I'm living proof that people can sleep in cars."

"I begged her to keep going."

"If she thought you were too drunk to drive, what made her think you were sober enough to make that kind of decision? She was a surgery resident. She should have been wise enough to figure that out."

"You have to understand the Mercer family Christmas—"

"I understand that if he doesn't love you enough to forgive you for what you did, then he doesn't love you. Period. He loves his own version of you. If he can't accept the real you, flaws and all, then you don't want him for a husband, because, sooner or later, you will let him down . . ."

Ruth's voice quavered and failed. She spread her hands and draped them over her knees. "You'll let him down."

For a moment, Jama pushed away thoughts of Tyrell and focused on the enigmatic woman in front of her. It didn't take a genius to realize Ruth was in pain, but Jama wished she'd seen it sooner.

"Is that what happened to you?" she asked Ruth.

The director closed her eyes, features contorting.

Jama felt sudden compunction. *Not your business, Jama Sue.*

"You've helped me realize how unfair I've been to Jack." Ruth's eyes opened, and a film of moisture dissolved into droplets that coursed slowly down her cheeks.

"How?" Jama asked.

"We had a five-year-old little boy. Our only child." Ruth's eyes closed again. "Benjamin." She said the word as if the very sound of his name caused pain. "Three weeks ago, Jack took him along on a call to a nearby village across the river near our home. He did this over my objections."

A deep breath, uneven and filled with anguish. "Their boat capsized, and Benjamin was swept downriver."

Jama felt the heat of her own tears once more. "Was he found?"

Ruth nodded. "Word spread throughout the area, and some people from a village far downriver brought his body to us. Our whole community turned out for a funeral, taking care of everything, while I hid out in the house, unable to cope, furious with God for allowing this to happen to us when we'd given up everything to serve Him."

Jama had always believed she'd endured a nearly unbearable load of guilt these past years; how must Jack feel?

"I've been so wrong," Ruth whispered, as if Jama's thoughts had been spoken aloud. "I've been so focused on my own loss and anger that I've given little thought to what Jack must be going through."

"Do you think you'll be able to forgive him?" Jama asked.

Ruth looked at her, touched her arm, leaned forward. "Thanks to you, I think so. It's going to take some time, but if he calls again, I'll have Chelsea give the call to me." She sniffed and dabbed at the moisture on her face, then stood, taking a deep breath.

She looked at the clock. "I'm going back to sleep. You want half my blankets?"

"No, thanks, I'm staying with Zelda across the street."

"Then get there and get to bed. We've got a busy day tomorrow."

Jama went. The boss was back on duty.

But she had brought up some pretty thought-provoking suggestions.

A missionary. Who'd've thought?

Doriann sat on the side of the exam bed, dangling her legs and swinging her feet back and forth. Her mother did the same, as the two FBI agents sat across from her, asking questions. She held on to Mom's arm. She couldn't let go.

"Clancy and Deb," the agent said.

"Yes, but Deb wasn't a killer." And once again, Doriann told the story. She'd told Uncle Tyrell about this already, but the agents wanted to hear it all again.

Mom still wore her dark blue scrubs from work, and tears kept trickling down her face. Dad sat on a chair next to the bed, holding Doriann's other hand.

Doriann had only been able to let go of Uncle Tyrell's hand when Mom and Dad arrived. Her parents needed her worse than Uncle Tyrell did.

And she needed them.

• • •

Jama walked across the chilly parking lot and paused at her car. She didn't make a habit of calling people at half past three in the morning, but she suspected Renee was still awake and on her way to the hospital—if she hadn't convinced the FBI helicopter pilot to fly her to Jefferson City with Heather and Mark.

Renee answered her cell phone on the second ring. "Jama? Why didn't you go to the hospital with Tyrell and Doriann?"

"I explained to the agents that I had a critical patient."

"But you were hurt."

"I've been patched back together. I have a question for you. Remember when Mark was dating Debra Benedict in high school?"

"Sure I do. She and Heather nearly got into a catfight over him. You remember how pretty Debra was, except she was all Goth, never wore anything but black. Mark only dumped her because she was using. That's when he started dating Heather."

"What was she using?"

"Speed. Why?"

"She's at her grandmother's, and she doesn't look the best."

"You mean she's still using?"

"Looks like it."

"Is she still as pretty as she was?"

"She looks twenty years older. Worse, she looks as if she's been beaten. She claims it's from a bike wreck, but I can't help wondering if she hasn't come into contact with an angry man. Was she extremely upset about the breakup with Mark?"

"She begged him to come back to her," Renee said. "She promised she'd stop the drugs, that she was just experimenting. You know how she loved to break the rules. Kind of like you."

Yeah, thanks for the reminder.

"He went back to her," Renee continued, "at which time Heather gave up on him and started dating someone else. I don't know what happened after that, because we went to college. Heather and Mark met again their sophomore year, and Debra was out of the picture. You say she's in River Dance now?"

"At Zelda's. She just arrived a few hours ago."

"And you called to ask me this because . . . ?"

"I was just curious and knew you'd be awake."

"And this patient you told the agents about, that couldn't possibly be Debra, could it?"

"That's the one, though she won't let me touch her until morning. She needs to sleep."

"Poor Zelda," Renee said. "She tried so hard with her grandkids. Then her grandson moves away as soon as he can after graduation, hardly comes to see her, and now this with Debra. Can I call you back? I'm not on my Bluetooth, and traffic's a little heavy."

"No need to call back. I plan to get some sleep. I'll see you soon."

"You did great today, Jama."

"Thanks. So did you."

"I'll give Tyrell your love when I get to the hospital." Renee disconnected before Jama could reply that Tyrell didn't want her love.

Chapter Forty-Four

On Tuesday morning, Tyrell woke up from a fitful three hours of sleep in the darkened waiting room. His sister Renee lay in the far corner on a futon. She must have had wings on her car, because she'd arrived at the hospital an hour and a half after Tyrell and Doriann.

It was growing light outside, and old habits died hard. He always rose with the sun.

He had been given a key card to the shower room upstairs, plus a toothbrush. He intended to use both.

He was halfway to the door when Renee yawned.

"Doriann's being released this morning, Tyrell. We can both go home and get some real sleep." She paused. "Well, anyway, *you* can get some real sleep. No way I'll be sleeping with four kids romping all over me."

"Somehow, I don't think the helicopter's going my way this morning."

Renee sat up, her short brown hair tousled over

her forehead. "Did you sit in on Doriann's debriefing?"

"Parents only, but Doriann pretty much told me everything on the way here."

Renee patted the seat beside her. "So spill, big brother. I want to hear it all."

He covered his mouth. "Morning breath."

She reached into her pocket and pulled out two sticks of gum, one for him, one for her. Then she crossed her legs and leaned forward, eager for news.

After a good, hard nap of four hours, Jama was up again and walking Debra across the street to the clinic. Zelda was snoring away in her bed.

Chelsea Franklin would be arriving in about ten minutes for X-ray. Debra had cleaned up and washed her hair, and was wearing some of Zelda's old scrubs that hung loosely on the skinny young woman's frame. She wore a jacket with the logo of Dancing River Winery. Though the swelling in her face had gone down, there was a lot of discoloration, and she walked slowly, as if in pain.

"Still have the migraine?" Jama asked.

Debra nodded. "It's worse."

"You've had them before?"

Debra nodded again. She stumbled when they reached the gravel, and Jama took her by the arm.

"Take your time. Can you tell me how long you've been using?"

Debra's steps slowed. She sighed and looked down.

"A long time, then," Jama said. "Since high school?"

"Don't say anything to Grandma."

"You don't think she already knows? Debra, we can get you help."

"I've tried to get off the stuff, but it's so hard. It's like chains binding me." Debra raised her hand to her neck and massaged it.

Jama unlocked the front door, wondering if Ruth was still asleep in her office. "I want you to get into a gown . . . if I can find one."

"I'm just wearing these scrubs. No metal. Do I have to change?"

"No bra with snaps?"

Debra held her arms out to her sides and looked down at her stick-straight frame. "For what?"

Jama's cell phone vibrated as she led Debra back to the treatment room with the most comfortable exam bed. She almost ignored the call—no personal conversations on clinic time, as per Dr. Ruth Lawrence—but she checked the screen. Sydloski.

She flipped open the cell. "Yes?"

"Dr. Keith, have you seen Debra Benedict?"

"Of course. That's the patient I was telling you about. I'm with—"

"If she's with you, please don't let on that I've called. We believe she was one of the kidnappers."

Jama closed her eyes.

"I was told that the female of the team may have

sustained some injuries around her face and abdomen from the hostile male. Can this be the same person?"

For a moment, Jama couldn't breathe. She shot a glance at Debra, who was watching her closely.

The atmosphere in the clinic changed as Debra's eyes widened.

"Yes," Jama said.

Debra shook her head and backed from the treatment room, stumbled at the door, turned and walked back down the hallway. Jama followed her, rushed to the door and locked it to keep anyone else from entering, and stood in front of it to keep Debra from leaving—not because she thought Debra was a danger to others, but she was in no condition to try to run.

Debra didn't try. She stood in the middle of the waiting room with her arms crossed over her stomach, shoulders stooped. Her face crumpled.

Jama could not believe it. Not Debra, who'd had such a soft heart, who'd rescued baby birds and baby rabbits, then cried when she couldn't keep them alive.

"We'll be there shortly," Sydloski said.

"Okay, then," Jama said into the phone.

Agent Sydloski was right.

"Jama?" Debra whispered.

Jama reached for her. "You need to be calm and sit down. We have no idea how much injury you've sustained, and we can't take any chances."

"They're coming to get me, aren't they?"

Jama felt such a weight of sadness. "Oh, Debra. How did this happen? Tell me what you've done."

"I didn't do what they think I did." She closed her eyes and swayed.

Jama noted that though Debra was crying, there were no tears. Dehydration.

"Help me, Jama. Please don't let them . . ." She leaned into Jama.

Jama tightened her hold around Debra's shoulders and eased her to a cushioned chair. "Tell me what's happening. I can't help you if I don't know."

There was a movement in the hallway, and Jama looked up to find Ruth walking toward them, wearing a fresh set of scrubs and a white lab coat.

Debra sucked in a breath at the sight of her.

"It's okay," Jama said. "She's my boss. She's a doctor, too."

There was a knock, and Debra jerked around to see who it was. She relaxed visibly when Chelsea Franklin stepped into view through the window.

Ruth joined Chelsea on the front porch, closing the door behind her, and leaving Jama and Debra alone.

"Now," Jama said. "Talk fast, because I need to get some fluids into you."

"The police don't understand, and they won't listen to me."

"I will."

"It was crazy. I heard over the grapevine . . ." Debra looked at Jama. "You know, the drug grapevine."

Jama nodded. She could guess.

"I heard there was a dealer in town who wanted revenge on a Dr. Streeter. That's all I heard. I didn't know the guy was a murderer, I just wanted to get more info. If it was Mark or Heather, I wanted to warn them."

"The police could have done that."

Debra gave a humorless snort of laughter. "I've been busted—the police don't ever believe druggies. I made an anonymous call, but it must've been ignored. Doriann wouldn't have been out on that street if anyone had paid any attention to me."

"How did you hook up with Clancy?" Jama asked.

"I made like a buyer and purchased a hit from him, then played around with him for a while, you know. Like I thought he was hot. Got high with him, got him to talking, convinced him I knew how to cook the stuff he sells."

"Do you?"

"No, but it wasn't as if I was marrying the guy, I just had to convince him to hang out with me long enough for me to find out about his plans for Mark." She paused, sighed. "I still love that guy, after all these years." She winced and leaned over. "It hurts."

"Let's get you back to the treatment room." Jama tried to get her up.

Debra pulled away. "Not right now. I'll throw up."

"That's exactly why—"

"I've got to tell you, Jama. Listen to me! I found out Clancy had a wicked-hot temper when he punched a hole in the wall where he was staying with some other guys. He needed some wheels, told me to come along, so I went. I was with him when he stole the truck."

Jama grasped Debra's wrist and took her pulse. Not good. It was slow. This didn't fit with dehydration or meth use. "He's the one who did this to you."

Debra nodded. "He wanted to case Streeter's place. We saw Mark and Heather each leave separately. I don't know why Clancy thought they were rich. They live in an apartment, nothing fancy. I thought Clancy was just going to check out their apartment, and I was going to try to call the police while he was inside. But then Doriann came out alone and started walking down the sidewalk. Clancy followed her in the truck."

"How far?"

"Only a couple of blocks. It was early, so no one else was around. I learned then that Clancy did just the opposite of what I told him to do. When he said he could grab the kid and make Streeter pay, I told him not to do that, because the cops would be all over him.

"Before I could stop him, he jumped out,

grabbed Doriann and hauled her into the truck, with me screaming at him, and the poor kid screaming for help. Then he lost it and said if I didn't shut Doriann up, he'd kill her right there. I slapped her until she got quiet." Debra shook her head. "That kid's a tough one."

Jama winced at what Doriann had endured.

"I know I wasn't using good sense," Debra said. "I was still high, trying hard to maintain. Clancy drove east on I-70, and Doriann started mouthing off, and I slapped her face again. Not hard enough to make a mark, but enough to sting so she'd shut up and stay alive.

"Since I'd learned that he . . . that the man . . ." She frowned, shook her head in confusion. "Since I learned that Clancy did what I told him not to, I told him we were low on gasoline, even though I knew there could be another full tank. It had dual tanks, but he's a city boy. He doesn't know anything about farm trucks. I told him not to stop on the interstate or we'd be caught for sure. So he stopped on Interstate. I called the police from there when he was in the bathroom. I'd hoped to be able to get help there and get away, but he caught me just talking to the attendant and flew into a rage. I'm telling you, that guy was on something more than speed. I knew I couldn't grab Doriann and run with her. Nobody'd stop for me, and he'd hurt us both. Even so, he suspected I'd done something, and socked me in the belly."

"How many times did he do that?"

"Twice. He's a strong man."

"I know. I took him on last night. You couldn't have explained the situation to the police when you called?"

"Not with that scanner in the truck. That was how I found out he was on the FBI Most Wanted list. Man! I was scared too many details would be given out about my call. I grabbed the steering wheel as soon as we heard the scanner report. I wanted to distract him. I got us off the interstate and headed toward River Dance. I figured I might be able to find somebody who knew me and would believe me."

Jama reached up and gently touched a bruise. "Where'd you get this?"

Debra raised her hand to her face and rubbed the spot. "We hit a swamp, and Doriann escaped. We followed, and I kept trying to stall. I spotted her trying to hide behind some bushes, and I started an argument to distract him. He slugged me."

She touched the other side of her face. "This one was when I saw a shadow moving past the cracks in the barn where we hid for a while. So I started another fight."

Debra paused, closing her eyes. Her face was losing color.

"It's time to get you onto a bed." Jama stood and took Debra's arm. Debra followed willingly. Her footsteps were slow. She stumbled, and Jama wrapped an arm around her.

"Debra, did you lose consciousness when he hit you?"

"Yeah."

"Do you have any idea how long you were out?"

Debra shook her head. "No way to tell. All I knew was that I said something that made him mad. I think I called him a moron, and he swung. That's all I remember until I heard his voice. I was lying on the barn floor in a pile of hay. He jabbered on, as if nothing had happened."

"But you do remember everything up to that point?"

"Yes, I . . . think so." Debra sank onto the exam bed.

Jama pulled off the jacket and helped her lie back. The woman felt so frail. So breakable.

"Clancy hated doctors," Debra said. "He hated anybody he thought was rich. Talked about it all the time, bragging how he took a sledgehammer to a Rolls, knocked the windshield out of a Porsche."

Jama placed a blood pressure cuff on Debra's arm and pressed the button on the automatic machine. "Why did he hate them so?"

Debra shook her head. Jama noticed that her eyes didn't focus. "He was crazy, you know? Grew up poor, to hear him tell it. Mother was an addict, died from withdrawal when he couldn't find any crack for her, couldn't con a doctor into writing him a narcotics scrip."

"That's why he went after Mark with such a vengeance, then," Jama said. Debra's blood pressure was too high. It didn't fit with the low heart rate.

The front door opened, and Jama and Debra heard footsteps, and the sound of men's voices, mingled with Ruth's.

Debra started to cry. "Oh, Jama, help me. I don't want to go to prison."

Jama called out the door to her boss and the agents. "Ruth, we need Chelsea for radiology, and we need a bag of saline. Debra's dry, but there's something else going on. I won't know if she can be moved until I do an exam and we take some X-rays."

She looked up when Agent Sydloski stepped into the room. He studied Debra's battered face.

"You should see her abdomen," Jama told him.

He nodded. "Do whatever you need to do."

Jama was attempting to establish an IV in Debra's needle-tracked arm when Debra spoke again.

"It hurts."

"I'm sorry, honey. I'm being as gentle as I can."

"My head. Hurt's so . . . so bad." Debra cried out, and then her body went limp. Her head flopped to the side. She stopped breathing.

"No. Debra!" Jama did a sternal rub to try to

wake her. There was no pulse. Jama checked her pupils. The right one was blown.

Jama looked around for Ruth. "I need a crash cart. We've got a code blue."

Chapter Forty-Five

Jama sat on Zelda's front porch swing, watching the morning rush-hour traffic pass by. Two school buses, three minivans, two cars in the space of ten minutes. A lot for River Dance. Everyone waved, and Jama waved back, glad she was far enough from the street that no one could see her tears.

They wouldn't stop flowing. It was as if she'd dammed them up all these years, and the dam had finally broken.

The worst part of the morning had been watching Zelda age and wither when Jama told her about Debra, when they watched Debra's body being taken away by Jim Wilcox from Berger Funeral Home.

A gentle south wind continued to blow this morning, warming the air with spring's touch. The tears chilled on Jama's cheeks, and she withdrew yet another tissue from her pocket.

She heard a familiar sound, and looked up to see Tyrell's Durango coming down the street. She looked away quickly as it parked in front of Zelda's house.

Why had she stayed here? She wasn't up to this.

Wasn't up to anything today. Ruth had given her the day off. Why not return home to Columbia? She needed more sleep. She did *not* need more grief from Tyrell. Hadn't she done that enough to herself these past years?

From the corner of her eye she saw Tyrell step from his Durango and walk slowly up the sidewalk. He stopped at the porch steps.

"Hi," he said.

She glanced at him, nodded, looked away. Didn't he have enough sensitivity to give her a break today?

He took the steps, hesitated in front of her, then sat down in the antique rocker. For a moment, he was silent, rocking back and forth, as if he had all the time in the world, as if they sat like this every day. Their knees nearly touched. He was close enough for her to catch the scent of the soap he'd showered with this morning. And yet she'd never felt so far from him.

What was he doing here?

She braced herself for more questions about the night of Amy's death, more anger that she knew he would have to work through. It was understandable, but not for her. Not today.

"I heard about Debra." His voice was surprisingly gentle. Not what she expected.

More tears flowed, no matter how hard she tried to stop them. She did not want to expose herself to him like this.

"Do you know what caused it?" he asked.

"There will be an autopsy."

"I know. I want to hear your opinion."

"Subdural hematoma."

"Okay, I'm a little rusty on that one. Remind me."

Jama didn't even want to think about it. "She took some hits to the head, and it appears one of those injuries knocked her out, possibly fracturing her skull. The trauma tore some veins."

"I heard she walked all the way to town," Tyrell said. "How could she travel so far with that much damage?"

"An injury of that sort is unpredictable." Jama could always talk about medicine, and some of the stiffness left her voice. "The blood vessels would have started bleeding, and kept bleeding after she woke up."

"But she would have been in pain, right?"

"She complained of a bad headache, but she described it as a migraine. I doubted her explanation last night as soon as I saw her, but she refused treatment. Nothing Zelda or I did could convince her to cross the road with me. Her headache grew worse this morning, and with the excitement of the FBI coming for her, she grew agitated. The veins blew."

"The ticking time bomb."

She looked at him. "Exactly. I don't know if the excitement this morning was what set it off or not, but once it happened, no one could save her."

Tyrell stopped rocking and sat forward. "How long from the time she refused treatment to the time you heard Doriann scream?"

Jama looked at him, startled when she realized what he was getting at. He held her gaze, and she saw the fatigue in his eyes.

"Several minutes," she said.

"So if Debra had agreed to go to the clinic with you, would you have heard the scream?"

Jama blinked as she thought of Debra lying on the bed, refusing treatment. Blast these tear ducts! She covered her face with her hand as the tears flowed.

"I couldn't do anything to help her."

Tyrell got up, opened the screen door of Zelda's house and stepped inside. A few seconds later, he came back with a box of tissues. He set the box on her lap and returned to the rocker.

"Could you have done anything for her if you'd gotten to her sooner?" he asked.

Jama shook her head. "It's a clinic, Tyrell, not a hospital. We don't have the capabilities everybody seems to think we have."

"Then Debra's refusal to go to the clinic last night probably saved Doriann's life. I understand she intervened a few times yesterday."

Jama nodded. "She told me about it."

"And Doriann told me."

Jama looked up at him. "She knew?"

"Yes, and she told the FBI agents about it. Renee

392

and I figured out who Doriann was talking about when we put our heads together this morning. Renee filled me in on your call to her. I think you guessed who Debra was when you saw her at Zelda's last night."

"She was never a killer."

"No, I don't think she was."

Jama wiped her face with a tissue, then looked up to find Tyrell studying her. The blue of his eyes was deeper today, and the dark lashes shadowed them.

"Did you get much sleep last night?" he asked.

"Apparently not enough. Ruth dismissed me."

"She's a wise director, then. She understands the need for sleep."

The words felt sharp and jagged to Jama, though he said them softly.

"Tyrell, it's been a long twenty-four hours, and we're both tired. Couldn't we—"

"You could have told me about Amy so much earlier."

Jama stiffened. Here it came. Calm. She needed to remain calm. She didn't look at him. Couldn't.

"I did tell you," she said.

"Sooner."

"Judging by your reaction last night, I don't think that would have been wise." She stood up. "If you don't mind, I could use a walk." She stepped from the side of the porch into the grass and strolled away, praying he wouldn't follow.

Tyrell had seldom felt so much regret. He thought about his niece, who wouldn't be alive now if not for Jama. About his father, who might not have made it to help in time.

Jama had tackled Clancy Reneker in the darkness like a mama bear, and Tyrell hadn't even asked how bad the knife wound was. She'd assured everyone she would be okay, but her focus was on getting Doriann to treatment as soon as possible.

It was Jama's way. It had been for years.

Tyrell closed his eyes and could almost read those passages of scripture against his eyelids this morning.

" 'Love is patient, love is kind,' " he whispered. " 'Love rejoices in the truth.' "

The truth was that he had searched his heart for many hours. He realized enough to know that the woman who had just walked away from him was not the confused young woman who had tried to drown the pain of her past with a few drinks.

He would not make excuses for Jama's actions all those years ago any more than he would excuse his own disregard for the feelings of others, the times he'd run roughshod over a sibling's wishes simply because he was the oldest brother.

He had some growing to do yet, and it seemed Jama was ahead of him. Maybe he should consider following in her footsteps. She'd had more experience swallowing her pride and searching out her own weaknesses. She'd made great strides toward becoming a whole person.

He got up and followed her. Whether she wanted to or not, they had some talking to do. And he would try not to disregard her wishes.

Unless that meant he couldn't tell her what was on his mind this morning.

It amazed him how the light of day served to clear a person's mind.

Jama strolled toward the back of Zelda's property, where a small stream trickled over boulders. She needed to soak up some of the ambience this place offered. She needed to calm down.

Far too often, she had placed herself in Tyrell's shoes, and realized it would be so hard for her to forgive the person who caused the death of a loved one. Of course, hadn't she proven that? She had never completely forgiven herself.

Perhaps it was time. Hadn't she been forgiven years ago by the Judge of all creation? Who was she to countermand an order from God?

She had just reached the stream, and allowed her senses to be filled with the sound of trickling water, the scent of fresh, moist earth and early spring flowers, when she heard another sound behind her. Footsteps.

She sighed. The man had no tact.

"How's Zelda doing?" Tyrell fell into step with Jama.

"She'll never be the same."

"Did you tell her what Debra did to save Doriann?"

"Yes, I told her that her granddaughter was a hero, but that doesn't bring Debra back, does it?" Jama looked up at him. "She made some mistakes in her life, and she died for those mistakes."

"And Doriann lived. Maybe because of those very mistakes."

Jama thought about that. And about Ruth's words earlier. God ordered their lives.

"Tyrell, I don't want to be rude, but I'm not the best of company right now."

"I think your company is great."

"Well, then, I'm not up to an argument right now. I'm not even up to a discussion. I just need solitude."

"Me, too. Let's have some solitude together, okay?"

Jama turned and walked away. She couldn't look at him. All the pain and regret of the past years welled up inside her.

The sharp edges of their situation overwhelmed her. Later, when she'd rested and was stronger, she would offer him another heartfelt apology. How was she going to face him—face his whole family—for two years?

"I was angry and hurt, Jama." He followed her. "You expected it. You knew me well enough to realize what my initial reaction would be. I know I was hard on you. I'm sorry."

"I remained a part of the family under false pretenses. You have nothing to apologize for. After this is over, after everything has settled down, I'll tell the rest of the family and take whatever comes."

He fell into step beside her. "What do you think will come?"

"You experienced it yourself last night. What do you think?"

"They'll be hurt. It's only natural. But I think they're going to draw the same conclusion I did after a long talk with God."

In spite of herself, Jama slowed her steps to match his.

He moved closer to her. She could feel him willing her to look up at him.

"What conclusion?" she asked.

"In the midst of my anger with you, I began to consider what you must have been feeling all this time. How you felt after telling me. How I'd hurt you. The horror you've lived with, the burden you've carried alone, because you've been abandoned so many times in your life, and you just didn't think you could face it again."

She turned and looked up at him. Tenderness in his eyes. Compassion.

"Jama, don't you realize that our family doesn't love you because you're Amy's friend. We love you because you're you. Jama Keith." He looked down, then away, almost as if he'd suddenly become shy—though there wasn't a shy bone in Tyrell Mercer's body. "Who I hope with all my heart will become Jama Mercer someday."

She'd been holding her breath. She let it out. She felt more tears warm her cheeks. "Don't you understand that this tragedy will always be between us?"

He reached up and touched the tears, caressed her face with his hand. "Don't you realize you're not the same Jama who made that disastrous mistake four and a half years ago? That tragedy was a pivotal point in your life. Just as you said, you sought God, and all this time you've been growing into the person He wants you to be. Your honesty with me proves it."

"I'm still Jama. I'm not some perfect, mature saint."

"Well, honey, you know I'm sure not one, either." Another step closer, until she could feel his warmth. "I'm in this for the duration, Jama Sue. I love you with everything in me, and I have no doubts. The rest of the family will feel the same once they've worked through the tangles. I'll stand beside you."

She sank down onto a boulder beside the stream and stared into the water. She couldn't think right *now*. She'd been so sure—

Tyrell cupped her chin in his hand and raised it until her eyes met his. Then he knelt beside her. "Jama, you told me last night that I was the only one for you. That there'd never been anybody else. Did you mean it?"

She nodded.

"You love me?" he asked.

"I love you." Drat the tears!

"Well, I'm a little bit of a rebel at heart, too, and I disagree with Dad about long engagements. How long will you make me wait?"

She couldn't speak. She could barely see him through the stupid tears. "Until everything's out in the open. Until everyone in the family can forgive me."

"That won't take long."

She closed her eyes. Caught the scent of flowers, heard the soothing trickle of the water and allowed herself to release the last of her fear.

She looked at him, reached for him. He engulfed her in his arms and kissed her, gently touching her lips, brushing his own lips across her tears, whispering his love into her ear.

"I love you with all my heart and soul, Jama Sue Keith. And I always will."

Center Point Publishing
600 Brooks Road ● PO Box 1
Thorndike ME 04986-0001 USA

(207) 568-3717

US & Canada:
1 800 929-9108
www.centerpointlargeprint.com